I0687638

What Reviewers Are Saying

The Wedding Rescue:
Love in Little Tree, Book One
"a full bodied romance filled
with a lot of emotional layers"
—Long and Short Reviews

Santa Dear
"an uplifting story"

Holly & Ivey
"Perfectly sweet Christmas romance!"

Stand-In Mom
"a charming romance"
—Romantic Times Book Reviews,
4 ½ Stars

"rich in emotional detail"
—Long and Short Reviews

Sign up for Megan's Readers' Group on her website,
MeganKellyBooks.com.

For my husband. Always.

This one is also dedicated to my patient readers.

And with thanks to my critique partners, beta readers, and proofreaders (you know who you are), without whom this book would have stunk to high heaven and been full of mistakes.

All rights reserved.
© 2016 by Megan Kelly

Cover design by The Killion Group, Inc.

ISBN 978-0-9886017-6-5

This book or any portion thereof may not be reproduced or used in any manner whatsoever without the express written permission of the author, except for the use of brief quotation in critical articles or reviews.

***

This is a work of fiction. Names, places, businesses, characters, and incidents are either the product of the author's imagination or are used in a fictitious manner. Any resemblance to actual persons living or dead, actual events or locales is purely coincidental.

RUNAWAY BRIDE

Love in
LITTLE TREE

BOOK TWO

MEGAN KELLY

CHAPTER ONE

Grace Marshall flashed yet another smile for the photographer, trying to disguise her yearning to escape. It was, after all, her wedding day.

"One more," the obnoxious man said. His stooped shoulders and squinty silver eyes belied his excellent artistic reputation. No one recommending him had mentioned he charted a negative two on the personality scale and looked like Gru from *Despicable Me*.

No one mentioned he made torturing the bride his personal mission. He didn't badger the rest of the wedding party—who were laughing and having a fine time off camera— with "just one more" picture. Grace swore she'd been in ninety shots already, as though only she needed re-takes.

Her groom-to-be, Jack Walker, tightened his arm around her as they posed on the altar. "Hang in there, honey. After the pictures there's only the wedding and reception and this will all be over."

If he felt the need to calm her, she must not have hidden her nerves very well. But Jack, more than anyone, would have an idea of her misgivings. When his head lowered, she kissed him, but her thoughts whirled. They'd seldom be together out on his ranch and alone even less often. *She'd* be at the ranch house all day, no doubt with her first baby by next year, while he'd be out riding the land until he stumbled back home at dark, too tired to mumble hello. She'd spend her time dealing with his correctly nicknamed uncle Crusty, raising Jack's sweet daughter Annabeth, and immersed in the other chores involved in ranching.

Her stomach hollowed out at this vision of her future. Despite growing up in Little Tree, Montana, she'd never pictured herself as a ranch wife. There would be no time for her to paint or sell to galleries or travel to unknown places for inspiration.

"Smile," the photographer reminded her.

Grace gripped the flower stems tighter in her clammy palms. When she'd suggested taking pictures before the wedding, she'd hoped Jack would appreciate the time saver. She needed to earn points now since she doubted she'd be an ideal wife. She wasn't obedient, and while she could provide dinner for them, she didn't really enjoy the "domestic arts." She was fond of his daughter, probably because the six-year-old tomboy reminded Grace of her twin sister, Lexi. And Grace was more than fond of Jack. He was handsome, strong, virile, fun on a date, a great dancer, and topped the charts in kissing.

But his ideal wife had died three years ago.

"How about a close-up of the rings?" the photographer suggested.

"I won't be wearing one." Jack took Grace's hand. "Did you want to put yours on now for the pictures?"

"No." Panic made her voice squeak. "Not yet."

The photographer rolled his eyes in an unprofessional loss of patience. "How about just your engagement ring then?"

Getting engaged was her own damned fault. Acting impulsively had landed her in trouble more often than she cared to recall. Trying to help Jack inherit the ranch from his ornery uncle, she'd proposed marriage. At the time, she'd wanted to be the helpful twin. Lexi made it look so easy, always ready to lend a hand and, most often, extending that hand to bail Grace out of trouble.

"These are wedding pictures, not engagement pictures." Grace sought to turn the attention away from herself so she could regain some control. "How about one of Jack and Annabeth?"

"We'd like you in it, too, honey." Jack smiled, his gorgeous green eyes shining. Happiness? Affection? Maybe the dawning of love? "You're family and will officially be a Walker in a few hours."

Even as Grace smiled for another photo, she couldn't imagine how she'd fit into her new life. Jack would never stop her from painting, but she sensed he regarded it as a lucrative hobby. He didn't understand the importance of galleries beginning to seek her out for showings. Her last painting sold well enough to buy about fifty head of cattle—or so she guessed, not really having any idea what one cow cost. But suffice it to say, she'd tucked away some money for a future land purchase, an idea for an artists' retreat that had percolated when she'd been studying landscape in the Australian Outback.

"Okay, now a picture with just the ladies." The photographer conferred with his anorexic female assistant, who wore a sleeveless tunic and leggings as black as her constant scowl. She eyed the proceedings with some dark humor only she understood.

Grace lined up on the altar step with her sister, Lexi, and little Annabeth. They wore goldenrod dresses to offset the yellow roses in the sisters' bouquets and the petals her future step-daughter would toss. Lexi had complained about looking like a weed, but the color complemented her blond coloring. Annabeth glowed with her almost-black sausage curls and shiny black Mary Jane shoes. Grace had consulted for hours with the designer about texture and colors to get just the right shade.

That part she'd enjoyed.

Positioned between Grace and Lexi, Annabeth tilted back her head and stared at Grace. Was the girl measuring her against memories of her own mom? Did she have any? Jack's first wife had died before the girl turned four. Grace and Annabeth hadn't spent much time together up till now, and the little one might need reassurance. Embracing the tender moment, Grace tucked a strand of hair behind the girl's ear. Kids weren't exactly Grace's strong suit, but she would try her damnedest to provide security and love. And siblings.

A cold shimmer of sweat coated her arms.

"If I have to smile any longer," Lexi said through stiff lips while the photographer's assistant fiddled with the lighting, "my face will freeze this way."

"That's not likely in June," Grace whispered back.

"It's not likely in here, either. I never realized the church was so hot." Lexi batted her lashes. "But your future brother-in-law sure is. Hot, I mean. Does Clint have a date for the reception?"

"He doesn't. Not for lack of female attention, though." Grace checked him over with a considering eye. Very dapper, but with his job in L.A., Clint had better not lure her sister away. Lexi wouldn't be happy in a big city, and Grace would be lost without her. "I wouldn't have thought he was your type."

The camera flashed and the sisters relaxed while Annabeth wandered toward her dad. So much for bonding.

Lexi's lips curved in amusement. "Do I have a type?"

"A cowboy," Grace replied without hesitation. "Someone who relies on the land, understands animals and nature, and wants to live that life. Here in Montana. In Little Tree, actually."

Her sister laughed. "Wow, I didn't realize I was so specific."

"You are." Grace tried to laugh. Lexi couldn't leave Little Tree, not now that Grace had returned from her years of studying and painting abroad. "You and I are going to raise our kids together."

"I need a minute to change film," the photographer said.

"Film?" Jack echoed. "What's that?"

"Philistine," Clint mocked. With some trepidation, he'd shown Grace his portfolio of landscape photographs. She'd been impressed. He had a sharp eye for interesting angles and a willingness to capture the unique shot. His camera rested only when he had to be in a picture. No doubt he'd produce some great photos at the reception.

The wedding, reception, and honeymoon night loomed closer, pressing on her and closing off her throat.

"I need to refresh my lipstick," Grace told Jack. Truth was, if she didn't have a moment alone to breathe, she'd probably faint. Her heart raced and she nearly panted trying to catch some air. Nerves didn't usually affect her, but then, she'd never gotten married before.

He barely turned from talking to Annabeth to smile at her rather absently, a blessing that would have irked her at another time. What kind of groom was he, anyway?

In case he remembered to look at her lips when she returned, she stepped into the dressing room and found her purse. The cool empty space offered exactly the respite she craved while she palmed her lipstick. The jingle of car keys in her bag made her glance at the outer door. A quick spin in the convertible would clear her head.

And mess up her hair. And make her late for the wedding if she traveled too far—like New York. Suppressing her longing, she cast away the idea of flying down the road, free from worry and doubt.

With more determination than conviction, Grace opened the hall door. She had made a promise. She had proposed. She—

Heard her name.

Pausing with indecision, she closed the door most of the way to hide behind. Although her mother had passed when Grace was twelve, her admonition about eavesdroppers never hearing good of themselves rang clear. As usual, Grace ignored it. Peeping between the door and the jamb, she saw the photographer and his assistant huddled near the water fountain.

"No, really, that's what I heard." The assistant's raspy tone confirmed her as a smoker, as did the heavy scent that hung on her dark clothes. "At the bar last night in town. I knew you should have come in from Billings earlier."

"The bride doesn't look very happy, you're right."

Grace winced. She'd have to do better at covering her doubts. She and Jack could work out something regarding her duties on the ranch and her need to paint.

"But her own sister?" the photographer continued.

She must have missed part of the conversation. What had they said about Lexi? Irritation crept along her skin. She didn't appreciate anyone gossiping about Lexi in a bar. Or in a church hallway.

"That's what I heard." The assistant halted near enough

to the dressing room that when she dropped her voice to a whisper, Grace heard the words clearly. "I can't believe that bride. She's in love with Walker. Has been for years."

Grace frowned with confusion. Why wouldn't the bride be in love with the groom? Although, they got the rest wrong. She hadn't even been in Little Tree until eight months ago, so she couldn't have been in love with Jack for *years*, as they claimed. She wanted to run out and tell them to get their story straight but hesitated. Why cause a scene? Still, what did her feelings for Jack have to do with Lexi? Gossip usually contained a grain of truth, but this assistant needed to sharpen her listening skills.

"So the bride stole him? That's just wrong."

Grace gasped and covered her mouth. They didn't move, indicating they hadn't heard her. Stole him? She stole Jack? From whom?

Then the jumbled pieces fell together. Did they seriously think she had taken him from Lexi? That Lexi was the one "in love with Walker?" Grace almost laughed out loud. If ever two people couldn't stand each other, it was Jack and her sister.

"She's been pining for him." The assistant made a repeated *tsk*. "The insensitivity of some people astounds me."

"Maybe the bride doesn't know."

"That one?" The snotty assistant snorted. "She knows."

Grace glowered as various curses ran through her mind. Having spent the past four years traveling Europe and Australia, she'd picked up a few that would curl even that woman's stringy black hair.

"Looks like the sister is holding up well," the over-priced photographer said. "Must be heartbreaking to watch the man you love marry your sister. Especially your identical twin."

The assistant's laugh grated down Grace's spine. "Maybe they'll all move to Utah and be real sister wives."

"Eew." But the photographer chuckled as they ambled off, their hateful voices fading with each step.

Grace slumped against the wall. Could it be true? Had she been blind to her sister's feelings since she'd returned? Did Lexi love Jack?

She'd never mentioned him in letters or phone calls during the years Grace had been abroad. She'd never even so much as glanced in his direction with longing, nor had her voice held a special tone when speaking his name. Unless she voiced disgust at his over-protective attitude.

But then, Grace recalled her own homecoming party where she'd pretty much locked eyes with Jack and tumbled at him. Tall, dark, handsome, manly. He'd made her knees weak.

Had Lexi noticed Grace's reaction and stepped aside? Were there certain looks between them Grace misinterpreted? But, no. Lexi couldn't stand Jack. He was the only man she'd ever reacted that way toward. The only person, actually. Lexi usually found something redeemable in everyone, from an ornery old codger like Jack's uncle to the meanest low-life cowboy. Only Jack could—

Only Jack. *Only* Jack.

Dammit.

Bile rose in Grace's throat. Lexi had given up her own chance at happiness. She rubbed a hand to her chest, easing down the burning. What a mess.

How could she ever be happy with Jack now?

Grace woke the next morning with her head pounding. Or did the pounding come from outside? One eye eased open to judge the angle of the sunlight leaking through the blinds. Low and soft. Maybe six or seven a.m. She raised her head, fuzzy from lack of sleep, and recognized her cousin Rachel's guest room in Longmont, Colorado.

Coming alert, she remembered all too vividly fleeing from her wedding. Tricking Lexi into trying on the wedding dress so she couldn't chase after her. Fleeing through the exit door—really, what genius had designed the bride's dressing room with an outside exit?—and driving as fast as she could before Lexi was discovered and the story revealed.

What were they thinking, doing, guessing back in Little Tree?

Jack would understand that her proposal had been impulsive, and a life without love had been too much to bear. He'd married the love of his life already. He wouldn't condemn Grace for wanting the same. Her dad would shake his head and worry until he heard the message she'd left on his home phone. And Lexi? She'd know, the way twins did, that Grace was saying "go after what you want." Her absence spoke more effectively than trying to explain it all. Words wouldn't have convinced Lexi that Grace was serious about stepping aside. If Grace told her she knew of Lexi's feelings for Jack, Lexi would think Grace was being noble.

Fleeing had opened the door for Lexi, but it had also freed Grace. A win-win for everyone, including Jack. He'd learn Lexi suited him better. She could only pray they found their way to each other soon. Then she could return home.

The tightness in her temples increased as Grace battled tears. She didn't need a crying jag to produce a headache. The awful pounding outside accomplished that.

Who would be hammering so early on a Sunday morning? A neighbor should have more respect for Rachel's sleep.

The neighbor might know Rachel had gone to Grace's wedding. Or rather, her non-wedding. Grace glanced at her purse and the cell phone she'd turned off after calling her dad at his house, knowing he wouldn't be there.

I'm okay, Dad. I just need to clear my head. Marrying Jack would have been a mistake. I'm sorry.

A pretty lame message but all she could share of her reasons, especially on the old-fashioned answering machine. She didn't want someone listening and learning Lexi's secret. Worse, if Lexi heard why she left, guilt might keep her from pursuing Jack.

Grace pushed out of bed to the window but couldn't see anyone. The noise grew louder, sounding as though it came from behind Rachel's garage. As the only one in residence, she would need to inspect. Pulling on the yellow sundress from the day before, she yearned for something to wear that didn't remind her of the wedding. Her clothes had been moved over to Jack's ranch.

Shaking off those thoughts, Grace swung open the back door and stepped gingerly through the tall grass of Rachel's backyard. Her white satin pumps would be ruined with grass stains. She scowled and blamed that on the noise-maker, too, even though she'd never wear these wedding shoes again. That bridge had been burned. Better for everyone this way, she reminded herself, and shook off her guilt.

Around the back of the garage, Grace spotted a man with a hammer. He wore faded jeans and a checkered shirt with the sleeves cut off at the seams, displaying his muscular biceps and forearms. Her fingers itched for her charcoal pencils to capture the curve of his hand on the hammer and the glisten of sweat on his sun-bronzed dark skin. He'd tied a folded, bright red bandana around his forehead to catch drips of sweat. His thick, straight black hair lay close-cut to his head. She'd seen gorgeous features like his when studying the ruins in Mexico. This guy exuded masculinity.

Three walls of a new structure stuck out from the back of the garage. Tin and wooden boards lay on the ground. "Good morning," she called.

He froze in mid-swing and turned in her direction. The hammer lowered, but his deep brown eyes remained cautious. "I didn't see you there."

But he saw her now. Grace held steady as his gaze seared down her bright dress to her bare legs and ruined shoes then back up to her face. Her body went on alert, even though she was used to male interest. When she and Lexi went out together, heads turned and men advanced. She'd always considered her looks just good genes, but with this guy's gaze on her, she thanked her beautiful mother for passing along that DNA. His stare sent tingles of anticipation running along her skin.

"Are you building Rachel a shed?"

"She's wanted one for a while. It's for her birthday."

Grace heard the slightest accent, which made sense given his Hispanic features and coloring. Someone else might miss the music behind his tone, but she'd developed an ear for language during her travels. "She's giving herself a present? That's very practical, and so like her."

"No, I'm giving her a present." He gestured to the structure.

"Oh, I thought she hired you."

His lips pressed together as though he'd taken her words as an insult. She hadn't meant he looked like a laborer, but that Rachel had hired someone to build the shed while she was out of town. For her birthday gift to herself. Ugh, Grace couldn't even make sense of it in her head, let alone find the words to explain.

His lean muscular body identified him as a man used to physical labor, so she could be forgiven for thinking him a handyman. Would the rest of him be corded and glistening? Would he allow her to sketch him? Maybe wearing a towel, rising from ancient baths in Rome. Or emerging from a jungle river, a white cloth covering his privates, contrasting with the darkness around him. The darkness *of him*, predatory and dangerous.

"I'm a friend," he explained, jerking her back to reality. "And you are...?"

Grace pushed away the images and the impression he embodied danger of some sort. Silly. "I'm her cousin."

"Ah." A smile lit his dark brown eyes as his stance relaxed. "You would be the bride's sister. Have you returned with Rachel?" His expression folded into regret. "I guess this gift is no longer a surprise. I'm sorry for the noise. I didn't realize anyone was home."

"No, no. It's fine. I was about to get up, anyway." A blatant lie. She'd rather pull the covers over her head for the next decade.

"I wanted to get this done before she returned, but I was detained yesterday." He winked. "A horse, you know, won't wait."

Grace nodded, charmed by this lighter side of him. Listening to her dad and Lexi talk about the veterinary practice had taught her a little about horses. She meant to ask, "Won't wait for what?" when he continued.

"But then, you know that better than I do. I understand you work as a vet in your father's practice."

Grace started to clear up his misconception but paused. Saying "I'm the bride" would require complicated explanations to this total stranger. Besides, she could no longer claim to be a bride. "It'll still be a surprise for Rachel. She isn't home yet."

His forehead creased. "Did something happen?"

You could say that. "No, she's fine." Seemed she'd have to explain, after all. "It's just, I'm not who you think. I'm Grace, the sister that was supposed to get married, not Lexi, the veterinarian."

After a second spent studying her, he stepped nearer and held out his hands. A little bemused, she placed hers in his hold. His nearness made her heart rate speed up. He stood just five inches or so taller than she, making him about five eleven, yet he seemed bigger. Solid. Sturdy. His rough warm hands held hers gently. His intent, concerned expression flattered, while at the same time puzzled her.

"He's a fool."

It took a moment before she understood. He extended all that sympathy and gentleness to a rejected bride. "Oh, no, no. He didn't jilt me. I..." No justification formed in her mind. She'd have to say it, blunt though it came off. "I'm the one who left. I realized we were better off not going through with it."

He dropped her hands and stepped back.

She frowned, her guilt putting her on the defensive. Then she felt ridiculous for the reaction. She didn't even know his name and certainly didn't owe him explanations. Nor did she care one whit about his opinion. Still, she'd been rehearsing what to say to her dad and the words wanted out. "We wouldn't have been happy. It was kinder to leave him before the ceremony."

Rachel's friend stood silent, and she forced herself not

to fidget.

"We wouldn't have stayed together long."

"I suppose not, if that's how you felt."

The words weren't cold, but his stiff bearing created more distance than the few feet separating them. Unnerved by his disapproval, Grace shot him a sassy smile. She'd disarmed many a snooty art gallery owner with her grin and eventually convinced most of them to show her paintings. Back in the early days, before galleries clamored for her work.

She stuck out her hand. "We haven't really met. I'm Grace Marshall."

He barely touched his palm to hers before retreating. "Mike."

She frowned when he left off his last name, as though he didn't plan to become further acquainted with her. Well, fine. Though he shouldn't judge her without knowing the circumstances. "How long have you and Rachel been friends?" *And why has she never mentioned you?*

A glint of humor hit his eyes. The man baffled her.

"I've known Rachel for many years."

They'd been lovers. Grace sensed it in her marrow. The humor, the shed, the sex appeal. It all made sense.

She couldn't blame Rachel for going after him. The guy was a hunk and a half, despite his disapproval. Since he didn't know the reason she'd left, his siding with Jack pointed to male solidarity. That smile earlier, when his dreamy dark eyes had gone all soft and supportive for the rejected bride, made her yearn for his friendship. She needed a friend. Lexi had always been her support, but Grace couldn't count on her now. Mike's shoulders looked broad enough to be her scaffold.

Realizing she stood gawking at the gorgeous male, Grace looked away. *Well, I'll leave you to your work then.*

Rachel should be home in a few hours."

"I hope to be done in less than that time. I constructed the roof but have to attach it now that I have the walls up."

She glanced at the tin and realized the boards beneath it had been assembled into triangles. Joists, she recalled. "Okay, then. Nice to meet you."

He nodded and turned away.

Grace frowned at his very broad back. He could have said he'd enjoyed meeting her, as well. Were he and Rachel still lovers, and if so, why hadn't she brought him to the wedding? Grace couldn't wait to ask Rachel about him.

Although, on second thought, that meant seeing her cousin, who had been at the non-wedding. While Grace wanted to learn what happened after she left, she dreaded the questions she'd face.

How could she explain how trapped she'd felt, even before learning Lexi's secret? How just the thought of a lifetime with a wonderful man like Jackson Walker—full of sexy, masculine confidence, but with her stuck on his ranch as a baby-maker and short order cook—had scared her into running away? Learning her sister had sacrificed her love for Jack had sealed the deal, especially when Grace already had doubts. Only Lexi would understand. Lexi had always been her best friend.

While traveling abroad, she'd devised a plan to fit into Little Tree without abandoning her art. Marriage to Jack would have crushed or delayed her plan.

But she'd learned her lesson. No more impulsive gestures to save someone else. She wasn't the good twin, and she might as well learn to live with that now, since she'd soon be back home. In Lexi's shadow.

Grace banished the worry about her eventual return to

Little Tree with a soothing shower, after which she dressed in Rachel's clothes. Her cousin's taller frame meant the sleeveless, button-down pink shirt engulfed Grace. She countered this effect by tying the ends around her midriff. The denim shorts hung a bit long on her, but they didn't require a belt. Grace paced the house, listening to Mike outside. Wondering about him.

After half an hour, the hammering and drilling sounds stopped. The silence distracted her as she tried to imagine his actions. Had he left? She peeked outside and saw a dusty black pickup parked at the curb.

Finally, she couldn't stand it. Feeling confined to the house by his presence ticked her off. She had no reason to hide from him. The rest of her family, maybe, but not Mike Whatever-His-Name-Was.

Considering the possibility of forgotten nails in the grass, she tugged on the ruined satin pumps. They looked ridiculous with her casual shorts, but she doubted Mike would notice the incongruity. Any shoes Rachel owned would have fallen off Grace. She eyed the flip-flops and sandals, but a nail would go straight through the soles.

With a twinge of misgiving for her welcome, she poured Mike a glass of lemonade. The heels made her feel like a repressed woman from the 1950s seeking excitement with the hired help. She only needed a short pearl necklace to complete the image.

She couldn't believe how uncomfortable his disapproval made her and tried to laugh it off. She wasn't used to being disliked. Even the condescending gallery owners had succumbed eventually. But then, they had coveted her paintings. Mike didn't seem impressed with anything about her.

Well, she'd grown up with people judging her and being disappointed.

She could never tell the townspeople back home why she'd run off, even to ease her way into their good graces. Her sister would be devastated.

Also, it didn't express the whole truth. She'd acted impetuously when she proposed to Jack, so it followed she'd be just as rash when it came to *not* marrying him.

She debated who she dreaded facing more: her father or Jack. Once Jack realized he and Lexi were perfect for each other, he wouldn't be angry anymore. Once she could tell her father she'd removed herself so Lexi could pursue her heart's desire, he would forgive her. But in the short term, she'd have to withstand their censure. Or stay in Longmont and avoid it.

Heat wrapped around her like a hungry cat the moment she stepped outside. Already in the high eighties, the day would turn into a scorcher.

"I brought you a drink," she called out as she rounded the corner.

CHAPTER TWO

Miguel Torres, known to people in these parts as Mike Thompson, paused in his painting to turn to Rachel's beautiful cousin. He'd finished the structure, a nice-sized shed with a secure hinged door. A layer of white sealed the boards, and now marine blue paint coated his brush, ready for the final coat. A battery-powered fan hurried along the drying. He wanted it done before Rachel returned from Montana. Yesterday, the boss's new horse had arrived from California, and during the off-loading, the skittish gelding had thrown itself against the trailer hard enough to need the vet. The boss said "stay" and Mike had, which delayed his start on the shed.

He reached his hand toward Grace, feeling her name coat his tongue, although he hadn't spoken it. She'd changed clothes. Before, she'd looked like cool citrus in that lemon yellow dress, tart and sweet. He'd wanted to drink her up. This new pink shirt made him think of a sharp rosé wine, tempting him to indulge, but sure to give him a headache in the long run. And those legs, tanned and strong, made other images swirl through his head. "It's getting hot. Thanks for the drink."

Her gaze stayed on him, and he forced the cool liquid down his throat.

"It was nothing."

He pressed the cold glass against his neck. "My parents

didn't believe in pop, so we grew up drinking lemonade. This is refreshing."

"We?"

Mike eyed her, considering whether to answer. He didn't want a woman like her in his life, not her opinion, not even her knowing about his siblings. She was too polished, too rich, too used to getting her own way. Too careless with other people's hearts.

He shook off his misgivings. More to prove something to himself rather than feed her curiosity, he answered. "I have three sisters and three brothers. We grew up running wild down in New Mexico."

Grace's eyes widened. "There were seven kids?"

He couldn't resist teasing her. "My parents were very expressive with their devotion."

"How nice for you."

He raised his brow at her odd reply.

"Having that many siblings, I mean," she clarified, her face pink. "I only have one sister, although she's my twin, so we're very close."

"They're a trial, but I'm glad they're around."

"Do they all live in Colorado?"

He looked into the glass, swirling the ice. Even after all these years, he found it hard to expose his family to questions. Telling her to mind her own business would be rude, and he owed Rachel more respect than to treat her cousin impolitely. Concentrating, he erased all accent from his words. "My siblings and I settled up here ten years ago. Two live on either coast, but the rest of us stayed around Longmont."

He could see her guessing his age and subtracting ten. How close to seventeen would she guess he'd been when his role changed from big brother to substitute dad?

"And your parents?"

"Papá had a heart attack and Mamá went the next month. She stopped eating." He shrugged. "She wanted to be with him."

"I'm so sorry. My mom died fourteen years ago, and I still miss her every day." She stepped nearer. "How old were you when your parents passed?"

He bent and set the paintbrush across the can, hiding his expression. She didn't need to see the pain thoughts of his parents evoked. After pressing a finger to a board, he adjusted the fan to dry the strip he'd just finished. "I was old enough to take care of the others. We have a place just outside town."

"You must miss the others who moved away."

"My youngest brother is at Bozeman, studying green architecture." He frowned. Why was he telling Grace any of this? "My brother still at home, Paul, hasn't decided what he wants to be when he grows up, even though he's almost twenty-one. I can sometimes get him odd jobs on the ranch where I work when the owner needs more hands. But Paul isn't happy being a cowboy."

"What do you do on the ranch?"

"I'm a horse wrangler." Mike stared at her, trying to decipher her thoughts. Would she comment on his job? Expect it of him, the way she'd picked up on his Hispanic roots and deemed him a hired handyman?

"Are you painting this blue?"

He blinked at the subject change and indicated the blue paint can. "Yes."

"Would you mind...?" She bit her lip then stood straighter. "I'd like to paint something on the side for Rachel. I'm an artist, so I can promise you it would look nice. A mural. Of horses."

Her expression turned soft and dream-like as though she pictured the mural complete in her mind. She seemed to have forgotten his presence.

"Wild horses in the background," she continued, her hand measuring out the space, "and Rachel's gelding, Curly, in a fence in the foreground here. I'll have to convey through Curly's body language and eyes that he wouldn't trade places with the wild horses for anything."

Rachel boarded Curly at a good facility and rode often. She'd probably love this idea.

The vista took shape in his mind as Grace spoke. He wanted to see what she would make of the shed walls. He gazed into her eyes, drawn into the sapphire depths as though falling upside down into the sky. He could get lost in there— even worse, he feared he wouldn't call for rescue.

"Maybe I'll put Rachel's hand holding an apple just at the side. I have to keep the majesty of the wild horses apparent, too. Maybe I'll call it *Choices*. The mustangs unfettered, running free." Grace frowned. "Maybe I'd better just paint the wild ones. Or put Curly on a side wall, giving him his own space so Rachel doesn't feel bad about keeping him."

That fast, Mike knew this woman's presence spelled trouble. She showed more understanding than he'd attributed to her. *Choices*. Yeah, that summed it up exactly. He'd made choices, bleaching all color from his past and from his siblings' pasts. For their safety. Horses also chose to be saddled or not, becoming a man's transport and partner out on the land. "Miss Marshall?"

Grace jerked back to the present. "Sorry, I got carried away envisioning the painting. If it's okay with you?"

Her finger tapped against her hipbone, waiting him out, her question more for form than any expectation of opposition.

Impatient and headstrong, she reminded him of a his horse, Libre, but he knew just enough about women not to tell say it. "I'm sure Rachel would be glad to have your mural."

"I'll see what supplies she has here. I leave some wherever I spend a lot of time, but it's been a few months since I visited."

He nodded once. "Would you prefer I keep the walls white then?"

Grace winced before her eyes went wide and her face slack, looking stricken. Her gaze darted between the shed and his face, as though she'd just realized she planned to take over his gift. The painting would overshadow the structure. He found he didn't mind.

"You know." She frowned and tipped her head as though studying the shed. "I'm not sure this is the proper canvas for what I have in mind."

Such a liar, he thought with amusement. Wild horses running across wooden walls in the outdoors would be striking. If she could paint half as well as she described it, the modest shed would become a masterpiece. But she'd give up her plans to prevent his feelings from being hurt? Yeah, she was trouble, all right.

"I think Rachel will want it inside where she can see it all the time. If you need anything," she said, "I'll be in the house."

He extended the glass to her but couldn't let her walk away. "Grace."

She turned, focused on him rather than a picture in her head.

"Do you know anyone in town other than Rachel?"

"No."

"Here." He pulled a piece of paper and a pencil stub

from his shirt pocket. After jotting both his phone numbers, he extended it toward her. "In case you need anything before she returns."

She stared at the paper as though not understanding. Her silence made him want to fidget. Good thing he never did that.

"The second number is my house. Cell service is sketchy depending where you are, probably similar to Montana's. So if you can't reach me on my cell, the top one there, you can leave a message at the house phone. One of the kids will relay your message."

"Thank you." She glanced at the paper where he'd written his name. "Mike Thompson. This is very sweet of you."

"Having an emergency contact is just common sense." He tried to downplay the gesture, as though he'd have done it for anyone. "Besides, I'd feel bad if something happened to Rachel's cousin."

Why did she frown as she turned away? Women. Figuring out this one would be harder than any other.

Fortunately, she was just visiting.

She wouldn't mess with his head any more than she had already.

"Lexi?"

Grace turned at Rachel's voice in the kitchen doorway and set aside the sketchpad. A glance at the clock confirmed she'd been drawing at the table almost all day. At some point, she'd finished iced tea and a sandwich, based on the crumbs on the plate and a glass holding an inch of watery brown liquid. The light outside had lost its intensity.

"Oh, my God," Rachel exclaimed, a hand to her chest

like the heroine in an olde-time melodrama, as her gaze swept over the sketchpad and pencils. "Grace? What are you doing *here?*"

Grace grinned at her cousin, feeling more nervous than she'd expected.

Rachel put her hands on her hips and frowned, looking every bit like the older sister Grace had never had. "I don't understand. I just saw you get married."

Grace's breath caught with surprise. "You what?"

"Although it couldn't have been you, could it?" Rachel squinted in thought. "Why did Lexi marry Jack? What's going on here?"

"She *married* him?" Grace's stomach tightened and she struggled for air. "She wasn't supposed to do that." *Not yet.* They were supposed to be thrown together, realize they were in love and *then* get married.

I ask her to do one simple thing, Grace thought with twisted humor. Now Lexi had complicated an already tricky situation. Or had she already declared her feelings for Jack? Had he reciprocated and they'd reached their happily ever after so soon? Grace doubted the perfect solution she envisioned had fallen together so easily.

But based on Rachel's announcement, it might have.

Hope surged within her. Was it over? Could she return home?

Rachel fell onto a chair and rubbed her temple. "For God's sakes, Grace, how could you leave Jack at the altar? And how could you leave this for Lexi to handle?"

"Hold on a minute. I never said, 'go marry him.' This was pure Lexi."

"You're right." Rachel scowled. "You left her with a different mess. Lexi just created this one trying to clean up yours. No wonder they didn't go to the reception."

"What? They didn't go?" Grace's head spun with all the information being thrown at her, but none of it made sense. "Just stop talking and tell me everything."

Rachel chuckled. "Not without a drink. Sounds like you need one, too."

Grace didn't want to wait to hear the details while Rachel mixed up banana daiquiris or some other current favorite. Grace couldn't wrap her mind around it. Her sister had married her fiancé. How could Lexi expect to be happy just stepping into his life? Shouldn't they at least have dated first? Given Jack time to adjust to a different wife?

That bastard had better not hurt her sister.

"It's been a long weekend." Rachel pulled the jug of lemonade from the fridge. No daiquiris then. "Do you want some?"

"Not unless it has vodka in it."

Rachel lifted an eyebrow.

"I've been waiting since yesterday for the fallout. I could barely sleep."

"How could you sleep at all?" Rachel shook her head then sipped, seeming to take forever. "I can't believe you, Grace."

Second-guessing had kept her awake until almost four o'clock. Then she'd slept like the dead, worn out from guilt over stealing her sister's love interest and from worrying over the way she'd handled giving him back. Running never solved anything. But if she explained it all to Rachel now, the story could get back to Lexi, who would feel guilty about coming between Grace and Jack. So complicated.

Grace changed the subject. "Well, I can't believe Lexi married Jack. Or no, on second thought, maybe I can. That's just the kind of hare-brained solution she'd come up with."

Rachel's empty glass *thunked* on the counter. "Watch what you say about Lexi. She just saved your fiancé from major embarrassment. God, I even saw her before the wedding. She was in a state. I should have realized it then. I thought it was you, upset Lexi had gotten ill and couldn't act as your bridesmaid."

"What? She didn't look sick."

"She must have invented that excuse to explain why you, why *she...* Oh, hell. Maybe I do need some vodka." Rachel grabbed some ice cubes and filled the glass with water from the faucet. After a long drink, she sat across from Grace, gaze serious.

"Let me get the facts out," Rachel said. "Lexi posed as you and married Jack. They didn't come to the reception, and no one knew where they went. We assumed that you and he had gone to the hotel to…start your honeymoon."

Grace stilled, the blood running from her face and leaving her skin clammy. Surely they hadn't had sex. Jack wasn't such a bastard to demand that from Lexi, to just exchange sisters, one twin as good as the other, and then expect Lexi to sleep with him.

Unless he hadn't known. What if Lexi had continued to masquerade as Grace, a prank they'd played on people in their youth? If Jack and Lexi had consummated, it would be a done deal. But her sister wouldn't trick him like that. Grace felt almost sure of it.

The *almost* had her heart racing. Lexi had married him, after all. But, no. Just *no.* "I can't believe it. Why would she marry him?" *So soon,* she wanted to add. But that would lead to questions, and Grace couldn't reveal there'd been a plan, at least in her head. "They don't even like each other."

Rachel smirked. "Maybe they do by now."

"That's not funny," Grace snapped.

"What's with you? You're acting like the dog in the manger. You obviously didn't want him."

"I...I do love him." Even to her ears, it sounded lame. But she had cared for Jack enough to propose and had planned to build a life with him.

She hadn't asked Lexi to make any kind of sacrifice. She'd expected them to...console each other, maybe. For Jack to have his eyes opened to Lexi as a caring and wonderful woman, more than just a thorn in his side. Grace tipped her head back, angry at this new layer of guilt.

"I doubt if Jack believes you loved him."

"Do you think Lexi revealed her identity?"

"Of course she did." Rachel paused, head tilted to the side. "Come to think of it, there wasn't time before the ceremony. I went to get you and walked out to the foyer with her. She explained Lexi had gotten sick. And, Lord, I bet the poor girl was."

"I'm sure she felt anxious, but Lexi is steady as a rock."

"I can't believe this. I blew off her illness to support you, so you wouldn't worry about the wedding continuing without her. Lexi probably thinks I didn't care about her illness. Though she wasn't really sick." Rachel rubbed her temples. "You twins and your convoluted schemes."

"Look, I never thought for one minute she'd marry him." Not for a while, at any rate.

"Now *that* I believe. What did you ask her to do?"

Grace shrugged. "Just explain that I couldn't go through with it."

"Oh, is that all?" Rachel sighed. "I love you like a younger sister, but sometimes I want to slap you."

Stung, Grace jerked backward in her chair. "Hey, I don't deserve that. I did him a favor. Or I thought I did. Are they even legally married? But if they slept together, I—"

"I didn't say they had sex. I said they didn't come to the reception."

Grace thought they'd have explained everything to the attendees. Smoothed it all out so by the time she went back home, it would be water under the bridge. How long would she have to stay clear of Little Tree to give Lexi the opportunity to win Jack's love? A few days? A month?

She could paint anywhere, but her longing for home had followed her through Europe and Australia. Despite the excitement of visiting beautiful cities seeped in art and history, she had yearned to walk through the dry scrubland of Montana. All too often, she'd mixed paint in shades of dirt brown and the yellow of stiff grasses. She'd painted a blue sky so soft it cushioned dreams. A sun that had no color, just dazzling brightness. Home. "Does Dad know about the switch?"

"I don't know. Uncle Kevin turned really quiet, obviously upset. We thought it was because Lexi fell sick and the bride and groom went AWOL. No one knew Lexi's whereabouts, and after the first time we asked, when your dad looked so pained, we stopped mentioning it."

"Don't lay a guilt trip on me, Rachel."

"I'm just telling you what happened."

So no one knew Grace had left or that Lexi had stepped in as the bride? "I need to call Dad again."

"You need to call Lexi and Jack."

Grace shied away from the idea. Jack was so overwhelmingly male, even when he wasn't angry. She couldn't imagine him really mad. His self-assurance had been hard for her to handle. She'd battled to get him to agree to take pictures before the wedding. It cemented her growing concerns that Jack hadn't been the right man for her.

While she regretted her escape, she didn't regret not being Mrs. Jackson Walker. She'd explained her need to paint, and Jack had nodded as though he understood. He would have had the same response to his six-year-old daughter explaining why she needed a puppy.

Grace couldn't go back to Little Tree yet, not until this mess got straightened out.

Were Jack and Lexi legally married? What a nightmare. "Can I stay here for a while?"

"Honey, I'd usually love a visit, but I think you need to go home and face the music."

"It'll be more like an orchestral concert, full of crashing cymbals. Since Lexi went to such lengths to save me and Jack from embarrassment, it wouldn't be very kind to show up now, would it?"

Rachel pursed her lips. "I can see right through you, but maybe you're right. You should stay until the rest of the manure falls off the fan blades."

"Thank you." Grace needed time to figure out what to do next. She needed to talk to Lexi so she could reassure their dad. She needed to finish her painting for Rachel.

Speaking of which, she also needed to prove to a certain disapproving, handsome friend of Rachel's that she could do better than paint by numbers.

Mike rested his boot on the bottom rung of the corral and watched as dusk covered his boss's ranch. He loved his job working with the horses, but today he'd been distracted when he checked on them. Before calling it a night, he'd given them one more look. Now he would kick back in the bunkhouse, too tired to drive home. His siblings would survive without him as they had on other nights when work kept him at the ranch.

Why did he feel itchy and restless? Only a greenhorn let himself be distracted around horses, but when he'd returned from Rachel's today, he couldn't concentrate. He continued to think of Grace Marshall alone at the house. It must be worry that Rachel hadn't returned safely that kept both women on his mind. A phone call would assure him Rachel had made it home. Then this tightness in his chest would ease.

Mike gave a low whistle and heard the slow, reluctant approach of a horse across the corral. His mare, Libre, stood facing him but had stopped a good ten feet distant. He considered it progress she'd come at all. A buckskin, her cream coloring made it easy to see her muscles quivering with the instinct to run. Almost a year after being rounded up by the Bureau of Land Management, she still yearned to be free, hence her name.

She shook her head, sending her dark mane flying.

He smiled. "You want to be admired, huh?"

The mare's legs tightened in preparation to bolt.

Since she'd refused his advances in the past, he remained still, just making eye contact. She stared back at him, not blinking and not relaxing. He thought of the blonde who'd stared him down today, the same woman whose image had distracted him from his work. A woman who seemed to want his attention but was so far out of his league, he knew not to touch her, either.

Slender body, eyes to drown in, and those legs. When she'd come out with her midriff bare and those white satin heels on, he could only think about taking her back inside and disposing of those clothes. Slipping off her shoes while she lay back watching him, anticipation running through them both.

A shiver of need spread over his skin. *Grace.*

He lowered his cheek to his arm, holding Libre in place with his gaze. What the hell was he thinking? A woman like Grace would never be with Miguel Torres, ranch hand, no matter if he called himself Mike Thompson or John Wayne. She was too cultured, too smooth, and no doubt too expensive for him. She could never be part of his world.

And yet, his gut ached like a horse had kicked him.

He wished she'd come out to paint that silly mural. Being around her for another ten minutes probably would have cured him of this...whatever he felt. Curiosity? Certainly not attraction, despite wanting her naked. A woman who'd leave her groom at the altar should repulse him.

But something about Grace called to him. Something about the expression in those dark blue eyes, the uncertainty, the yearning for approval. That need didn't fit with the kind of woman who jilted a man.

The contradiction made him uneasy. He didn't like puzzles, much preferring firm footing. Fortunately, he doubted he'd see her again, even if she remained until Wednesday for Rachel's birthday. He'd planned to just call Rachel, but now he wanted to assure himself in person that she'd returned.

Who was he kidding? He wanted to see Grace, which only proved how stupid he could be. If he didn't stop thinking about her, he'd try to figure out why she'd left the groom and why she looked so delicate under the blazing sun.

"I don't want to break your spirit," he whispered. Libre's ears twitched, but Mike's mind filled with the sunlight gleaming off Grace's hair. Her hesitant smile as she handed him that lemonade. The taste of the drink came back to him now, sweet yet sharp. Addicting, like the woman herself. He wanted more, despite the eventual stomachache.

He shook his head. "I won't hurt you. Trust me."

The mare twitched and trotted to the far end of her enclosure.

A skittish wild mare and a wary, fragile woman. Both would cause him trouble. He could feel it in his bones.

Despite knowing better, anticipation licked through him at the challenge they each presented. He turned toward the bunkhouse, a smile spreading across his face.

CHAPTER THREE

Grace climbed inside her car later that evening and engaged the lock, then glanced at the scruffy gang of boys hanging around the convenience store before checking her cell phone. The ringtone had sounded an incoming call as she stood at the cash register, but she hadn't wanted to stay in the store any longer than necessary. The sticky floor and strong smell of over-cooked corn dogs made her question her candy bar purchase. The gas station on the edge of town might not have been the safest choice with its potholes, loose gravel and seedy customers, but she'd needed gas. Unfortunately, the service at Speed-Ease had been neither fast nor easy. Unless "Speedy" owned the place, the sign totally lied.

She'd told Rachel she needed a drive to do some thinking, but she'd actually come out to escape Rachel's condemning gaze. How long before her cousin would demand she go back to Little Tree and face the consequences? Lexi and Jack needed time together, not her interference.

As she listened to Rachel's message on her phone, her confusion grew.

"It's Rachel. I can't meet you for that movie, after all. You'll have to go without me. I'm going to be busy at home for a few hours. I'll call you later, when I'm free to talk."

Grace frowned in bewilderment. What movie date? They hadn't had plans. If this was a code, Grace sure couldn't decipher it. She pulled out of the gas station, cursing as she hit a deep hole then bounced out of it only to hit another. The convertible's undercarriage scraped on the concrete.

Since the message said not to return to Rachel's for the time being, she headed away from town again toward the foothills. Did the bit about the movie mean someone had been listening?

Grace froze as, for a panicked moment, she wondered if Rachel had called her for help. Just as quickly, she dismissed the idea. Why would a burglar let her cousin make a phone call? The fake message only meant Rachel didn't want Grace to return while someone was there.

Her heartbeat stuttered. *Jack? Dad? Lexi?* No. Grace calmed her breathing. None of the family would drive all this way when they could call to ask if Rachel knew Grace's whereabouts. The visitor would turn out to be someone from Rachel's school or a neighbor, just come to visit.

Rachel saying she'd be busy for several hours provided a time frame for Grace to return. She could buy some sandals to replace her wedd—

A *thunk* had her gaze flying to the rearview mirror. Nothing came out from under the car and no animal or debris lay squished behind her. She exhaled with relief, hoping it had only been a small bump in the asphalt.

Rough through here, she noted, as her grip tightened on the steering wheel. The narrow road cut through fields of scrub and rock. Uneven and noisy, a repetitive *ka-thump* reverberated from the rear of the car. She glanced at the dashboard, relieved her gas gauge indicated Full. Thank God, she hadn't scraped a hole in the gas tank in that awful parking lot. A wire fence stretched along one side of the road, but she couldn't see whatever animals it enclosed. Cows and horses meant people to care for them, but how far away?

As she started uphill, the car wanted to pull to the left into the other lane. She fought the wheel, grateful there weren't any vehicles to worry about. Everyone must be home for Sunday dinner. Her stomach rumbled. The last car she'd seen had been at that rundown gas station. Had they watered down their product?

Resigned, she pulled over as far as she could onto the tiny strip of dirt that served for a shoulder before it fell away into a ditch. The other side of the four foot wide gully rose into a gradual slope. She couldn't see the top of the road.

But stepping out, she could see her rear tire almost flat against the road. Thank God she'd stopped before she destroyed the rim.

Grace fought to recall a mile marker or a recent sign of life. Nothing came to mind. She was stranded, and she feared Speedy owned the nearest tow truck. What if those hoodlums followed the tow truck out here to the middle of nowhere?

She'd have to change the stupid tire, provided she could remember her dad's lessons from a dozen years before.

First, open the trunk. Okay, she'd need a jack, and that lever thing to pump it. And something to remove the screws—or wait, wasn't that part of the pump handle thing? She seemed to recall that it was, even if she couldn't recall its name.

Grace didn't like standing behind the car as its nose pointed uphill. She'd need some rocks to shove behind the front tires to keep it from rolling. Looking around, she didn't figure finding rocks would be a problem, though hauling over a couple big enough to do the job might be.

It took her a good ten minutes to drag over enough

large rocks that she felt secure in jacking up the back end of the car and placing herself in close proximity to it. She dusted her hands together, pretty pleased with her work, and turned to drag the spare out of its cubbyhole.

The graying sky made her nervous. "Better get started."

Nervous enough to talk to herself, apparently.

After much swearing and smearing black rubber onto her clothes, she wrestled the spare tire out of the trunk and onto the gravel. She set the jack in place and turned for the lever. A jack handle! That was it.

"No wonder I couldn't think of it," she muttered as she pawed through the detritus in her trunk. "I never could handle Jack."

Her weak chuckle died. Where in the heck was that handle? Unease crept along her skin. She moved things she'd moved once already. Then twice, three times.

It simply wasn't there.

Grace kicked the flat tire and slumped against the car. Of all the stupid things to go missing. She took two full minutes to feel sorry for herself before straightening. This problem wasn't going to fix itself, and she didn't have the tools to fix it. She had a phone, though, and, yes, thank God, a signal. One bar, but she'd take it. She shouldn't call and disrupt Rachel's mysterious plans. Grace didn't have car insurance that would send a tow truck to find her on a Sunday night. Which meant Speedy and the thugs.

Unfortunately, she only knew one other person in the state. Calling Mike for help galled her, but she had his cell phone number. He would come to her aid as a favor to Rachel.

How would he feel if Rachel's coded message involved another man? How would *she* feel if Rachel's coded message had involved Mike?

"This is Grace Marshall." She listened to silence. Was the connection bad? "Rachel's cousin. We met earlier today."

"I remember."

His deep voice gave her a purely feminine chill. *Dammit.* She didn't want to be attracted to a man who didn't like her, especially if he had been or currently was her cousin's lover. Okay, maybe she could justify it if their relationship had ended.

"My car has a flat. Rachel has company at the house and can't answer the phone. I don't know anyone else..." She gritted her teeth and hoped he'd jump in with an offer to assist. She waited. No sound. Her pride wouldn't allow her to ask him for help, after all. And she definitely wasn't telling him about the missing car part. He'd condemn her as a typical useless blonde. "I could look up a mechanic's shop on my phone, but I don't know what's close by me or who to trust in this area." She waited a beat more. Stubborn man. "Do you know someone who can fix my tire?"

"Yes." Was that a sigh? "Of course. Where are you?"

He *would* have to ask that. "I left the Speed-Ease gas station and drove west for about fifteen or twenty minutes. It's a two lane road with a ditch on my side."

"You don't know where you are." His statement came out as flat as her tire and totally unsurprised.

She bit her tongue. One shouldn't yell at the person coming to save her. With a smile in her voice, she replied, "Of course I do. I'm west of the gas station, up in the foothills. The flatirons of Boulder are to the south, but I can't see them anymore. I might be past Lyons, but I don't think I'm in National Park lands yet. Do you need me to GPS it for you?"

A sound came she couldn't distinguish. A sigh? Teeth grinding?

"Stay inside your vehicle."

She scowled at the disconnected phone, wishing he could see her expression. Did he think she'd stand in the road, waiting to be run over like some stupid mule deer? Yanking open her car door, she said a few bad words about Mike What's-His-Name and his ancestry, just to get them out of her system before he showed up.

But he didn't.

Fifteen minutes later, a blue pickup truck with a yellow passenger-side door stopped behind her. Ten minutes after that, she followed Mike's brother to their house. Seemed he wouldn't get out of seeing her, after all.

Even a saint would forgive her for the smirk she wore.

"What are you doing here?" Mike couldn't believe Grace had come to his home. Wasn't it bad enough she'd invaded every thought that afternoon? After her call about the tire, he'd come home rather than remain at the bunkhouse, needing to hear of the incident directly from his brother.

Yet here she stood in the doorway, pretending to be uncertain, using her considerable charm on his gullible brother, Paul. Women like her were never uncertain. She knew that powder blue top fit her like a wet T-shirt and made a man's hands itch to unbutton it.

He scowled. Paul better not be thinking that—though who could blame him, green kid that he was?

"Mike," his youngest sister, Anita, admonished. "How can you be so rude?" She ushered Grace into the kitchen. "Just ignore my bear of a brother. Come and sit. Please."

Mike glared at her then turned to Paul. The almost-twenty-one-year-old had no doubt taken one look at Grace's curves and fallen for every word from her lips. Paul couldn't know the woman had dumped her groom at the church steps, breaking her promises. Knowing better, Mike still had to remind himself those alluring lips told lies, such as those to her groom. "I said change her tire, not drag her back home with you."

Paul glared, obviously not liking to be reprimanded in front of company. "I thought she was a friend of yours."

Grace stepped up close to him, but not so near she had to tip back her head. He could smell a trace of a thick flower scent like hyacinths or gardenias. The challenge in her eyes made his groin heavy.

"He didn't have to drag me," she said. "He invited me when he learned I couldn't return to Rachel's right now." Her gaze moved lower. Was she staring at his chest? Mike fought the urge to inhale, to puff out his upper body, and felt like an idiot.

"I can't go home." She picked her words as though tasting each one before releasing it. "Rachel has company. I hope I'm not imposing."

Hell, yes, you are.

Anita and Paul rushed to assure her of her welcome. "A relative of Ms. Rachel's is a friend to us," Anita said.

"How do you know my cousin?" Grace asked.

"Let's take our guest into the living room." Mike preferred that Grace continue to believe he and Rachel had been lovers. Perhaps it would curb any interest she had in him. He didn't need to be tempted into becoming a wealthy bride's rebound lover.

His mouth went dry. He could picture her in his bed, wild golden hair across his pillow, welcome in her eyes.

Oh, hell no. Mike pulled back. He wasn't getting caught up in her drama.

He ran his gaze over the living room as his siblings made a fuss over Grace, assuring she had a pillow for her back on the lumpy sofa. Though tidy, the shabby dark room needed an overhaul. A makeover, like on the shows Anita obsessed about.

He'd been meaning to get to it. Right after he finished paying for Robby's college and saved enough to send sixteen-year-old Anita to college next. Right after he helped Paul figure out what he meant to do with his life, and then financed the beginning of it. After he helped June pay for the renovations her house had needed to accommodate her husband Jimmy's wheelchair. After he made enough extra cash to buy some lumber for fences and a barn for that forsaken piece of land he had his eye on north of town. After he bought horses and hay and feed. Provided, of course, he could obtain a loan for the land in the first place.

Home improvement inched farther down on his priority list every day. Only Frank in New York City stood on his own feet, even sending money home on occasion. But given he lived in an expensive town and had an entry-level job and school loans, Frank's contributions to the family couldn't be counted on.

Mike hated for Grace to see the drab brown room. He'd been embarrassed enough for her to see his small house without her artist's eye assessing the lifeless interior. He didn't give it much thought other than its upkeep and cleanliness. The roof didn't leak, the appliances worked, they had power, water, and satellite TV. He and Paul helped Anita keep it clean.

It wasn't enough.

Clean and safe were adequate but not anything to take pride in. He saw that now, through Grace's eyes, even though she'd seated herself without comment. He'd thought he'd done a good job, providing a home for his six younger siblings. Now he could only see where he'd fallen short.

He wanted her gone. Away from here. Her bright perfection highlighted his deficiencies. Everything he'd built, accomplished, fought for, and made for his family jumbled up inside him. In her eyes, he felt common, and he wanted her far away.

She listened to Anita and he realized too late his sister had answered Grace's question. As Anita's third grade teacher, Rachel had tutored Paul. She'd also tutored Anita two years ago, helping her scrape by with a C average and advance to high school. Mike suspected Rachel hadn't charged them a proper fee, despite her taking on students to earn extra money. The family had done odd jobs for Rachel for the past several years to make up for her kindness. Even Paul would work without complaint for her. She still smoothed out Paul's English when he started talking ghetto like his worthless friends.

"So you and Rachel were never romantically involved?" Grace asked.

The kids laughed as though she'd mentioned the impossible. He shrugged. "I never said we were."

Her eyes narrowed, and despite wanting her gone, he enjoyed knowing she felt...something. She thought her cousin could have been his lover. Had she considered the possibility for herself? Did she find him handsome? Desirable?

He held her gaze, watched the annoyance fade from her expression. He let a smile curl his lips, reach his eyes. Paul and Anita remained oblivious to the byplay as Grace blushed. His body hardened.

Paul offered a toothy smile. "Big brother doesn't have time for a long-term relationship like Ms. Rachel would require because of us. But for the short term?" He shook his hand against his chest as though it were on fire. "Doubt he can remember them all."

"Paul." Mike stared down his brother. The little twerp liked to stir up trouble. "My brother's imagination is larger than any list of my dates."

Why did he need her to know that? Too late to haul the words back.

"I'll give you a pass on your dating record, as that's not anyone's business but yours."

The playful smile in her eyes made him want to capture it from her lips. He could imagine her playful in bed. He just wasn't going to find out.

"What are you doing in Longmont, Miss Marshall?" Anita asked.

Mike quirked an eyebrow at Grace. He couldn't wait to hear this answer.

She stared, as if daring him. Oh, she'd have to learn not to do that. If they were alone...

"It's something like a vacation," she said.

"A vacation?" Anita asked.

"What's that?" Paul shot Mike a look. "We've never been on one."

"I don't think that's true." Anita tilted her head as she did when puzzling something out. Mike didn't have to think about it. Another place he'd failed his family, and Grace had to witness Anita's realization. Dammit.

Paul crossed his arms over his chest in his usual chip-on-his-shoulder posture. "Name one place we went."

Grace watched the interplay as though she sat at a ping pong match, but warily, as though afraid of getting a ball in her eye.

"We went to the rodeo," Anita crowed. "Last year."

"We went to the rodeo grounds," Paul corrected, "because we had to pick up Libre. His wild horse," he added for Grace's benefit before turning back to his sister. "And we didn't get to go in and watch the rodeo."

"But we watched through the fence. We didn't have to help. It costs a lot of money to go in, and Mike needed it to board the horse."

"He always needs the money for something other than us. For something other than fun."

"Watch it, boy."

Paul's jaw clenched and his chin jutted out. "Deny that it's true."

"Have you gone hungry? Naked?" Mike dragged in a breath and turned to Grace. "I apologize. You didn't come here to listen to us argue."

Grace shot him an apologetic glance. "I was wrong to call this a vacation. I'm really here hiding from the rest of my family. I left my fiancé at the altar, and I don't want anyone to find me yet."

The kids' mouths dropped open and their eyes bugged out, making Mike wish for a camera in his hand. Dragging out his cell phone would jar them out of their momentary surprise.

"Oh," Anita said. "I'm so sorry to bring it up."

"That's so cool," Paul spoke at almost the same time. "Why'd you do it?" He had the grace to blush and rush on with, "Not that it's any of our business. But, wow. I mean, that takes guts."

Guts? As though this was an act to admire? What kind of mind-set was that? Mike hid his dismay behind a bland expression. His disapproval would only make the exploit more appealing to Paul.

Grace looked at her hands in her lap. "It wasn't easy."

Mike blinked, his mind a-whirl. He'd had a different picture of the event in his head, maybe Grace laughing as she zipped off in the sporty red convertible he'd seen in front of Rachel's house.

"We have brownies, if you're hungry," Anita said into the silence. "Or dinner. Gosh, I didn't even offer you anything. Were you stranded for long?"

"I'm fine, but thank you."

"She can't stay," Mike said at almost the same time.

Grace and Anita both glared at him.

"*Mike.*" His sister leaned hard on his name in reprimand. "It wouldn't be right not to feed her. *I* was brought up better than that. You were the one to teach me manners, though no one here would believe it."

"That's enough, Anita." His little sister could get wound up like a mustang, and all hell broke loose when she let her anger take the reins. Fortunately, it didn't happen often.

At the moment, she leveled him with wounded eyes rather than a kick to the teeth. She turned her shoulder to him and addressed Grace. "Would you care for something to eat or drink, Miss Marshall? I'd be happy to get you anything."

To give her credit, Grace hesitated before agreeing. She glanced in his direction, taking in his glower and body language that shouted for her to refuse. "I'd love a brownie, but let me come with you to get it."

They rose, tight as co-conspirators should be.

"My cousin doesn't keep chocolate in the house," Grace said. "She can't resist temptation."

Anita's eyes went wide and she commiserated as they left the room.

Movement from the corner of his eye had Mike looking

at his brother. Paul's shoulders shook. A hand covered his mouth.

"What?" Though Mike wasn't sure he wanted to hear it.

"Man," Paul said through his laughter, "you are so screwed."

"What are you talking about?"

"She ain't likely to give you the time of day, let alone...anything else."

Mike lowered his voice. "I'm not looking for 'anything else.' Not with her. Don't be saying that around her."

Paul's laughter cut off into a dark glower. "I ain't stupid. No matter how they treat me at work."

Not this again. "Don't let anyone treat you like you're stupid, Paul."

"They put me on nights with the morons. They think I can't do more than mop floors."

"Prove them wrong." How many times had he and Paul rehashed this conversation?

"Ain't no way to. I never see the bosses."

"Start with removing 'ain't' from your vocabulary. When you go to the office for your check, be especially polite. When—"

His brother jumped up. "I ain't bowing to nobody. It's enough I scrub their floors. I don't have to kiss their asses."

"Paul."

But he was gone, the slam of the door underscoring his youthful anger.

Mike closed his eyes and sent out a quick prayer that his brother wouldn't do anything dangerous tonight. As the truck engine gunned to life, he wondered whether Paul had money enough to buy any trouble.

Mike walked into the kitchen to find Grace and Anita

bent over Betty Crocker's recipes. "Did you pay Paul for his help?"

Grace drew upright, looking affronted. "Of course."

Anita's gaze met his. "Oh, no."

He nodded reassurance he didn't believe. "It'll be fine."

Grace looked between the two. "What's wrong? He did me a favor coming out and changing my tire."

"Mike?" Anita now shared her gaze with the outer door, watching for Paul to return.

"It's fine. Our brother," he told Grace, "sometimes has more emotion than sense."

"He'll buy beer," Anita said, her voice whispery with fear. "He's driving and he'll buy beer."

"He'll be fine." Mike doubted the truth of that, but Anita needed the words. Their brother-in-law, Jimmy, had been in a bad accident after drinking, winding up in a wheelchair. For a while, no one in the family had touched alcohol, as though the drink itself were the problem. "We were talking about him getting his paycheck. He probably just went in to work to see if his check is in his mailbox."

"He works nights," Anita said to Grace, "but not Sundays."

Grace frowned. "I'm sorry if I made things worse. I didn't know not to pay him for his kindness."

"You should never pay for kindness. It's a gift." Anita sounded older than the Rocky Mountains—and she was quoting him. Did he sound that ancient?

It took a while to pry Anita away from Grace, but after another fifteen minutes, he followed Grace out to her car. The night closed in around them. "I heard you say something to my sister about a recipe. You can just mail it. Rachel has our address."

"I don't mind bringing it. I'm pretty sure I can find my way back."

"It's more practical."

She narrowed her eyes. "You're uninviting me to your home."

He crossed his arms to combat the need to touch her. He should push her away, but he wanted to pull her close. He couldn't make up his damned mind. She couldn't become involved with his sister, especially making plans for the future. Anita took such things to heart and would be devastated when her "new friend" forgot, broke dates, and headed home to Montana without a backward glance. Grace had broken the most important promise she'd ever made. How could he trust her to keep her word to Anita?

Grace would be Trouble for him, not some one-night stand he could remember with a smile or forget if he wished. Being Rachel's cousin put her in a box marked *Do Not Open*. He had to make his position clear. "Don't make promises to my sister, Grace. Not about sharing family recipes. Not about anything."

"Is this because I gave Paul money?"

"It's because you don't keep your promises."

Her indrawn breath sliced sharp in the night air. "That's not true."

He steeled his resolve, not giving in to the hurt in her tone. The woman was a danger to his family in so many ways. "Isn't it? Go ask your fiancé for his opinion on that."

CHAPTER FOUR

Grace wandered into Rachel's house, stewing over Mike's words. Despite the twenty minute drive from his place and stopping to buy shoes and clothes, her anger hadn't abated. Maybe if he knew she'd jilted Jack to help Lexi, Mr. Family Man wouldn't be so fast to condemn her.

So, if she could rationalize his words away, why did they repeat in her skull like a jackhammer?

"Grace."

She turned at Rachel's call from the living room. "Sorry, I didn't see you there. How was your meeting?"

"Good." Rachel's lips curved. "Very good actually, but you'd better sit while I tell you about it."

Halfway across the room, Grace froze as a chill ran over her. "Why?"

"My visitor was Clint Walker."

Knees weak, Grace dropped onto the couch before turning to face her cousin beside her. "How did Jack's brother know I was here? Is he going to tell them?"

"Hold on. You've got hold of the wrong end of the stick."

"I do? Is that good news?"

Rachel see-sawed her hand back and forth. "A little good and bad. The good news is Clint doesn't know you're here."

"Then why did he come?"

Rachel shrugged. "He took a guess. A good guess, as it turns out."

"And here I thought you were having sex."

"What?"

Grace laughed at Rachel's surprise. "I didn't know it was *Clint* coming to see you. He's nice enough and great looking but not really your type."

Rachel's lips firmed as she withdrew. "Because he's younger."

"I hadn't thought of that, but yeah, now that you mention it, he's about five years younger than you. More my age."

"If it's not his comparative youth," Rachel asked, "why don't you think he's my type?"

Grace paused before answering. Her cousin's stiff tone took her by surprise. She didn't want to hurt Rachel's feelings. "He's living the bachelor life in Los Angeles, and he wants to be a professional landscape photographer. That's a very difficult profession. I can't imagine anyone less suited to living a quiet life in Longmont."

"By bachelor life, do you mean he's a player?"

Grace recalled what Paul had said about Mike's list of one-night stands. She couldn't believe it of either man. But she wasn't about to bring up Mike until she knew the extent of Rachel's feelings for him. She'd interfered with her sister's feelings for Jack; she didn't intend to do the same again with her cousin. "Knowing his brother, I doubt Clint is dishonest with women, but that doesn't mean hearts aren't broken. He's like Untamed Sex wearing boots."

Rachel's eyebrows rose. "You're attracted to him?"

"No, I just noticed because *I'm breathing*." She smiled. Rachel wouldn't consider bedding a guy without knowing him for a year and having met his family first. "Clint's still finding his way, building his career. Actually, he's deciding what career he wants. You're more steady."

"Steady." The word came out flat.

"Yeah, you've made your life here. You're dug in." Grace didn't want to talk about Clint as a prospective bed warmer, which *so* was not going to happen for either woman. "Anyway, forget him. You weren't having sex with some neighbor, and I'm sorry I thought so. Although, I'm also sorry it wasn't true."

"Grace." Rachel exhaled the word as a sigh. People did that a lot.

"Well," Grace needled her cousin, "it would be fun to watch you fall in love."

"Sex and love aren't always the same thing."

"They're not mutually exclusive either." Grace slowed her breaths, not wanting to give any importance to the question. "Are you dating a guy now?"

"Just Clint."

Grace relaxed at her cousin's joke. "Okay, fine, don't tell me about your love life. Why was he here?"

"He came looking for you. I didn't tell him you were here, of course."

"Thank you."

"Up until this point, I had been tempted to tell you to go back to Little Tree and face Lexi, Jack and Uncle Kevin."

Grace's stomach cramped just thinking about it. She hung her head and nodded. "I know."

"But."

Hope flared. Grace focused on Rachel. "But?"

"Clint's visit changed my mind."

Amazed, Grace considered the possibility. Unassuming Clint, practically a poster model for "Hot in Bed," convincing practical, composed Rachel about anything. Grace couldn't imagine it. "How?"

"He reminded me of the way Lexi looked at Jack when she said her vows."

"How did she look?"

"Like she meant them. Is that possible?"

Grace didn't know how to answer. Should she expose Lexi's feelings for Jack? No, she couldn't do that. If things didn't work out, Lexi would need her pride.

"It's crazy," Rachel continued, "to think their marriage might work out, but I want you to stay here. Give them a chance to figure this out. To see if there's a future for them."

Grace stared. Rachel wasn't sending her home? "You really think she looked like she wanted to marry him?"

"I thought it was you, remember? I was thrilled you'd found a man to put that look on your face."

The conversation had turned unbelievable, yet at the same time, gave Grace hope that she'd done the right thing. "What look?"

Rachel sat silent for a moment before nodding as though the right word had made itself clear. "Adoration."

"Really?" Relief swept through Grace. She'd helped her sister marry the man she adored.

"Yes, and I think you need to respect that. Give her a chance to see where it goes. I don't know how she wound up in your wedding dress, but Lexi's no pushover. If she hadn't had feelings for Jack, she wouldn't have gone through with the wedding, even to save you."

Grace couldn't reply without giving away her sister's

secret. "Okay, I'll stay. Thanks for putting me up, and putting up with me."

"Of course." Rachel hugged her. "You're always welcome here. Do you see the sense of leaving them alone?"

Grace nodded. "I hope it's the right thing to do."

"Well, you going back now won't help Lexi, not if she's trying to build a relationship with Jack."

"He knows it's her, not me?"

"Of course. She told him right away, according to Clint."

"Good. They must be giving marriage a shot." Grace crossed her fingers.

Rachel smiled and did the same. "We can only hope."

"To hell with him," Grace muttered as she stomped up to Mike's porch Tuesday afternoon. He didn't want her to visit, but she hadn't come to see him. She balanced the strawberry rhubarb pie on one palm and knocked. Hopefully she'd timed it so Anita would be home from school and Mike would be at work. She wasn't afraid to see him, but why poke the bull?

She'd waited a day, debating, then decided dithering made him too important. Her mind made up, she'd felt bold while baking, hoping he had a strawberry allergy.

The door opened. Anita's wide smile made the trip and the baking worthwhile.

After half an hour of testing the dessert and ruining their dinner, their friendship warmed like the pie had in the microwave. Anita clapped her hands with excitement at the idea of decorating the room Grace had reserved at a restaurant for Rachel's thirtieth birthday party the next afternoon.

"You don't think your brother will mind you helping?" Grace asked.

"No, Paul will help us, since he's coming to the surprise party anyway. He can do the heavy lifting." Anita leaned back in her chair. "Oh, you mean Mike and how he doesn't want us to spend time together. He won't mind, since it's for Miss Rachel."

Grace considered that. Mike seemed to make a lot of concessions for Rachel. Maybe he had feelings she didn't return. A crazy idea because what sane woman could resist—

She cut off the thought. "This would be better with homegrown fruit."

"The crust is amazing. You have a secret. I won't ask." Anita smiled then glanced at the plate. "I'm sure it's a family recipe you only pass among yourselves. It would be wrong for me to put you on the spot about it."

Grace suppressed a smile. "Thank you for understanding." When Anita's head jerked up, she couldn't help laughing. "That was pretty good, Anita. Does that trick work on your brothers?"

Anita grinned. "On Paul, always. On Mike, I'd say ninety percent of the time."

"Not bad, especially for so young a girl with no mother to teach you wiles. You show promise of becoming formidable."

Anita folded her hands in her lap. "It isn't proper for a lady to always ask for things. She should wait to be offered, and that way, shown respect."

Grace snorted. "Quoting from the Book of Mike?"

"He's no Miss Manners, but he tries."

"Right." Grace hesitated then came clean. "He doesn't want us to be friends. I think because I'm only staying a little while, he's afraid you'll be hurt when I have to go home."

"Well, that's stupid."

Grace almost fell off her stool with surprise.

"You're visiting your cousin," Anita said. "I'm old enough to realize that means you're leaving. Why shouldn't we be friendly in the meantime?"

"I can't think of a single reason."

"Then maybe you could give me a list of ingredients and a date when you can teach me to make this crust. You know" —the girl stopped to bat her lashes— "as a sign of friendship?"

Grace laughed. "We can swap recipes."

Anita's grin disappeared. "I don't have any. Mike didn't think to pack Mom's recipe binder when we moved. We just took clothes."

"Oh. I'm sorry." Feeling clumsy, Grace scrambled for an idea. "We'll find something on the internet to make together then."

They were still plotting when Mike and Paul came in the door. One of the men didn't look happy.

"Pie!" Paul reached for the knife before he even had a plate.

Anita swatted his hand. "Go wash up."

He looked pained but turned to the sink.

"What are you doing here?" Mike's tone conveyed curiosity instead of displeasure, but the tight set of his jaw spoke volumes.

"She brought us pie," Anita said. "Strawberry rhubarb."

Paul groaned as he brought down two plain white stoneware plates. He set one in front of his brother then cut a hearty wedge for himself.

"The pie is to thank you," Grace told Paul, "for helping me out the other night with my tire."

Mike folded his arms across his chest. "That wasn't

necessary. You already paid him."

The younger man flushed and ducked his head. "I appreciated the money."

"Hey." Grace laid a hand on his arm. "You came to my rescue. In olden days, I'd have given you a small plot of land in my father's kingdom. Today, I can only give you some paper with our forefather's picture on it."

Paul and Anita laughed.

"Now it sounds like you were cheated," Grace said.

"Trust me," Paul replied, "I know what to do with the paper. It's a much better reward."

"That's settled then." Grace turned to Mike. "I'm surprised to see you here so early."

"I have to head back out. I only took a break at work to bring the kid home."

"Here." Anita shoved a forkful of pie toward Mike, who instinctively opened his mouth. His face softened as he savored the sweetness. Grace's chest nearly burst with pride.

"I was working at the ranch today." Paul held out his hands, bent at the fingers. "Filly about pulled my knuckles off fighting the rope."

"I told you," Mike said, "you can't yank them around like they're little red wagons."

"I never had a toy wagon," Paul taunted his brother.

"Do you want me to make a plate for you?" Anita cut off Mike's response. "I made stew. It should be okay if you warm it up a bit."

Mike glanced from Anita to Grace, and scowled.

"He can't stay." Paul wore a pleased smirk as he leaned against the table. "Taking time out of his day to drive me home was inconvenient enough." He also obviously quoted his brother. The Book of Mike was a tough read. It would never hit a bestseller list.

"Why didn't you drive your own truck?" Anita asked as she lifted the pot's lid. Thick luscious scents almost made Grace's knees buckle. She peeked in at beef, carrots and potatoes in a gravy so glossy it looked like caramel sauce. She couldn't remember the last time she'd had stew. Would Mike invite her to stay to dinner?

Fat chance.

"Got towed," Paul said. "I worked for Mike today because I needed the fast cash to go get it out."

"I can give you a ride into town on my way," Grace offered.

As one, the family glanced at the clock over the harvest gold refrigerator. "Four-thirty," Mike read with some satisfaction.

"Oh, man," Paul groaned. "I got towed in Lakewood. I checked already. The police station will process me 24/7, but the impound yard is in Denver. It closes at five, way past the time we have to drive down, go through the paperwork in Lakewood, then get down to the tow lot." Paul's shoulders fell. "Thanks anyway, Miss Marshall."

"Can you stay to eat with us?" Anita asked her. "Just because Mike won't be here doesn't mean you can't enjoy some stew."

Grace almost laughed at the consternation on Mike's face. He didn't want to leave her with the kids nor could he stay and guard them. Did he regard her as some wicked witch? Just for spite, and because she sincerely liked the kids, she agreed.

"And you can make out that list for me," Anita said.

"What list?"

The suspicion in Mike's tone made Grace want to

smack him. She smiled sweetly. "Arsenic, hemlock, and wart of toad."

Anita chuckled. "Miss Marshall is going to teach me to make this amazing pie, just like her mom used to make it."

Did Mike's glower mask his worry over the cost of extra groceries? Grace sought to allay his concern. "I'm sure you have everything in your kitchen already. We'd just need the fruit."

"We'll see," Anita said, "once you list the ingredients."

"Anita," Mike said, "scoop me a bowl to go please. Grace, I'd like to talk to you privately. Would you step outside with me?"

She nodded but he'd turned and walked out, assured she would follow his suggestion. "Should I bring my six-shooter?"

Paul, at least, thought it was humorous.

Mike didn't stop on the porch, or the steps, or the near yard. He stalked to his truck, parked halfway to the road behind hers. A quick pivot on his heel had her stumbling back a step. "What are you doing in my house?"

"Bringing a pie to your family." She tried to match his scowl but couldn't possibly make her face that disagreeable. "She understands I'm leaving soon. There's no reason we can't be friends in the meantime. I like her."

"Great. Then stay away from her."

"That's not very nice."

"I don't care." He looked across the horizon and swore. "I didn't mean that. But I asked you to stay clear of my family the last time you were here."

"No, the last time, I very distinctly remember you said don't make her promises."

"Well, hell, Grace, what do you call what you just did?"

"I'm making a date to bake with her."

"That's the kind of promise I meant."

Grace nodded. "I never agreed. You just assumed I would follow orders." She showed her teeth in a smile. "Seems like I don't."

Before she could blink, his hands gripped her upper arms, and he leaned so near her, she could have counted his eyelashes. If she had the time. He had lovely thick lashes.

"Listen to me. You're going to go in the house and remember a previous engagement." He sneered. "Oh wait, an *engagement* wouldn't stop you from doing whatever you wanted."

Grace refused to rise to the bait, although kicking him in the shin had its merits.

"Let's say you're having your nails done. I doubt you'd *run out* on that."

He'd be lucky if she didn't run her nails down his face. "No."

That stopped his nasty tirade. "What?"

"No," she repeated. "I won't cancel on Anita."

"I don't want you here."

Pain sliced through her and she lost her breath. Lost her ability to speak. Tears pricked her eyes, and she blinked them away.

His words hurt more than she would have imagined. More than his hands tight on her arms. More than the intensity of his dark brown eyes.

"I don't care what you want," she said, forcing her voice to remain steady. "Did you ever think maybe Anita needs a woman to talk to?"

His face fell slack with surprise but his hands didn't loosen. He stared into her face, emotion rising dark under his skin.

"Damn you." Then his hands yanked her close and his mouth landed on hers. It wasn't a gentle kiss. It could barely be called a kiss but more of a punishment for saying the one thing he couldn't fight against.

She tasted sweat, strawberry, rhubarb, and Mike. Undertones flavored the kiss as it stretched on. Resentment, dislike. Hunger.

Grace didn't want to feel anything, but dammit, his kiss stirred her. Her legs shook and she clung to him. She responded to his primitive-level intensity, to a male protecting his clan. To his sheer masculine allure. To Mike.

He thrust her at arm's length, his gaze scouring her face before his hands opened. Stepping back without losing eye contact, he found the door handle and climbed in his truck. She didn't stay to watch him drive away from her.

"I didn't want a celebration."

"Tough." Grace pushed Rachel into the back room of Vincenzo's, the Italian restaurant Rachel frequented. She pasted on a smile as people applauded. Anita had tied balloons to some of the chairs and Paul had strung streamers. White LED lights trailed across the ceiling, adding to the restaurant's intimate lighting for their party room. Festive, fun and still classy, the decorations fit Rachel's personality.

"You'll smile and enjoy yourself," Grace warned her without moving her lips from their fixed smile.

Somehow Paul, Anita and Mike had helped spread the word so that the small space now filled with teachers, friends, and neighbors. A surge of satisfaction swept through Grace as Rachel relaxed. A brown-haired male handed them both white wine. When Rachel laughed at something he said, Grace eased away to give them room to talk.

"She looked surprised."

Grace stiffened at Mike's presence beside her. She'd hoped to avoid him for the few hours of the party. His kiss had replayed in her dreams—or rather, her nightmares. "I can keep a secret."

He sighed. "It was a compliment. Let me try again. You look very nice tonight."

"Thank you." She shook her head at herself. "I thought maybe you'd stay on your own side of the room."

He cocked his head. Maybe he thought of this as neutral ground. Grace couldn't get his words out of her head. She'd begged off eating stew with the kids the evening before but had promised to bring the ingredients with her for pie on Saturday. And Mr. "I Don't Want You Here" could just shove his bad opinion and his great kiss.

"I appreciated Anita and Paul helping with decorations this afternoon. Did you know about that?"

"They told me."

After the fact, she'd bet, and she'd lay odds he hadn't liked it. Or maybe doing something for Rachel was allowed, despite Grace's involvement. "I made sure Rachel saw your gift since we couldn't bring it along."

"She hadn't seen the shed yet?"

"She didn't know anything was behind the garage."

"Did she like it?"

Grace relaxed a bit and gave an exaggerated eye roll to emphasize her point. "She's delighted. I'm sure she'll tell you herself. I have a picture of her face when she first saw it. Remind me to show you, or I could text it to your phone if you'd like."

His eyebrows lifted. "That was thoughtful of you."

Jerk. He didn't have to sound so surprised. She took a

sip of her wine so she could form a calm reply. "I can be thoughtful. It takes a lot of effort, of course."

"I didn't mean it that way." He took a calming breath. "Did you paint your mural on it?"

"No, I gave her a preliminary sketch as a present. I can't just slap a painting together. Now that she knows, I can paint without hiding from her." She smirked. "So the shed is just from you."

"From my family." He put his hand on her arm. "I didn't mind if you wanted to paint your horses on it."

Paint her horses? Grace almost laughed. He didn't know her reputation and hadn't seen her work, so she forgave him. After all, he sounded just like everyone in Little Tree, except her family.

She shrugged his hand off. His touch reminded her of that bone-shaking kiss the night before—the kiss she daydreamed about. "Just what is your problem? From the first moment, you've had a burr up your backside. Right after you found out I left Jack." She stopped, the light dawning as a cold ball knotted in her stomach. "Is that the problem? Did some woman jilt you?"

"No."

Grace didn't welcome the relief that washed over her. It implied she was concerned for his feelings, and she didn't need that complication.

"I've never been engaged." Mike scowled. "Though I don't know why I'm telling you that."

"Do I physically remind you of some woman who hurt you? Some blonde who didn't keep her word?"

"Nothing happened to me, but yes, breaking your word is a worry. I have to think of Anita and Paul."

"I won't break my word to either of them." *Or you,* she

wanted to add.

He shrugged. "Things happen, sometimes out of our control."

She stared for a moment. He didn't say she'd be careless with Anita's feelings, but Grace heard the words nevertheless. It hurt, despite being unspoken. She refused to let his silent accusation make her cry.

His gaze met hers, and his eyes darkened. He leaned close. "That doesn't mean we couldn't...have dinner sometime."

So he didn't consider her a danger to himself?

Mike leaned closer, a hair's breadth from her lips. His gaze held her spellbound, wanting to fall into their depths. "I find you very attractive."

His declaration thrilled her, God help her, and she tamped down that traitorous emotion. How could she feel so many things toward the man?

He'd already shown how he truly felt, and she wouldn't put her heart at risk. Being attracted to him was daunting enough. Part of her wanted to say yes, to enjoy him while she visited Colorado. Since she planned to go home in a few days, "dinner" with him didn't sound that threatening.

But she knew better. She couldn't afford a gamble like Mike Thompson.

Summoning up enough backbone to resist temptation, she said, "Look, Mike, we don't get along very well. Why don't we agree not to antagonize each other on Rachel's birthday, okay?"

She could feel his gaze on her as she walked away. For once, she'd rejected him. It should have made her feel victorious.

She only felt hollow.

CHAPTER FIVE

Grace spent three days painting Rachel's gift on canvas. She often thought of Anita but resisted the urge to call her. Not usually one to follow orders, Grace tried to respect Mike's place as the head of his family.

On the other hand...

His worry about her and Anita being friends was so off-base, she couldn't take him seriously.

By Saturday morning, she'd had enough. She slapped the kitchen table, making her coffee cup tremble. She'd like Mike to tremble.

Better yet, she'd like to forget how his angry kiss had made her tremble and shiver, though not with fear. Despite his rough hands, he hadn't hurt her or left a mark. While she didn't appreciate man-handling in general, she'd thrilled to his controlled passion. Images of him losing that control in the midst of another kind of passion had disrupted her sleep. She hadn't forgotten his kiss nor forgiven his words.

By God, the man couldn't have it all his own way. He had no authority over her. That kiss had meant nothing to him other than an outlet for his exasperation. And maybe some lust.

A smile grew across her face as she imagined taunting him. And nothing would drive him crazier than her spending time with Anita, whom she genuinely liked. Grace had meant what she told him about the girl needing female company. Though he wouldn't consider her a role model, Mike couldn't deny she was female.

Maybe she'd do a makeover on Anita. That ought to twist his testicles.

Not testing her luck, Grace started by taking pie fixings to Mike's house. Her little car climbed the narrow roads while rough scrub pushed through the hard-packed dirt on either side. Although glad of the air-conditioning, she considered lowering the top on her convertible for the ride home. It would still be hot in the sun, but the freedom of the wind whipping across her skin excited her. Her hair would be a mess but it wasn't as though she had a date later.

As a matter of fact, she was off of men until she got her head on straight. Jack's pursuit had been exhilarating. Her marriage proposal to save his land and then jilting him to clear the way for her sister had both been out of character. If she'd stopped to think, she wouldn't have done either. Being impulsive had led her into trouble. Again.

From now on, she'd think before she acted. Right after she gave Anita a baking lesson and ticked off Mike.

She pulled into the yard and the house door flew open. "I didn't think you'd come," Anita said.

"Why is that?" Grace piled groceries into the girl's arms.

"Mike said you were busy with a painting for Miss Rachel."

Grace hid her grimace. The jerk had banned her from his house then blamed her for not showing. "Well, here I am. I brought makings for two kinds of pies. Since two large men live with you, I figured two pies would give you a fighting chance for having a slice."

Anita grinned. "Oh, I have places to hide the things I want to keep to myself."

"I imagine you've had to develop some survival techniques." Grace stepped into the house. How many other strategies did the girl employ to endure living with an overbearing father figure and an immature boy who worried the family to pieces?

For the next thirty minutes, they mixed the dough, then ate the fruited chicken salad Grace had brought, and talked fashion. Anita absorbed every feminine trick and tip that Grace imparted. Flattered by the attention, Grace added makeup tips for Anita's complexion and gorgeous dark coloring. "You could be a model."

Anita snorted as she set cheesecloth on the counter. "Mike would have a heart attack. Then he'd lock me in my room and brick the house closed."

Grace laughed. She liked having a younger friend and listened a little too avidly while Anita filled her in on the other siblings.

"Robby is my next older brother. He's almost nineteen, at college in Bozeman. Is that near you?"

"Not close, but in Montana, distance is relative. In good weather, we could drive there in a few hours."

Anita nodded as she rolled out the dough. "I'd like to see Robby. He has a job and won't be coming home this summer. Frank—he's next older after June—he could make it in less time probably. He drives real fast. Or he did, but now he's in New York City, and doesn't even have a car. His twin is a speedster, too. I mean, she'd have to be, to compete with him."

Grace chuckled, distracted from keeping track of the family names. "No joking? I'm a twin."

Anita stopped rolling. "You're kidding me."

"No, really. My sister, Lexi, is a veterinarian."

"Did you two compete over everything?"

Grace dropped some flour on the round for her. "Watch that sticky spot there. You don't want to tear the crust. It can be pinched back together or patched, but it's better to do it smoothly."

Anita nodded, her concentration intensifying.

"And no, we didn't compete. Maybe because we were each other's best friend. I was jealous, though, when she and a classmate named Carrie Moore started hanging out together. I competed with Carrie, trying to be more important to Lexi. Which is silly. Who can be closer than your own twin?"

Except a husband. Grace hoped Jack could be Lexi's new best friend—or, she amended, her Lexi's new best, non-blood-related friend.

"My sister Ceeley—I mean, Lilly, that's what she changed her name to— is trying to be an actress." Anita wiped her eye on her shoulder. "She doesn't stay in contact with us, only with Frank. Then he calls June. She's our sister whose husband was in the car wreck and is now in a wheelchair. Do you remember we mentioned them?"

Grace nodded, though her head spun with all the names. She'd given money to Paul, and Anita had gone pale to think of him drinking and getting in a wreck.

"June calls me or Paul with news, so if Lilly ever asks, June can say she didn't call Mike. But everyone in the family understands we're going to tell him. Still, it's a sad way to keep in touch when you have the same parents."

"Let's see if I can get this right," Grace said to distract the girl. "Mike's the oldest. Then June?"

Anita nodded like a proud teacher. Distraction

accomplished.

"Then…?"

"Frank and Lilly. Frankie by eight minutes and seventeen seconds."

Grace chuckled. "I'm older, too, and my sister and I can both tell you by how much. Okay, that's four. Then Robby—no, Paul, then Robby and you?"

Anita nodded. "We're a big bunch. Like a circus, Mamá would say."

"Do you remember your mom?" Grace figured out Anita had been six when her parents passed.

The girl sobered. "Some. We have a few pictures, so I can keep her in my head. But she's always in my heart." The girl put a floury fist to her chest.

"I know exactly what you mean. My mom died when I was a girl. Older than you, but her absence always hurts."

Anita nodded. "You're lucky to have memories, and I'm lucky to have such a big family. Especially Mike. I don't know what would have happened to us without him."

Grace's chest ached. Memories. That was all her mom had left her with. She wasn't there when Grace had been a teen, finding her way in the adult art world. A young girl whose good looks had been trickier to deal with than the harshest comment from an art show judge. She'd had Lexi, going through the same thing, but no Mom.

The afternoon sped by. As she drove home, Grace wondered what she could do to make Mike realize she was no threat to Anita.

Threat? The word brought her up short. Jilting Jack didn't mean she'd hurt Anita. Who was Mike really worried about? Himself?

Or was she projecting her own feelings? Because Mike

could hurt her, deeply. His words had wounded more than her pride. She already felt more for him than she'd ever felt for her ex-fiancé.

Grace walked into the house and heard Rachel's voice. Her cousin spoke quietly but clearly. No one replied in the pauses, so she must be on the phone. Grace eased the outer door closed, her heart pounding. Was it someone in Little Tree calling?

"I'm having a baby," Rachel said. Then a little metallic click as she set the phone on the table.

Grace could barely breathe. A baby? *Mike's* baby? She eased into the room to see Rachel on the couch, head bent.

"You're having a baby?"

Rachel swung around, tears on her cheeks, a hand to her breastbone in surprise. "Oh, crap, Grace. I didn't know you were home."

Grace walked over and pulled Rachel into a hug. "Are you happy about it? Because you don't look happy."

Rachel shook her head but didn't pull away. "I'm very happy."

They made it to the couch, arms around one another. Grace wasn't sure who was bracing up whom. She felt as unsteady as Rachel. "Who is it? Was that him on the phone? Is he—?"

"Wait." Rachel mopped at her tears with a tissue she pulled from the box on the coffee table. "First, there is no guy."

Grace's stomach sank. She clenched her teeth to hold back the swearing going on in her head. Some sonovabitch had knocked her up and left her? Cussing wouldn't help, and if Rachel got back together with the jerk later, harsh words now could drive a wedge between the two cousins.

But Grace knew Mike wasn't the father. Mr. Family Man would never walk away from his child or the woman bearing his baby. If he knew about it.

"I'm no biology expert," Grace said in an attempt to lighten the mood, "but I'm pretty sure there has to be a guy in this equation. No guy, no sperm. No sperm, no baby."

"You're so old-fashioned." Rachel's tears had dried.

"Alien technology?"

"Sperm donor."

"Ah." Grace thought about it for a moment. If her cousin wanted a baby but didn't have a guy in her life, Rachel would consider a practical solution like this. And if she'd considered it, she'd probably researched and planned it all out. Given what she'd said on the phone, she'd implemented it. Successfully. The only question left was, "Why now?"

Rachel shrugged. "I'm thirty. I have a steady job and money saved up. I don't have a man in my life. The last couple of guys made me lonelier than being by myself."

"I think we've dated the same guys."

"So you know. Sometimes a man isn't the answer."

"But a baby is?"

"For me, anyway." Rachel took Grace's hand. "I'm ready for the next stage in life."

"Motherhood?"

"Yes."

"It's going to be harder to find a husband once you're a single mom."

Rachel shook her head. "If the right man comes along, it won't matter. No, I take it back. If the *right* man comes along, he'll be thrilled to be a dad to my child."

Yeah, right. "It'll be harder to date to find that right man."

"Then I won't date. Being single isn't the end of the world."

"Have you thought this through?"

"For about two years. First, it was just a 'what if.' What if I have a baby? What if I stop dating around and start living the life I really want?"

Grace squeezed her cousin's fingers. "And single mother is the life you want?"

Rachel stood, paced a few steps, then turned. "No, of course not. I'd like to be in love. I'd like a man to love me forever. Someone to build a family with. But that man isn't here." She gestured to the room before letting her arm fall against her thigh. "I can't wait forever for Price Charming to come along. I want to start my life now."

"What about that guy the other night?"

Rachel turned away.

Interesting.

"That was Clint Walker," Rachel said. "He came looking for you."

Hope of a romance deflated. "Oh, right."

"I'm doing this on my own." Rachel sat beside her again. "I've saved for the insemination and put away money for childcare. If I get pregnant by the end of July, or the beginning of August at the latest, I can take maternity leave at the end of the next school year."

"So you're not pregnant yet?"

Rachel shook her head.

Could Grace talk her out of this crazy plan? Should she? Was it even crazy if it made Rachel happy?

No one ever looked to Grace as the voice of reason. The very idea made her laugh. She'd never had this kind of responsibility thrust upon her. Lexi was good at this stuff.

But Lexi wasn't here.

Grace held up her hands and counted on her fingers. If Rachel got pregnant when she planned to—and if anyone could do it, Rachel could—the baby would come in May. School would probably end in June. Six weeks of maternity leave would probably see her through the end of the school year. She might have to take an extra week of sick leave, but it was doable. "Then you'd have the first two or three months of its life off work next summer."

Rachel nodded. "I had a family from Lyons stay here after the big flood destroyed their home. Their middle daughter graduates from high school next June. She's happy to have a job lined up."

"Is she experienced?"

"Very. She saved up for her first two years of tuition by babysitting, all while still paying for her own movies, clothes, and stuff like that. That's a lot of experience."

Grace gave a low whistle. "Impressive. And after the college year starts?"

"She had planned on going to community college while she figures out her major. If I get pregnant, she's going to look into night classes."

"You've been planning."

Rachel blew out a breath. "This isn't a whim, Grace. I've got leads on live-in nannies. I've looked into local childcare facilities that take infants, though I'm leaning toward a couple of women who have home-based care."

"Okay."

Rachel had the practical aspects covered or at least set up as best she could this early in the process. What about the emotional aspects? "Are you prepared to raise a child alone?"

"I have to be. No one wants to be a single parent, but

I'm trying to get my ducks in a row the best I can."

"Your ducks are fine, sweetie. I'm thinking about the rest of you."

"I don't imagine it's going to be easy." Rachel put a hand flat on her chest. "But it feels like it's the right time. This is what I'm supposed to do. Now is when I'm supposed to do it."

Grace thought for a second before engulfing her cousin in a hug. To hell with being practical. Sometimes a woman just had to follow her heart. "Then I'm happy for you. I don't have my life as organized as yours, but whatever I'm doing next year, I promise you at least a week of help."

Rachel chuckled. "You sound more terrified than I am."

Too true. Like the character from *Gone With the Wind,* Grace didn't "know nothing 'bout birthing babies" or about caring for them. But she figured she could live through helping for a week. "Okay, then. What's the first step?"

Rachel burst with laughter. "Well, that'll be up to the sperm. I'll let you know when I need you."

A reprieve. Grace tried not to show her relief. Hoping for a negative answer, Grace offered, "Do you want me to go with you and...you know, hold your hand?"

Rachel bit her lip, eyes dancing with laughter. "Are you sweating?"

"Probably. But I'll be there for you, Rach, any way you want."

Rachel pulled her into a hug. "Come back next year with diapers and chocolate."

Maybe in that amount of time, Grace could sell a few extra paintings and hire someone for the actual childcare. Then Grace would come with donuts and pamper the new mom. Manis and pedis were more in her ballpark.

***

Grace jumped as someone pounded on the front door Friday night. She looked at Rachel, who shrugged.

"I'll step into the kitchen, just in case." Grace grabbed her purse. She needed to make another run to the store for chocolate bars so if this meeting went long, she wanted to be ready.

"It's probably the newspaper carrier, collecting."

"Call me if there's trouble."

Rachel smiled. "My carrier is fourteen. I think I can take her."

Grace slid into the kitchen, staying close to the doorway. The door opened and a male voice rumbled. Not the papergirl then.

"This is quite a surprise, Clint." Rachel's voice came loud and clear.

Clint? Was he *still* looking for her? Grace hadn't known bloodhound traits ran in his veins. She sidestepped to the outer door. Rachel offered everyone drinks, and Clint might become suspicious if she didn't. Though he wouldn't know that, would he? Grace shook her head. Adrenaline made her thinking fuzzy.

The outer door creaked as she pulled it open, and she froze, heart pounding. When no one came to investigate, she slipped outside and eased the door shut behind her. The latch hitting the jamb reverberated in her ears like a gunshot, though she knew it was only her guilty conscience.

Thankfully, Clint had parked his rental car on the street, leaving the driveway clear. Now she only needed to back her convertible out of the garage and clear the window view before he saw her. The open garage door gave her a moment's pause. If he'd walked around to the side of the house, he would have spotted her car. While she didn't doubt she could get away, she didn't want to reveal her whereabouts or put Rachel on the spot, having to answer questions.

She blessed her quiet motor and put the car in neutral to let gravity take her down the driveway. With an eye on the house, she shifted to reverse and inched away from. No movement at the front window. The door remained closed. With a sigh of relief, she headed out to...

Good question. Candy bars didn't that long to buy. She could have dinner and bring back carryout for Rachel. Grace pulled over on the next block and counted her cash. Fifty-eight dollars and change. Looked like those candy bars wouldn't have to be her dinner, after all, and she could buy something healthy for Rachel. But she worried over her shortage of cash.

Turning on her phone, she called galleries exhibiting her work. Two hadn't sold a painting of hers recently, but the third had sold one that morning. If she hadn't been sitting in her car, she'd have collapsed with relief. "That's great news, Mr. Willard."

"Not really, Ms. Marshall. It was the smaller piece, *Ayers Rock at Dawn.* It brought just under the list price, but more than your stated minimum."

Grace couldn't be bothered to care. She couldn't use her ATM or credit card without Lexi finding her. She had money saved toward building an artists' retreat, but she couldn't access it. "I understand. Do you think that buyer would be interested in the Mala Walk series if I drop the price a bit? Bundle it and offer him a deal?"

"Ms. Marshall." He sounded scandalized. "I'm sure we can get full price for the other Ayers Rock paintings. Your perspective is unique and—"

"Yes, thank you, Mr. Willard. See, the thing is, I need

the money."

Humiliating silence thrummed through the line. *How the mighty are fallen.* May as well get it over with. "Have you sent my check to the bank?"

"Not yet. However, I will do so immediately."

"Thank you, Mr. Willard, but can you mail me a cashier's check or, better yet, wire me the money?"

Once Grace convinced the man to help her in "this highly irregular" exchange, she felt more able to deal with the problems at hand. Money always eased the road. She could get candy bars and dinner, then takeout for Rachel. Clint shouldn't be there long. Rachel just had to convince him she hadn't seen or heard from Grace. He wouldn't need to linger after that. Half an hour, tops.

Grace splurged on several varieties of candy bars to replenish her stock, then took the bag into the restaurant so the chocolate wouldn't melt while she enjoyed nachos carnitas with the works and honey-covered sopaipillas for dessert. The sale of her sunrise painting deserved a celebration, though Grace mourned the loss. She half-hoped the Mala Walk paintings wouldn't sell for cheap. Though it was stunning, viewing Ayers Rock from a distance had left her unmoved artistically. Spending time studying and painting it, however, had sent thrills through her veins like jingle bells on Christmas Eve. She'd had trouble enough leaving the paintings at the gallery. Imagining them stuck on a wall in someone's home depressed her.

So she concentrated on the money and hoped for more sales. Next time, she wouldn't ask the gallery owners which piece had sold. If there had to be a next time. Hopefully, she'd be heading back to Little Tree before she had to make another embarrassing phone call.

Speaking of which, she pulled out her phone to text Rachel and ask what she wanted Grace to bring for dinner. Maybe she'd head to the Albertson's grocery store and spend last twenty-eight dollars on milk and vegetables for Rachel.

A text returned almost immediately. STILL HERE. COME AT TEN.

Ten? Where did Rachel imagine Grace would go for another three hours? And *why* would Clint take three hours to leave? Had Lexi or Dad been in an accident? Jack? Surely, if something had happened to someone in the family, Rachel would have texted the information. Grace would rush home to Little Tree and deal with the fallout of jilting Jack.

She took a breath. Rachel would have said so. She would have called or texted the minute Clint told her. It wouldn't be Jack because Clint would have gone straight to Little Tree, which left— No. She couldn't think that way. Everything was fine. Everything had to be fine.

As a distraction, Grace sat in a dark movie theater with a horror movie playing. Summertime limited her choices to slasher films or teenage-boy-humor. Not that she saw enough to be frightened. Her own imagination of trouble at home scared her more than a maniac with a sharpened screwdriver.

Grace checked her phone as soon as the credits rolled. The one text from Rachel chilled her blood more than the screwdriver-wielding psycho or anything from her imagination.

CLINT STAYING HERE. MIKE'S EXPECTING YOU.

If she had two cents to her name, Grace thought as she pulled into Mike's drive, she'd be anywhere but here. But no, she'd run away from home without a plan.

The Thompson's house door opened while she stewed. A rectangle of light shown around a tall masculine figure. If she was lucky, it would be the screwdriver-wielding psycho.

"Grace?" Mike called.

Luck was never on her side.

"Why are you sitting in the car?"

She waved then grabbed her purchases from the seat beside her. No way could she face tonight without chocolate.

"Hi. Thanks for letting me come by." She approached the wooden steps with all the enthusiasm of a French aristocrat climbing the gallows to greet Madame Guillotine.

"Rachel arranged for you to stay the night." His tone exuded all the warmth of the masked Executioner.

"I'm sorry to impose." *I've got to meet some new people here.* She didn't want to admit why she couldn't use her credit card for a motel. "If I had another option, I wouldn't dream of asking you for a favor." She winced. "Sorry, that was rude."

A rumble came from Mike and she waited for him to cart her back to her convertible. When the sound broke out of him, it was laughter. Deep, from the belly, genuine amusement. She relaxed, glad he found humor in her gaffe.

"I'm glad we can be honest with each other. You don't want to be here anymore than I want you here."

CHAPTER SIX

Grace stopped short, breath leaving her as though he'd delivered a physical punch to her stomach. Tears pricked at the corners of her eyes and she blinked, grateful for darkness. Feeling like the dirtiest beggar, she ducked her head. "I'll try to stay out of your way."

"Just stay out of Anita's." He held open the door and waved her into the house. A single lamp cast a faint yellow glow from the corner, leaving most of the path a brown mystery. He pointed to the couch and left her to its lumpy solitude.

She would not cry. Would not.

Half an hour after she heard the last sound from the house, she crept outside to her car. The yard provided the safest parking spot she knew other than Rachel's house, and she wasn't likely to sleep anyway. She had chocolate. What else could a girl want?

Because, by God, she wasn't staying in that man's house for even one night. When daylight broke—and she'd probably be the first to see it—she'd be out of there.

Ten minutes of adjusting the seat didn't provide comfort. She moved to the passenger seat, hoping the lack of steering wheel would allow her to curl up or stretch out. It would lessen the temptation to start the vehicle and drive home. "Home" in this case meant Montana where she longed for her sister's smile and her father's embrace.

The house door opened, darkness spilling into darkness. Grace tensed and rechecked the locks.

In a few long strides, Mike stood by the driver side door. He had to bend in half to peer inside. They stared at one another for a few moments. "What are you doing in there?"

Since the answer was obvious, Grace said, "Go away."

He stared a little longer.

She stared back.

A thin waning moon disturbed the black of night, making his features indistinguishable. She read his stillness and interpreted it as anger. He wouldn't like being thwarted.

Mike stood upright but didn't move away. Now she gazed at his ribs, the loose, half-buttoned shirt over his muscular abs, the zipped but unsnapped jeans. The view annoyed her and she figured he'd done it on purpose. She sat braced, ignoring the shadows across his abdomen, ignoring that zipper. Ignoring her imagining of what lay beneath.

Even angry with him, she had to admit he made a glorious specimen. She let herself off the hook. As an artist, every aspect of her being responded to his male beauty. One could admire the strength of a lion without wanting to cuddle with it. Okay. Better. He was just...gorgeous. That didn't mean she had to like him.

"Unlock the door."

She jumped. He hadn't moved; he hadn't yelled. What would he do, yank her out? Tear apart her roof? She unlocked the doors.

Mike folded himself inside, and she wished she hadn't left the seat so far back. Watching him struggle into the cramped space would have given her an edge. *My car, my rules*. He looked at her in the overhead light, gaze roaming her eyes to her lips. Still watching her, he shut the door.

She waited for his argument, but he didn't speak. Their eyes adjusted back to the darkness and features blurred. Sight diminished, her sense of smell took over. The clean scent of Dial soap. The cotton of his shirt. Heat. Perspiration. Man. She didn't want to react to his masculinity.

Her body didn't give her a choice.

"Come back inside."

Though worded as a command, his voice held supplication. She shook her head.

"I apologize if I was rude."

If? A thousand recriminations raced through her brain. Steadying her voice so it wouldn't break, she said, "How many times do you plan to say you don't want me here?"

"I never plan to." He sighed heavily. "Or maybe I should keep saying it as many times as it takes for me believe it."

Her mouth gaped and she snapped it shut. What did that mean? "You do want me here?"

"Yes. No." He shook his head. "Yes, if it was only me to consider."

"Just what do you think I'm going to do to Anita or Paul?"

He had no answer. It was almost an admission. He used the kids as a shield, pushing her away for his own sake. She took solace in that, in him knowing she wouldn't hurt his sister or brother, and in him caring enough to need to protect himself.

Moments passed while she wondered what tactic he would employ to convince her to go inside. Would he bring the kids into this? Picturing Anita's confused and wounded expression almost made her guilty enough. What explanation could she give? *Your brother is an ass, but I had nowhere else to go.* While true, it wouldn't comfort Anita.

He sighed in defeat. "All right."

The last words she expected from him.

Mike turned to her and she held still, braced as he leaned closer. She shrank back but there was no room to evade him. His hands reached out. She waited for him to put them around her neck, but they cupped her jawline, eased her closer. His head descended.

Seriously? Did he really believe she'd—?

It was her last thought as his lips brushed hers. Once, twice. He nuzzled; she loosened. He smelled good, like a man should, with a little leather and mint toothpaste mixed in. Her hand found his hair, black as the darkness, silky between her fingers. He coaxed her lips apart—no hard feat—and his tongue played with hers. Her stomach went liquid, and heat drizzled down as her blood pulsed.

The kiss went on and on, and she pulled him in. His hand caressed her ribs, his thumb just grazing the curve of her breast. Her breathing labored. Her body grew soft, making a pillow for his descent.

Heat and need. She wanted to pull him down onto her, to ease the ache inside her.

Mike drew back, half an inch. They panted as though they'd just crossed the finish line at the Kentucky Derby. She searched his face, deciding between desire and sanity, wishing she could make out his features better. But she could only see by touch. She sat frozen with indecision. Would she go back in with him, to his room?

"Good night."

She lay against the seat, surprised and bereft as he eased out of the car. Arousal made him move with difficulty.

The knowledge gave her little satisfaction. Arousal wasn't doing her any favors either as she lay limp and pulsing with need.

He adjusted his erection, walked onto the porch and into the house.

The bastard.

Did he think she'd follow him? Ticked off at the thought, she pulled herself upright. The ache would subside. She could wait it out. Not that she'd sleep but—

The house door opened and Grace braced herself. As much as she hated to admit it, she probably couldn't withstand another attempt at seduction.

A large object appeared in the doorway, moving outside. She frowned. When it took shape with Mike behind it, she blinked. An armchair? She'd seen it in the living room, upholstered and cushy and old, covered in a thinned material, sandy brown darkening to oak.

Mike set it on the porch with the slightest thud that wouldn't disturb anyone not already awake. She eyed him with bewilderment. He sat down and stretched out his legs.

Did he mean to intimidate her? Because it wouldn't work. She could out-stubborn anyone she'd met, especially when she knew she was right.

A minute passed. He didn't move. Two minutes. Five.

What was his game? This wasn't seduction.

Then it hit her.

He was watching over her, like Atticus Finch at the jailhouse. If she meant to stay outside, he meant to see she stayed safe. If his gesture hadn't been so overbearing and high-handed, it could almost be called gallant.

The warmth of near-affection followed her into sleep.

Mike hid his relief as Grace strolled into the house in the morning. She didn't speak or look at him but made straight for the bathroom.

How could she look so appealing after such an uncomfortable night? At least he'd had the chair, short and lumpy as it was. Grace had been squashed into the front seat.

He'd moved the chair back inside as the sky lightened to gray. She could leave if she wished. Maybe it would be better that way, not upsetting the kids.

He should make her breakfast. She was a house guest, of sorts, and he owed her an apology. He hadn't wanted her at his home, but he shouldn't have said so. He'd been rude and he could only blame it on his attraction to her. Having a brief sexual relationship while she visited appealed to him. Making her part of the family was out of the question.

The refrigerator offered sufficient milk and eggs for four people. He could shred the three red potatoes for hash browns. They didn't have ham, bacon or sausage, but a cup of bacon grease waited to flavor a skillet. A loaf of fresh bread with jam would fill them.

Would it look like he was waiting until his next paycheck to go to the grocery store? Anita and Paul understood most of his pay went into savings, to pay for their brother at college, to save for the horse rehabilitation farm Mike dreamed of building. They always had sufficient, if not plentiful food.

Grace's footsteps made him turn. Her face shone and she smelled of his soap. She'd brushed her hair and straightened her clothes. A reminder of how the shirt had become loose made his blood pound in his ears.

"You didn't need to watch over me all night."

Mike held back a grin. So much for gratitude. "I didn't want the bears and mountain lions to eat you."

A brow lifted. "No tigers? Oh, my."

Her skepticism enchanted him. As did the look on her face. Her body. Her sass. She *overall* enchanted him. He stomped it down. "You're a guest. It was my duty."

That ought to disillusion any white knight ideals she had of him.

"You're an ass. Guilt, not duty, had you on that porch."

Okay, so maybe she didn't have any illusions about him. He'd made sure of it with his boorish behavior so he couldn't complain now. "I don't want you to get the wrong idea about that kiss either. I don't intend to be your rebound man."

Her face went blank and her mouth fell open, almost as wide as her eyes. Was she surprised he'd seen through her plan? Or that he didn't jump eagerly into bed as other men she'd enchanted?

He admitted to being tempted. She was a looker and soft under his hands. The kiss had aroused him, but also tightened a place his chest. He'd wanted her to come inside, to his bed for sex, sure, but also to comfort her. She'd seemed so hurt and defenseless. That had made him pull away and leave her. He knew better. Grace Marshall was as defenseless as a puma.

He'd lasted thirty seconds inside the house before he knew it wouldn't work and he'd grabbed the chair. Sat all night in the cool outside air like an idiot.

"I'm not interested in a one-night stand," he assured them both, knowing it was half a lie. He wanted more, and on the other hand, he wanted nothing from her. "You might need a guy in your bed, but I don't need the headache."

Her blue eyes flashed anger and rejection. "You're not that lucky. Thinking of going to bed with you *gives* me a headache."

The time-worn excuse made him smile. He couldn't believe the things he said to push her away. He couldn't give her the life she was used to, and they'd only wind up miserable together.

She carefully closed the screen door, and he whistled with appreciation at her restraint. The woman had spirit and cold control.

Too bad—and thank God—she would leave town soon. He got churned up every time they stood within shouting distance. If she hadn't just dumped her fiancé, Mike might have reconsidered a relationship. Short term, no strings. It might have been fun if he could keep her away from his family. If he could protect his heart.

As it was, he considered himself lucky. Forewarned was forearmed. And he needed all the help he could get to withstand her charms.

"More coffee?"

Grace waved away the waitress, who'd been refilling her cup since just after dawn. Sunrise over the mountains could only be considered breath-taking if one had a full night's sleep. Today, it just came too early and too bright.

Later this afternoon, she'd have money wired from Mr. Willard for her painting and she'd never, *ever,* be beholden to Mike Thompson again, not even for a safe place to park overnight. The jerk.

She kept hearing him say he didn't want to be her "rebound man." As if she'd put up with his bossy, mocking, arrogant lack of manners. And rudeness, she reminded herself with a thump of the coffee cup on the table. Even suggesting she wanted him, that she intended to use him for sex, made her want to scream.

If she wanted a man in her bed right now, which she did not, it would be as much about comfort as sex. His having big muscles and a handsome face—and okay, being a fabulous kisser—weren't enough. Sex for her meant connection, affection, and plain old liking the guy, if not loving him. Mike failed on all three measures.

Well, she sometimes felt a connection, like when he locked gazes with her and pulled her close. She even admired his protectiveness toward the two kids at home, though unwarranted in her case.

So, okay, she could sometimes see herself sleeping with him. If he'd keep his mouth shut.

When the diner filled, Grace paid, leaving a bigger tip than she could afford. Hopefully, the rental car would be gone when she arrived at Rachel's. Grace needed a few hours in a real bed then she'd clean up and pick up her wire transfer.

She should pay Mike for parking in his driveway overnight, she thought while in the shower later. She scrubbed at her hair, trying not only to perk up some energy but to wash away any memory of the man. She would check the fee for overnight parking at the airport and then send him the cash in a thank you note so sweet he'd choke on it.

Her rebound man. The more she thought of it, the angrier she grew.

Soap dripped in her eye, and Grace swore as she rinsed it out. The sting reminded her of his rejection. She should be used to it, she thought as she dried off. He'd told her he didn't want her at his place each time she visited. And each time it hurt.

Was it just her pride? Why couldn't she laugh it away? She didn't win over every man she tried to attract. What made

Mike's rejection different?

She'd been around more handsome men. Some better built, though that was a narrow field. Certainly more charming. She didn't even like the man, so why should his dislike bother her?

Despite Rachel's advice, Grace wanted to go home. She wanted to be around people who loved her. Which, sadly enough, didn't include Mike.

Wait. What? Grace gripped the counter and stared wide-eyed into the mirror. Mike?

Oh, God. She couldn't have those kinds of feelings for Mike Thompson, of all people. Was she that big of an idiot?

There wasn't anything lovable about him. Sexy, yes. Admirable, okay, in the way he'd taken responsibility for raising his siblings. He still protected Anita and tried to guide Paul and did who-knew-what for the rest of them. She'd give him a point for being a family man.

Sweet? He'd built Rachel a shed, knowing she wanted one. So one more point in his favor.

That made three: sexy, admirable, sweet. Kisses that rocked her to her toes didn't count. *They certainly don't count against him.* Okay, she told her conscience, one point for kissing.

Funny? Not that she'd seen.

Reliable? He hadn't come when she'd had a flat. *But he sent someone,* that pesky voice reminded her.

Grace scowled and stopped assessing his virtues. He had more of those than flaws. But his attitude toward her definitely counted against him.

Falling for Mike would be even more foolish than proposing to Jack. Worse than jilting Jack, which she'd done for an almost-noble reason, although the timing could have been better. She'd only met Mike two weeks ago. Maybe loneliness overruled her better sense.

She wanted to go home. Lick her wounds and forget those dark brown eyes that always found fault.

***

Grace spent two weeks creating new paintings. She needed more sales to buy land when she returned to Little Tree. The townspeople might forgive her for jilting Jack, their golden boy, if she brought income to the town. An artists' retreat, with classes and maybe a gallery later on, would bring painters, maybe with their families. That should secure her place in a town that had never understood her.

Sitting on the guest bed, Grace gripped her cell phone as Lexi's phone rang in Montana. And rang again. If her sister didn't pick up on the next ring, Grace might lose her nerve and disconnect.

But Lexi answered. "Where are you? Are you okay?"

"I'm fine, don't worry." *Liar.* Grace felt anything but fine. Confused, hurt, angry, lonely. Hearing Lexi's voice served as a balm. She dug out some cheer for her tone, trying to fool the one person who could probably hear the deceit. "What's going on there?"

Lexi gave a half-laugh. "Are you really okay?"

"Yes, Lex." Her sister sounded tense rather than happy to hear from her. "Why are you so upset? What's happened?"

"A lot, considering it's been less than a month. I want an answer this time, Audrey Grace. Where are you?"

Grace sighed, acknowledging the reprimand. She was only "Audrey" when in big TROUBLE. "I had to get away, you know that."

"Old news. Update me."

Grace couldn't implicate Rachel, especially when her

cousin had covered for her twice with Clint. "I don't want to say."

"Grace, I want whatever's best for you. If that means you need to stay where you are, you should. Just call Dad again. He's worried sick."

"I will." *Dad.* Grace gripped the phone, squeezing her eyes shut against tears. She really wanted to see him, to be in his arms. She could almost feel his kiss on her head as she burrowed into his chest. "I wanted to call you first, find out who's angrier at me. So-o-o, how is Jack?"

"Jack's handling things." Humor came through Lexi's words. "We might need you to sign some papers. Will you promise to leave your phone turned on so I can contact you?"

"If you promise not to hire someone to trace me through the GPS."

"Deal."

"What papers?"

"Just some things having to do with the marriage."

The marriage? Grace hadn't been the one to marry the man. What could she have to sign?

"Grace, are you still there?"

"Yeah. And so are you," Grace hinted. "Still at the ranch, I mean." *Tell me it's working out.*

"Yeah."

Grace waited for more. How did Lexi feel about Jack? Did they have a chance together? *Please, don't let all this be for nothing.* He had to realize what a great catch her sister was. But since that sister wasn't forthcoming with details, Grace sighed. If there'd been anything good to report, Lexi would have shared it. "I might be able to sign those papers in person. I'm thinking of coming home."

"Coming home?"

Lexi sounded more panicked than pleased, which must be due to the phone connection. Her sister would be thrilled to have her back.

Almost as thrilled as Grace would be to escape Mike's vicinity. To flee from the temptation of having him near but not wanting her. From the danger of becoming any more enamored. Though how she could even like him made her question her sanity.

"That's not a good idea."

"What?" Grace squawked in surprise. "Why not?"

"You said you needed space. You should wait until you have your head on straight. Know what you want. What you want to do next, I mean."

Grace's head grew light. She felt as though she might faint and grasped the sheets in her fist. Never had she considered Lexi would say not to come home. Tears burned; her nose tried to leak. Mike didn't want her, and now Lexi had built this barrier. Grace had no place to go. No anchor.

Panic rose in her chest, just as it had when her mom died.

Before she could summon words, Lexi spoke again. "Give Jack some more time, Grace."

"I'm surprised he'd need it." Her voice cracked and she held the phone away for a second as she regained control. She didn't want Lexi to hear her cry. "I thought you'd want me home."

"I'm glad you're safe. Call Dad and tell him that. But don't come back yet."

And the phone went dead in Grace's hand.

CHAPTER SEVEN

"I have a donor."

The bite of toast stuck in Grace's throat. She quickly forced it down and chased it with orange juice as she eyed Rachel standing in the kitchen doorway. Heck of a way to start a Sunday morning. Grace had stumbled through the last week since her phone call with Lexi, anchorless and drifting. She'd obviously not been paying attention to Rachel.

One last swallow and she found words. "That's great. Right?"

Rachel nodded, smiling with her entire body. "I'm so excited. It's the right thing for me and the right time to do it."

"And the right guy to do it with?"

"Definitely." Then Rachel shrugged. "I think so. No, I *believe* so, which is more important. I've thought this thing to death, saved the money for so long. I'm tired of thinking. It's time to—"

Grace chuckled. "Get busy?"

With a giggle, Rachel pulled out a chair and sat. "I planned to say, it's time to enjoy it. But, yeah, getting busy with this guy won't be a hardship."

"And you're sure about him?" Grace filled a glass and passed it over. "What does he want afterward? Or does he just... I don't know, get paid now and you never see him again?"

"Like a gigolo?"

Grace reached for Rachel's hand, and after a hesitation, her cousin grasped it. "Sorry, Rachel. But I'm new to all this. You've had time to think it through."

"And have second thoughts. And third and fourth," Rachel agreed. "That's how I know this is right."

"So walk me through it."

"This guy is healthy, sane, and handsome, which doesn't hurt in the baby-making process. I've saved up enough to pay for *in vitro*, and now I won't need that. I'll be able to keep that money for raising my child." She paused. "God, that sounds good. *My child.*" Rachel shared a smile with Grace.

"What is this guy asking from you?"

Rachel's expression closed. "Don't worry, he's not taking advantage of me. Just the opposite."

Grace wanted the glow back in Rachel's eyes but she couldn't help worrying. She forced enthusiasm into her tone, hoping the words didn't stick in her throat like the toast had. "So he's someone you know and trust, and he's willing to help? That's great."

Rachel relaxed back in her chair. "You don't have to fake excitement. I would think I was crazy, too, if I didn't know the story."

"How did you find a baby daddy? I mean, you don't just take out an ad in the classifieds for this." She hesitated, uncertain. "Do you?"

"He volunteered. And I admire the heck out of him for offering to be my partner. He's taking as big a chance on me as I am on him."

"And he's willing to...donate and then just disappear? Not see the kid or anything?"

"He's going to be a distant parent."

Alarm bells rang in Grace's head. "How's that going to work?"

"He's the father. A role model. Like we're divorced, only without any bitterness."

"Joint custody?"

Rachel shook her head. "No. We don't have all the details in stone, but he's being very reasonable. He's supportive without trying to take over."

Grace would keep an eye out for this guy. He sounded too good to be true. But for now, she raised her OJ glass in a toast. "Well, then, here's to the baby daddy. And his successful cooperation."

Rachel clicked her glass against Grace's. "Don't worry. It'll work out. I'm more sure about this than I was about becoming a teacher."

"You're hung up on this guy."

"No, I'm not, but, yes, he's sweet and kind and fun and a good lover."

Shocked, Grace blurted, "A *what?*"

Rachel blushed but held her gaze.

Grace hooted. "You took him for a test drive?"

"No. I mean, yes, although he wasn't going to be my donor then. It was just for fun."

Grace couldn't help teasing. "Rachel Jane, you devil."

"He was going to be a fling." Rachel rubbed a finger through the condensation on the table, concentrating on the pattern. "One last fling before I became a mom. Now he's more. He's special to me. It's not love, and that would just complicate things."

Grace nodded and hid her expression by taking another drink of juice. Her face had probably turned green with envy.

Rachel obviously cared for him, and he must secretly be in love with Rachel to be willing to give so much and ask so little.

Would she ever find a man who felt that way about her? Jack hadn't loved her, but he'd been willing to try to build a future together. Mike didn't like her, despite wanting her.

Grace set her shoulders and firmed her resolve. She wanted a man who loved her and would be committed like Rachel's donor.

And next time, she wouldn't settle for less.

Mike hadn't seen Grace for four long weeks. Anita chattered about their phone calls and outings, so he couldn't get Grace out of his head. He'd hoped time would lessen the ache of wanting, but it hadn't healed his wounds, as promised. He'd done nothing but miss her. He'd take whatever she offered for as long as she stayed in town.

He forced his feet up the path to Rachel's house. He had to see Grace, to undo the mess he'd made. His big mouth, protecting... What? His pride? The woman wanted a little male attention to prove she was still desirable. Maybe something had happened with the groom to make her call off the wedding. Hell, Mike didn't know what to think.

Because he'd never asked. Maybe she'd discovered the groom cheating on her. Though Mike couldn't imagine what kind of jackass would want another woman with Grace about to become his wife.

He took a breath and plodded up the three stairs to the porch, feeling every one of his twenty-seven years.

She didn't seem like the kind of woman to stick with a cowboy, and he had no business coming here, hoping to improve her opinion of him. She oozed polish and sophistication, even when she brought sunlight to his small drab house. Maybe he could've had her in his bed by now if he'd tried, but he'd taken one look and craved her with an intensity that shook him. So, he'd built instant walls and pushed her away each time they met.

Damn it, why couldn't she have been the veterinarian twin? They would've been on common ground. Shared the same interests. Most importantly, an affair with her wouldn't have turned his life upside down when she left.

He knocked, hoping no one answered. As much as he wanted this off his conscience, he equally didn't want to see her. The curtain at the side window twitched then parted. Grace stood full-view in the opening, staring at him. Debating whether to answer the door. He held her gaze but didn't smile, didn't try to convince her. She had to make up her mind without coercion. If she opened the door, she might be half-way to forgiving him. He'd be her rebound man in a heartbeat, if she'd let him.

The curtain fell.

He put on a pleasant expression, waiting for the door to open. A smile would look cocky. He was going for contrite. Did he know how to do contrite?

And why hadn't she opened the door yet? She knew he stood out here.

Perspiration beaded on his top lip. The sun, not nerves. Long years around skittish horses had honed his patience. He could wait her out.

Sweat trailed from his temple to his cheekbone and he wiped it away. The July heat seeped through his T-shirt. Maybe he should let her be. Her silence spoke for her: she wasn't in a forgiving mood.

Still he stood there. Another minute passed before the door opened.

A hand to her hip, Grace looked him up and down and back up. "You might as well come in since you're here."

Damn, if he didn't admire her spirit. He had sense enough not to grin and merely tipped his head in acknowledgment as he passed by her into the house. "Is Rachel home?"

Her mouth firmed. "You came to see Rachel?"

"No. I came to see you." He held her gaze. "I want to know how much privacy we'll have."

"Enough for whatever you came for."

He waited out her dismissal.

She gestured him into the living room and then curled herself into the corner of the couch. With her knees between them, the position kept him an arm's length away.

It also limited her escape options.

He kept that to himself and eased onto the middle cushion, close to her. He turned his body to face hers and saw by the flare of her nostrils she felt trapped. Like his wild horse, Libre, Grace in a wary mood could be dangerous. He knew better than to move: even a backward shift might make her bolt. "I want to apologize."

She reared back as though surprised, narrowed her eyes as though wary. "You're sorry?"

"Let me say it." He let a smile grow on his lips and seep into his eyes. Keeping his muscles relaxed, he used the same techniques he used on the horses he tended. Not that he'd tell her that either. With the slowest of movements and the gentlest of touches, he placed his fingertips on her calf. The smooth skin made his fingers itch to capture, to claim, but Grace would balk if he tried it. With women, the words had to come first. "I was an idiot."

She blinked. "Which time?"

He couldn't hold back a chuckle. "I deserve that. I've been unrecognizable even to myself since we met. Surly, rude. That's not me, Grace. Not usually."

"So it's my fault? I bring it out in you?"

He skimmed his fingertips up her leg to her knee and trailed the back of his nails down to her foot. She brushed his hand away, swiping the goose bumps from her leg in the process. Knowing he affected her made his heartbeat pick up. "Not your fault in a bad way, but yes, you bring out...something in me. I act before thinking. React, really, and not admirably."

Her frown made a crease in her forehead. He wanted to smooth it away.

"Why?"

A shrug would have to suffice as explanation because he felt equally confused. He wouldn't speak of his suspicions. Not yet. "You're different from what I'm used to. Beautiful, classy. You don't fit anywhere in my world—" He saw the hurt in her eyes. "And yet, I want you in it."

"Why?"

He raised to his knee on the cushion, levered over her, hands to either side of her on the back and arm of the couch. This close, he saw her eyes darken, black overtaking the blue as awareness struck her. Her breathing changed and blood rushed under her cheeks. "I want you, Grace."

She swallowed and wet her lips. "You do?"

"You're in my head. Have been since we met." Another inch and he laid his mouth on hers. A nibble. A taste. A tease. Her lips softened in acceptance. He sucked her lip, pulled, before sinking in for a long, soft, soul-stirring kiss. Well, maybe not his soul, but something in him stirred. Heat rushed across his body, under his skin, underscoring his need. Trailing his lips to her ear, he whispered, "From day one," he repeated, "you've been in my head. Now I want you in my bed."

Her palm cupped his jaw, held him while she found his mouth with her own. His blood pounded in his ears, and he wouldn't have been surprised if steam rose off their bodies. He shifted his weight to one arm, freeing the other to touch her. The softness of her cheek, the taut cord of her neck, the curve of her shoulder. Dare he trail his fingers lower? Would it distract her, sober her to the moment? Would she stop him?

He didn't want to interrupt the connection between them. Finally, they were communicating, on the same page, and hopefully with the same outcome in mind.

"Grace." The moan escaped him.

"Hmm?" Her lashes lifted to reveal dazed, unfocused eyes. So blue, so beautiful.

"Where's your bedroom?"

Grace's eyes snapped wide open at his question. Her heart raced faster than her thoughts.

He hovered over her, braced on the couch, while she lay like a melted ice cream cone. Which was a pretty apt description, given what he could do with his tongue. But a few minutes of lust, even with his knee-liquifying execution, didn't mean she welcomed him in her bed. "You want to go to my bedroom?"

His lovely brown eyes crinkled at the corners. "I thought you'd never ask."

Handsome, sexy, a great kisser. Now, funny too. She could see having a fling with him—if only they got along better. If only her heart wasn't in danger of becoming his.

Though he did have his good qualities. Devotion to his family. High moral standards. Protectiveness. Responsibility.

Strong work ethic.

She could do worse.

But she'd promised herself she would do *better* next time. And here was "next time," smiling into her face, promising her hot sex.

"But you don't even like me."

Mike jerked backward, sitting on the cushion beside her. He took her hand and caressed the back with swipes of his thumb. "I'm sorry you think that. I've been an idiot, as I said. I happen to like you very much."

"Name three things you like about me." When he opened his mouth, she added, "Other than my looks."

"Lots of things, of course, but your beauty is the most obvious. The first thing a man notices, so the first thing I thought of."

He was intelligent enough to smooth talk her while stalling for time. "Okay. What's the second thing that pops into your mind?"

"Your artistic ability."

She waved it away. "I was born with it, so I can only take credit for developing my gift." Dammit. Couldn't he think of anything? Just three legitimate traits he admired and she'd be in his arms.

Maybe she needed higher standards.

"Okay, your tenacity."

She pursed her lips with doubt. "That's something you admire?"

"Another woman would have stayed away when I told her to. You continued to visit my sister, despite me telling you not to."

Grace leaned forward, jabbing her finger at him. "Remember that. I *kept* my promise to Anita."

"Jilting your fiancé was all I knew about you."

Okay, she could see that. All she'd known about him was he was smokin' hot and a good builder of sheds. She'd assumed he was Rachel's lover or ex-lover because...well, face it. He was smokin' hot, and no woman in her right mind would turn him down if he offered.

So what did that make her?

"Now you know better." She hat to wait for his nod. He sure wasn't trying very hard to talk her into bed.

"Keeping your promise to my sister changes what I thought of you. Maybe if I understood why you left the guy at the altar...?"

Grace shook her head. "Take me as you find me."

His eyes darkened, if that was possible, and she realized what she'd said even before he replied. "I would." His deep tone ran across her skin with little thrills of pleasure. "I'll *take you* any way you want."

She should have found him too overbearingly male. Was "too sexy" even a thing?

"Sorry." She gave him a flirtatious smile. "We're so not there yet."

Mike blew out a breath and retreated the tiniest bit. She admired his restraint. "Okay, can I admire your baking?"

She couldn't hide her wince, making him laugh. "That's not really a personality trait."

He put his hand back on her calf and she shivered. The warmth of his hand soothed while the calluses spoke of his barely tamed nature. There was something elemental about him, earthy and raw. Her ancient female genes recognized him as Protector, and her womb tightened. Stupid, and counter to every feminist ideal she held, but part of her basic nature. She couldn't deny she responded to him on a primitive female-to-male level.

Fortunately, she'd evolved slightly more than her cavewoman ancestor. "No baking."

"Can I change it to thoughtfulness? You saw a need in my sister for a woman's understanding, and you reached out to her."

She nodded, a satisfied ribbon winding through her. Trying to bind her to him?

"So that's two," he said.

Grace could have let him off the hook because he'd mentioned her perception and her taking action, which were technically two things, but she wondered what else he would mention. After his lack of appreciation for her in the past, his admiration would salve her wounded ego.

"It's not looking good for you, Mike, how you're struggling to come up with three likable things about me."

"You're pretty, feeding my attraction to you." He rose to his knee again. "You're a good baker, feeding my body." He ran a fingertip from her temple to the now-very-sensitive corner of her lips. "You're kind and thoughtful to my family, which..." He closed his eyes for a split second before searing her with his gaze. "Means more to me than I can put in words. You reached out to my sister, but you also bonded with Paul, which isn't an easy task. He talks about you. I think he has a little crush."

Something melted inside her at the words. "I like them. You should give Paul more lead rope, see what he does without you controlling his every step."

"With more rope, he'd hang himself."

"You don't know that. Give him something to be responsible for, to be proud of achieving, and let him know you believe in him." She bit her lip, afraid of going too far, but doubting she'd have another opportunity with him being so agreeable. "He wants to please you. He wants to live up to your expectations—or he'll live down to them. Trust me," she went on as his face closed, "I can identify with that. Just give him a chance, okay?"

Before he could comment, she took a chance of her own. "And take them on a vacation. They need to see something other than this town." She saw his expression closing against the idea. "I'm not talking about Europe or Australia. Just a city bigger than Denver."

She held her breath and would have crossed her fingers if she thought he wouldn't notice. The kids needed greater exposure to the outside world.

It took a minute—or two—as he digested this advice. Emotions simmered in his eyes: denial, hope, regret. Others she didn't know him well enough to identify. Finally his face softened and he focused back on her. "Not all women would take the time for half-grown kids."

She arched a brow at him, hiding her relief. "Not all women get a glimpse into that side of your life. I barged in."

He gave her a half-smile of acknowledgment.

"If not for that flat tire, I never would have met your family."

"I wouldn't say *never*."

"Never," she insisted. "You would have kept the groom-jilter at a safe distance, despite" —she waved a hand between them— "your other feelings."

"Doesn't it mean something that I want you despite what I thought? Despite what I know of your recent actions toward a man?"

Ouch. But she couldn't deny he was justified. She *had* embarrassed Jack. "You want me despite your better instincts?

Yeah, that means something. It means I ought to kick you in the privates and out the front door."

His legs flinched together and she had to chuckle.

One of his eyebrows lifted in challenge. "You think that's funny?"

The severe tone made her hesitate, but she spotted the twitch of his lips, suppressing laughter. His brown eyes lit with laughter, and she relaxed, nodding.

"I can see we're not headed to the bedroom today." He ran a finger along her cheek. Grace restrained an urge to nuzzle into him like a cat being stroked. She feared she would purr and humiliate herself.

Recalling their conversation, she had to shake her head, regret real and probably visible in her eyes.

"Will you think about us getting together?"

Getting together. She couldn't help but compare that to Rachel's mysterious donor's offer of support. Sure, the donor would bed her cousin, but he planned to be there for her afterward. While "getting together" with Mike sounded heavenly, Grace couldn't help but wish for more.

Here he was, her "next time" man, smiling hopefully, caressing her like a lover. He was handsome, sexy, and a family man. But he lived in Longmont, while she longed for home, for Little Tree. He proposed sex while she wanted... She wasn't sure what, exactly, just...more.

Still, she had to be honest. "I'll think about it. About us. Together."

After all, she'd thought of little else since meeting him.

She found herself trying to paint him two days later. Tried, but she couldn't get his expression how she wanted it.

"Grace!" Rachel's call held a strident tone of urgency.

Grace dropped her paintbrush, rushed out of the guest bedroom, and flew down the stairs. Heart pounding, she nearly tripped on the steps and forced herself to slow. She couldn't be helpful to her cousin if she was unconscious. "What is it?"

"In here."

Grace propelled herself around the newel post toward the kitchen to find Rachel staring at her cell as though she didn't recognize the instrument. When her head came up, her wide eyes met Grace's.

A quick inventory showed neither blood nor bruising, and Grace let out her breath. "What's going on?"

"You need to charge your cell phone."

Grace stared. "Is that why you called me downstairs, screeching like you'd severed an artery?"

Rachel laughed. "No. Sorry. Lexi's getting married."

Grace's knees gave out and she went a little light-headed. Fortunately, a chair waited nearby or she'd have wound up on the floor, after all.

Lexi. Getting married. Again. Or for the first time? "To Jack?"

"Well, of course, to Jack." Rachel put a hand to her hip. "What are you grinning about?"

Grace hadn't realized she was. A chuckle escaped, became a hoot of laughter and she was gone. *Married.* She held her sides as she rocked with joy, barely aware of Rachel joining in.

"What are you laughing about? What are *we* laughing about?"

It had been a long six weeks. "I'm just happy for them."

Which didn't start to describe how she felt. *Relieved* that the wait was over. The other shoe—in this case, a wedding slipper—had dropped. *Thrilled* that her plan had worked, that sacrificing what respectability she'd earned in Little Tree had paid off. *Ecstatic* that her sister finally had won the love of the man who held her heart.

Grace sobered. He'd better love her. What if this wasn't a fairy tale wedding?

"And now you're scowling," Rachel said. "I swear, your emotional mood swings are going to give me whiplash. I hope I'm not as crazy as this when I'm pregnant."

"What? Oh, no, sorry. I was just thinking. Maybe it's time for me to go home."

CHAPTER EIGHT

Mike rapped on Rachel's door, feeling ten kinds of a fool. Grace had been pretty plain two days before about not wanting a short-term relationship, yet here he was, chasing after her for just that. His dad would have kicked his butt for pursuing a woman who'd said no already.

But she hadn't said no, exactly. Which gave him enough hope to be on the doorstep. Again.

This time the door opened right away, and Rachel smiled out at him. "Mike, how nice to see you. Come on in." She stepped back. "We're in a tizzy today. Grace is packing to go home."

His heart jumped a beat. His vision went white. His throat closed.

Swallowing a lump of what tasted like panic, he stepped into the house. Must have been the mid-July sun causing those reactions. Dehydration maybe. "Why's she leaving?"

His voice came out as a croak but Rachel gave no notice.

"Her sister is getting married."

He nodded. "This is her twin sister?"

"She only has the one. No brothers."

He nodded again, a plan formulating in his racing brain.

A crazy plan, but she wasn't leaving him. "Where is she?"

Rachel gestured with her head up the stairs. "Her room."

"Can I?" But his foot was already on the bottom step. It would have taken a stronger force than Rachel to stop him. Like Grace herself.

"Sure," Rachel's voice followed him up the stairs, a little laugh behind the word.

He disregarded that. Maybe him making an ass of himself was funny. He didn't know, never having chased a woman before. Wanted, invited, and enjoyed, sure. But if a woman in the past hadn't shown interest, he hadn't tracked her down, cornered her and tried to persuade her otherwise.

And there he was, back to Grace being interested. Or not.

He had to believe she was. It couldn't be just hope coloring his interpretation of her responses.

He heard a click which he identified as a medicine cabinet shutting. Tinny with glass around it. Anita made that sound ten times every morning.

The reminder of his sister drew him up outside the door. *Anita and Paul.* What was he thinking? He couldn't carry through with this half-baked idea. He had responsibilities.

He saw Grace then, emerging from the bathroom, he supposed, with both hands full of little tubes and a deodorant bottle. She dropped them on the mattress and stared at them with her hands on her hips.

And, just like that, he embraced the craziness of his plan.

With an inner smile of certainty, he cleared his throat.

Grace spun, a hand to her chest. "Oh. I didn't know you were here." She drew breath to calm herself. "What *are* you doing here?"

Claiming you. But he wasn't clueless enough to say it. "I just stopped by. Rachel says you're going home."

She gestured to the pitifully few things on the bed. "I'm packing." Beside the toiletries sat a pile of three folded shirts, some satiny stuff he guessed was underwear sticking out from under two pairs of shorts, and a bra. He spotted yellow fabric on the far side and recognized her dress, the one she'd worn the first day they met. And yep, there on the floor lay those silly grass-stained wedding shoes. Was that all she'd had to wear these past weeks? He'd never paid particular notice to her clothes. She looked enticing all the time, but that wasn't due to her clothes.

Today she had on a form-fitting tee in bright rainbow colors that made him think of her personality—exuberant, full of life and joy. Her modest, cut-off jeans shorts exposed long tanned legs down to strappy sandals with a heel high enough to trip her up. *At least they would make running difficult.*

"Why are you going home now?" His mind raced as he searched out convincing words.

She beamed at him, and his chest went tight. "My sister's getting married."

"That's great. Has she known the guy long?"

Grace's chuckle made him want to join in. She fairly glowed with happiness. "You might say that. It's a small town and we all kind of grew up together. I was actually going to marry him."

He stared, his head filled with the whoosh of ocean waves, or at least the sound of a seashell. It made his stomach roll. "Marry him? When?"

She threw back her head in a full laugh, and the creamy length of her throat snared his gaze. He'd like to sink his teeth in, nuzzle her scent, trail his tongue to just behind her ear. He jerked back to the present to find her looking at him questioningly.

It took Mike a second to remember their conversation. "Not the guy you just jilted?"

"The same."

He searched her expression. Clear blue eyes, lit with happiness as far as he could discern. A smile on those alluring pink lips. Ease in her stance. If she was a horse, he would have felt confident approaching her. But with a woman, and Grace in particular? No rules applied.

"You don't seem upset." He leaned against the doorjamb.

She studied her hands, withdrawing from him. Had she planned to go back and marry the guy? Was her original flight only a case of cold feet?

What about the attraction that simmered between himself and Grace? He knew she felt it; he'd seen it in her eyes and tasted it on her lips.

"I only want Lexi to be happy," she said so softly he might have missed it if he hadn't been fixated on her every nuance right then. "So," she straightened and spoke in a more steady voice, "I'm going home to make sure that's true."

To see her ex-fiancé? Not a chance in hell. "I'll drive you."

Grace's mouth dropped open, and her eyes grew enormous. He couldn't help but grin, never imagining he'd see her speechless.

"Makes sense." He shrugged as if it were "no big thang," as Paul would have said. "Two people will make the drive easier."

"That's not necessary."

"Is Rachel going?"

"No. she staying clear of this one."

"Then I should come, ensure you make it safely." When she looked to protest, he added, "And Rachel will be reassured, too."

"That's very...kind of you, but I can't ask you to drive me."

"You didn't ask."

"I don't need help. I drove here by myself. But, I mean, thank you."

He straightened from the doorway and stepped into her room. "It's no trouble. You're the one who told me I should take a vacation."

"A vacation with Anita and Paul."

Gotcha. He smiled, perhaps a little too victoriously since she slid backward a step. "Good idea. I'll have them drive up as soon as Anita's summer school class ends."

"But—"

"You said I need to give Paul more responsibility." Even though the idea of them on the road alone made his gut hurt. "You suggested I let him prove himself. I've been giving a lot of thought to that."

"You have?"

He moved in until he could have touched her but kept his hands to his sides. Loose, as though he was relaxed, when in fact, he felt just the opposite. One short lean forward and he could touch his lips to hers, try to convince her in the most basic way. But he wanted her to accept him with her brain as well as her hormones. "I think about everything you say, Grace."

"You do?" Her expression showed equal parts doubt and surprise.

"Of course. From our first meeting when you thought I was your cousin's handyman."

"I didn't... Okay, I did, but you *were* building her a shed."

He nodded. "And then you decided I was her lover."

She went pink and looked away.

"Why is that, I wonder?" With a finger on her chin, he turned her face back to his. Inches separated them. He stood close enough to see her pupils dilate, her cheeks flush deeper, not with embarrassment, but, he hoped, with desire. He lowered his voice to a whisper. "Why would you have looked at me and decided I was someone's lover? Because you were attracted to me?"

She firmed her lips as though to keep words inside. It was enough of an admission to renew his hope. They'd met the day after her wedding to another man. Too soon to feel attracted to him. Too soon for the pull he'd felt for her.

And yet, there it was, timing be damned. They'd met at an inopportune hour, but it hardly mattered. They were meant to be lovers. Aligned in the stars or drawn from the earth, their meeting was fated.

"Tell me," he said, a hair's breadth from her mouth. "Tell me you don't want me."

He took her lips then, hard and insistent. She might have expected him to coax and convince, but instead, he overwhelmed and demanded. She tasted sweet, like promises of tomorrow, just out of reach. She tasted of desire, as though he could have her now, on this bed, on this pile of clothes, obliterating her plans to leave him behind.

She tasted like she was his.

"Tell me you don't want me to come with you."

Somehow, two hours later, Grace flew down the road, laughing at the sheer freedom of the wind in her hair and having a handsome man riding shotgun. She'd thrown her belongings into a canvas tote bag while Mike called his sister and his boss and explained things. How he'd done that, what he'd said to make it sound less crazy, she didn't know.

It *was* crazy.

It was also wonderful and exciting. And it hadn't taken much convincing on his part.

Tell him she didn't want him? Not possible. She wanted him in all sorts of ways.

"But I can't take a man home after I just left one at the altar six weeks ago," she'd said. "Everyone will think I'm flaky. Or that I was cheating on Jack all along." Not that the town didn't consider her flaky already.

"What do you plan to tell all the fine citizens about why you left?" he'd asked.

She didn't have an answer because she didn't plan to tell anyone anything. She needed to check that her sister was happy, that this marriage—and second wedding—fulfilled all of Lexi's dreams. That Jack had flown over the moon in love this time.

"Trust me," Mike had continued when she didn't reply, "it's easier on a guy to be dumped for another man than to be dumped for no reason at all."

She'd had to grin. "How would you know? Have you ever been dumped?"

"Of course. Hasn't everyone at some time?" He raised a brow. "When you turn a guy down for a date, don't you make some excuse?"

She had to admit it. "Okay, you've made your point. I guess it's better for Jack if I have another man in tow. I'm not

sure it matters what the town thinks of my reasons anyway."
She rushed on before he could ask her to explain. "But why
should you come?"

"You don't have another guy to fill this role, do you?
Besides, you convinced me I needed a vacation."

Grace smirked. "Little Tree isn't exactly the tourist
mecca of the West."

"Do I look like a Vegas kind of guy?"

And that had somehow been that.

According to Mike, the kids had been thrilled to get
him out of their hair. Grace heard the guilt and worry under his
light tone, and she appreciated his gesture even more. She
wasn't sure she wanted him to witness her return home, but
he'd serve as a distraction.

Sometimes they drove in silence, sometimes they—
okay, *she*—sang along with the radio. "I missed American
music while I was abroad." She told him about Paris and the
French countryside, about all the picturesque towns in Italy and
the grandeur of Rome. The bustle of Sydney and the vastness
of Australia. Being behind the wheel made it easier for her to
open up to him, given she didn't have to make eye contact.

"Everywhere I went was so beautiful, small town or big
city or lonely countryside. There was so much to paint, so
much to see and learn."

He shot her a glance but she didn't look over,
pretending to concentrate on driving. Few cars shared the road,
and fences in this stretch kept antelope and other wildlife from
jumping into her path. In her mind's eye, she revisited the
places she'd traveled, feeling a little nostalgic. But of all the
fond memories, no place called to her like Little Tree. As a
teenager, she'd longed to travel, to escape. She smiled at the
irony. "No matter where I went, no matter how beautiful, I

could only think of coming back."

"Like Dorothy."

Surprised, she said, "From *The Wizard of Oz*? I guess so. There's no place like home."

"Tell me about Little Tree."

She took a minute then shrugged. "It's just my hometown. It started as a settlement built to serve the surrounding ranches. My dad's the vet." A surge of pride filled her. "Up until a few years ago, he was the only veterinarian in the area, but a young guy opened a place in the next county. Fortunately, Dad has Lexi to help him keep the business running."

"How is she viewed by the ranchers?"

Grace whipped her head toward him, taking a moment to search his face. Not finding any sign of disrespect toward Lexi, she relaxed and turned her attention back to the road.

"I only meant it's hard for a woman to be accepted." Mike read her reaction accurately. "Some of the old-timers can be set in their ways."

"What about you? Are you comfortable with a female vet? Or horse trainer?"

He grinned. "I love working with women."

Grace bit back a smile. He was different in the car. Relaxed and talkative. He'd lost that air of judgment she hated, or maybe, about to face her father, sister, and the town, she had ceased to worry about Mike's opinion.

Nope. That wasn't it. The thought of him hearing all about her antics from the good citizens of Little Tree made her anxious. Mr. Responsible would turn tail and walk back to Longmont to get away from her. But it couldn't be helped. She couldn't erase her past, and the chance to get in the town's good graces by marrying Jack Walker had sped off with her in the convertible last month. Mike hearing about her misspent youth would only confirm his original opinion of her. Flaky. Inconsiderate. Heartless.

Unfortunately, she had a heart. And the man sitting beside her claimed too big a piece.

Night had fallen before Grace drove through Little Tree, past the feed store, the pharmacy, the library, and the school she and Lexi had attended. Past Kerr's Grill and the Mountain View Hotel where she would have spent her honeymoon night. Past The Diner where Lexi's friend, Carrie Moore, worked. Past Buck's Bar—where she really wanted to stop for a little Dutch courage.

Grace parked the car in front of her dad's house instead and stared, trying to drum up the courage to face him. She couldn't bear to see disapproval on his face, and she wouldn't be able to explain her way out of her actions without exposing Lexi's feelings for Jack. And maybe not even then.

"Are we getting out?" Mike asked after two minutes passed.

She turned to him then shrugged. "I guess. This is my dad's house."

He rounded to her side of the car before she blinked. Mike opened her door, fairly shimmering with energy. "What?" he said when she didn't move. "You don't want me to meet him? Do you want to drop me somewhere else before you go in?"

"Of course not." She climbed out, reluctant to be pushed along at his pace but amused by his eagerness. Maybe he considered it an adventure, meeting new people, seeing new places. But this wasn't a vacation for her; it was face-the-music time.

The house door opened and her father stood on the porch. They stared at each other, frozen in their own thoughts. Although still muscular from wrangling animals in his vet practice, he seemed to be holding on to the house for support. A hand gripped either side of the door frame, while the light from the entryway highlighted the gray at his temples.

Grace searched his expression, looking for disapproval, annoyance, or even resignation. After all, he was used to her hijinks. She'd wanted to show him she'd outgrown her rebellion, but jilting the local golden boy at the altar probably hadn't been the best illustration of her maturity. She couldn't read his thoughts from across the length of the yard.

Just as she managed to buck up her courage, her father straightened. And smiled.

"Daddy!" She didn't remember racing across the lawn, only felt magically transported when his arms enclosed her in a tight hug. He rocked her side to side, and she didn't know whether to laugh or cry.

He kissed the side of her head. "Don't do that again."

She hugged him tighter, trying to shake her head in a promise not to. "I called," she choked out.

He snorted and set her back on her feet, keeping an arm around her waist as though not quite ready to relinquish his hold. Not quite ready to believe she wouldn't flee. "Who's this?"

Guilty to have forgotten her companion, she waved Mike forward from the side of the car where he'd politely waited out their reunion. Two minutes into her homecoming and she'd shown total disregard for another person. Damn.

"I'm Mike." The men shook hands, and her father made no pretense of not weighing him up.

"He's a friend," Grace said to warn him off. "He was

good enough to drive home with me."

"We're kind of dating."

Her jaw all but dropped off. "What? Why would you say that?"

Mike winked at her. "Wasn't I supposed to tell him?"

She turned back to her dad. "I didn't know him before, I swear. I met him at Rachel's."

Her father nodded with the expression that had won him a reputation for being a savvy poker player. That is, no expression at all. "Might as well call me Kevin. I'm not ready to answer to you calling me Dad yet."

Grace shrieked with irritation as Mike chuckled. "Dad! He's not likely to call you that. Good grief. We barely know each other."

Her father's gray-blue eyes assessed her hot cheeks and Mike's lazy insouciance. He grunted. "Might as well come in before the neighbors start talking."

They followed him into the kitchen where all important conversations took place. After handing around cold drinks, she nearly burst. "Tell me about Lexi, about what's been going on." She glanced at Mike but continued, "I know she married Jack, but Rachel said they're having a second ceremony. What's that all about? Is he treating her well? Is she happy?"

"That's a lot of questions," her dad said.

"I just need to know Lexi is happy."

He rubbed his chin, studied the scarred wooden table, then sighed.

Oh, God. It hadn't worked. Lexi and Jack hadn't found their forever love. Grace had felt pretty full of herself, thinking she could bring that about. "Dad?"

He put a hand over hers on the tabletop. His mouth drooped at the corners. She wanted to reach for Mike's hand for support.

"Well," Dad dragged out the word. "She's marrying him quietly, in the judge's chambers tomorrow."

Grace gulped. Not the celebration she'd hoped for Lexi to have.

"They both seem willing to do it." He eyed her. "*Willingly* and *knowingly* this time."

She ducked her head, unable to tell him why she'd put Lexi in that dress. Then he laughed.

She shot upright. "Why are you laughing? What's funny?"

"You."

She glanced at Mike, who looked bemused. Poor guy was ten steps behind her, and it seemed, she was quite a few behind her dad. "Why am I funny?"

"I can read you like a book, little girl. And the good news is, it worked. Lexi loves that hard-nosed rancher, and he seems to love her even more."

She wilted. "That's good. Great. Why's Jack a hard-nosed rancher?"

Her dad's face closed. "It hasn't been all smooth sailing out at the Rocking W. But that's your sister's story to tell, if she chooses." He turned to Mike. "How did you meet my girl?"

"I'm a friend of Rachel's."

They passed information as though drinking coffee at The Diner. When Mike mentioned horse training for his boss, their bond snapped closed. She could have been invisible. After a few minutes of watching them talk over her, she walked out to the living room and stared at the telephone. Would Lexi pick up if caller ID showed their dad's number?

She couldn't believe how nervous she was about talking to Lexi, especially after the reassuring news that her sister and

Jack had fallen in love. Jumping in the car to attend the wedding had taken no thought at all. Back in Longmont.

Her hand shook as she reached for the phone and she pulled it back, laughing a little light-headedly.

Tomorrow would be soon enough. She'd go to the wedding with her dad—and take Mike along as a beard.

Lexi would be thrilled to see her.

***

"What time are we leaving in the morning for the wedding?" Grace asked her dad as she cleared dishes from their late meal of warmed-over mostaccioli.

Her father's poker face abilities deserted him as he gaped at her. "You're not going."

"Of course I am. My sister's getting married. That's why we sped home. I wouldn't miss it for the..." She cleared her throat. "I didn't know she was getting married last time."

"Last time?" He snorted. "Last month, you mean?"

She avoided Mike's gaze by setting the dishes in the sink.

"Wait," Mike said behind her. "I'm a little lost. Your sister is marrying your ex-fiancé, right?"

She nodded without turning, waiting for her dad to spill the story. When silence pulsed behind her, she searched for words to explain without exposing Lexi's secret. She faced them, leaning against the countertop. "Lexi married Jack, my groom, last month when I left. Now they're having a second ceremony, a wedding they're choosing because they're in love."

She waited. She and Poker Face watched Mike, who did a pretty solid "no comment" expression himself. Her shoulders ached with tension.

Mike shook his head. "There's never a dull moment

around you, is there?"

The men erupted in laughter. At least Mike wasn't judging her harshly. There'd be enough of that to deal with from the townsfolk.

"If you're uncomfortable with the situation, you could stay here," she told Mike reluctantly, "and not come to the wedding."

"I wouldn't miss this for the world," he echoed her earlier comment. "Besides, it would look strange if your *new* boyfriend wasn't on your arm, wouldn't it?"

She threw in the towel, literally, leaving the drying up for her dad. "It's been a long day. I'm turning in. It is okay if we stay here, right?"

Her dad...didn't answer. Didn't say "of course." He looked at the wall clock. "Well, you might stay at your own house."

Grace gawked. Was her father sending them away? Suggesting she and her "boyfriend" shack up at the house she'd once shared with Lexi? But before she could find breath to comment, he continued. "No one's there, and we wouldn't want a break-in."

"A break-in? In Little Tree?"

"Someone broke in a few weeks ago."

"Oh, my God. Was Lexi home?"

He slanted her an ironic look. "She lives with her husband."

Grace's glare didn't curb his chuckles.

"We should bunk over there," Mike put in. The men eyed each other for a long moment before her dad nodded.

"And you're okay with that?" Grace asked. "Us alone. Unmarried."

"You're a grown woman, Gracie, and a headstrong one.

Whatever you plan to do, you'll do, whether here or over there."

If she'd been a cartoon character, her eyes would have popped out of their sockets on bouncy springs. He hadn't been that understanding when she'd been a teenager.

Truth be told, it hurt just a little that he didn't seem to care what she did with Mike. As though he shouldn't expect any better of her.

"Sir," Mike said, "we aren't that far along in our relationship. If there isn't a second bedroom, well, it won't be the first time I've slept on the floor. Your daughter is safe with me."

"If Grace didn't trust you, you'd be going alone. She's a sound judge of character, though a little impulsive at times."

She couldn't decide if she was miffed at being called impulsive—although she couldn't deny it—or tickled at being determined a sound judge of character. She hadn't realized Dad viewed her that way. She eyed Mike and wondered about her judgment. She considered him a responsible family man, a hard worker, true to his word, and loyal to his friends. Dependable. Like a work truck.

She grinned, glad she hadn't been so blinded by his sexy-red-convertible exterior that she missed the reliable core. Maybe Dad had it right. She'd known Jack had been wrong for her, despite his excellent qualities. But on first meeting, she'd been drawn to Mike. Maybe using her dad's evaluation of her abilities just rationalized her desire, but she felt better about seeing what would develop between them.

Now if she could only get Mike to realize *she* was a catch.

Which wasn't helped by his comments on their way over to Lexi's house.

"You're okay with us staying together, right?" he asked too late. "We need to bolster the impression we're a couple."

"Sparing Jack's feelings and all that."

"Right." He sighed in evident relief. Like he thought she'd take advantage of the situation and jump him.

He should live so long.

She pulled up in front of the house before she realized they had a problem. "Oh, shoot. I gave my house key back to Lexi."

"Would your dad have a spare?"

"Maybe, but give me a minute." After flipping on her cell's flashlight app, she walked up to the house and glanced around, sure she'd know the hiding spot Lexi chose.

"The turtle?" Mike took a step toward the ceramic figurine on the side of the porch.

"Don't bother." She stopped him. "Too obvious." But his idea brought her attention to the side of the porch. Walking over with certainty, she located the extra key in a fake rock by the ferns. She'd known Lexi hid it there, but Grace couldn't remember any such conversation.

"You know that's not normal, right?" Mike's voice vibrated with amusement. "Just suddenly finding a hidden key in a hidden rock in an overgrowth patch of ferns in the dark."

She shrugged. It wasn't the first time a similar connection had occurred.

The house looked the same, and she realized she'd missed the hominess of those ugly tan loveseats with their colorful mounds of pillows. Lexi's yarn bag was gone, probably with her at her new home.

A pang of separation made Grace's chest ache. Miles and continents had divided them before, but now Lexi had left her in a different way. She loved someone else; Jack had become important, maybe *more* important to Lexi. While it was expected and hoped for—and heaven knew, Grace had worked hard to arrange just that—she still felt left behind. Abandoned.

She led Mike to Lexi's room and found him sheets.

He insisted he could make a bed. "Better than I'd hoped for," he said. "Your dad didn't reassure me I wouldn't have to sleep on the floor."

Grace hid her hurt expression. "Because he thinks we're sleeping together."

All of a sudden, Mike's arms went around her, pulling her close. His lips closed over hers, stealing her gasp of surprise. He molded her against him until she relaxed and returned his kiss. The sunshine, wind-blown smell of him from the car ride filled her senses. She caressed his broad shoulders and thought again of how reliable he was. She felt secure and cherished in his arms.

And crazy-aroused. The sexy-red-convertibleness of him couldn't be overlooked. His stubble scraped her skin, igniting her desire like steel on flint. His taste and scent fanned the spark.

He nuzzled her neck, sending shivers to all her womanly parts. "You're a siren, Grace, luring me to my doom. But I'd go with a smile on my face."

She laughed. "Is that a compliment?"

"Meant to be." His chuckle warmed her skin. "I want you to understand why I'm sleeping in here, alone, tonight."

She pulled back and looked into his eyes, trying to assess his intention. But those dark brown eyes only distracted her without revealing anything. "You're safe. I didn't plan to sleep with you. We're not there yet."

"I agree." He nodded. "Reluctantly."

"Then why are we in each other's arms?"

"I told you, you're a siren. But your dad knows you're not stupid or reckless, despite what he calls 'impulsive.' That's why he trusts you, Grace. Trusts you to be sure of your feelings before you sleep with me. Trusts you to be sure of me, too."

"Maybe."

"He may barely trust me not to take advantage of the situation, of us sleeping in a house alone together, but he trusts you to make the right decision—right for you, not him—and be persuasive enough to hold me off."

"He taught us to defend ourselves." She ran her knee along his inner thigh in a caress that hinted at just what she would do.

Mike's face screwed into a wince. "Yeah, I get it."

"And I get what you're saying." She kissed his chin. "I hope you're right, and thanks for the reassurance."

"Hey, I'm in a parental role, too. I understand the way he thinks."

She bit back a smile. "So, how long before you tell Anita it's okay if she spends the night with a guy?"

He growled and she broke away, laughing.

"Don't even joke about that. Now, I'm going to check your locks and make sure this place is secure after that break-in."

Grace sobered. "I don't understand that. Little Tree seldom has crime."

"You said you've been gone. Maybe it's changed a little." He held up his thumb and forefinger a quarter inch apart. "Just this much."

"Maybe. I hate the idea it changed, at all."

"Change is inevitable."

She slanted him a glance. "Remember that the next time

Anita wants to do something that doesn't fit your little-girl view of her."

His brows lowered. "Don't poke the bull when there's a flimsy wooden fence between you."

"You're the bull, all right. But your promise not to ravish me isn't flimsy." When he raised a brow, she added, "If I couldn't trust you, you wouldn't be here."

Mike kissed her. "I don't know that I've earned your trust yet, but I appreciate it."

She left the room before she revealed more of her feelings.

CHAPTER NINE

Since there was no food in the house for breakfast, Grace realized she'd have to face the townspeople. Had to be done, and a small step like The Diner was enough of a challenge before coffee. Thankfully, she had her choice of battle gear, as her clothes had been brought back from the ranch. She donned a comfortable blue blouse and shorts and took Mike on a brief tour of the town, after which they found a table at The Diner.

It remained as unpretentious as its name, with classic red vinyl booths and stools at the counter, and the best comfort food this side of mama's kitchen. At least, so Leo, the owner, claimed, and Grace had never had cause to disagree.

A waitress stopped by their table and Grace looked up, apprehensive to face her first challenge. She froze. Carrie Moore wore her nearly black hair in a ponytail, and her white short-sleeved shirt exposed slim, muscled arms. A black apron covered her shorts. Grace groaned. Wasn't it just her luck Lexi's best friend would be working today?

"Can I get you some coffee?" Carrie glanced up from her order pad and met Grace's gaze. Her brown eyes widened with surprise. She went still for a split second then shot a questioning look at Mike. "Lexi?" She frowned. "No, I don't think so. Your face is just that tiny bit different. But he's definitely not Jack, which means you can't be Grace. That makes you Lexi, I guess." She assessed Mike again. "So, is this the hot drifter?"

Outraged on Mike's behalf, Grace burst out, "He's not a drifter."

Carrie winked. "But you don't deny he's hot."

Grace's face heated.

"Everyone knows you left town with a hot drifter."

Panicked, she appealed to Mike. She didn't want this idea in his head, compounding her sins. "I didn't leave town with anyone."

Mike shook his head. "No sense denying it, darling. Here we are, having breakfast together."

She gaped. "What are you talking about?"

Carrie scowled. "That sounds just like how Grace would say it, but she should be having breakfast with Jack. I know all the Marshall relatives, and all Jack's cousins, and this guy isn't one of them." She tapped the pen on her pad. "Grace should still be in the honeymoon phase, not off with some other guy. Except... I think you are Grace."

Grace debated for a half-second. Carrie had always kept their secrets, but The Diner didn't offer any privacy for explanations. Plus, she had to see Lexi before telling anyone anything. "What makes you say that?"

"Twenty-six years of knowing you two and your antics," Carrie shot back. "I just can't figure out how you ended up with Lexi's hot drifter."

"Give it a rest, Carrie."

"Just promise me you're not cheating on Jack."

"I'm definitely not."

"Okay then. Be whoever you want, but it's kind of crazy to be parading the Hot Drifter right in town."

"Stop calling him that."

"I really don't mind." Mike shot Carrie a dazzling smile.

Carrie smiled back, a little too friendly.

"Oh, sorry," Grace interrupted their moment. "This is Mike."

"Are you a painter, too?"

Mike coughed but Grace heard the snort behind it. She narrowed her eyes at him.

"I'm a ranch hand."

"Is Jack hiring?" Carrie asked.

Grace had to reroute the conversation off this track. "You haven't seen Lexi lately?"

Carrie's demeanor brightened. "Is she back?"

"Uh, yeah. We're both back in Little Tree."

"Tell her I never really believed that story about a hot drifter—well, until today. I'll have to call her," Carrie said, "and get the real scoop."

"It should be a good story." Grace shifted in her seat. Where did a guy figure into this? "But not today. Lexi's busy. I'll tell her to call you tomorrow."

Carrie slanted her body and attention toward Mike. Grace didn't care for that, for several reasons. Jealousy definitely not being one of them.

"Did you ever hear about the time Lexi posed as Grace to take a test in high school? She did well, of course, and the teacher praised her up and down. Lexi couldn't take it. She's the nice one." Carrie shot a mischievous smile in Grace's direction and missed Mike's frown. "Anyway, Lexi felt so guilty she burst into tears and confessed."

"And I got in trouble."

"You let her pretend to be you and take your test. That's cheating."

Grace sighed. "It was ten years ago, for Pete's sakes."

Carrie raised her brows. "And you've changed so much?"

"I'd love a coffee," Mike cut in. "Black, no sugar, and as strong as you can carry."

Blessing him for his perception and quick thinking, Grace ordered her coffee, then turned away as though she needed to study the menu. The offerings hadn't changed since The Diner opened, but the large page provided a handy cover. "The pancakes melt in your mouth."

"It's going to take me a minute to decide," he said to Carrie with a blinding smile. "Since this is my first time here."

Carrie nodded. "I'll be right back with those coffees."

Grace watched her sharp retreat. "I bet she will be, too. Thanks for saving me."

"Do you want to eat somewhere else?"

She shook her head. "I've got to face the music sometime. I just want to see Lexi before anyone else discovers I'm back. Try to explain to her."

Mike took her hand in his. "Do you want to practice by telling me?"

The warmth of his hand and the intimacy of the public act made her wish she could confide in him. "No. Lexi needs to hear it before I tell anyone else. Even you, and I know you wouldn't blab the story around."

He quirked a brow, his eyes twinkling. "Do I look like a blabber?"

She relaxed at his humor. "You're a nice man."

One side of his mouth lifted. "It doesn't count as a compliment when you sound so surprised."

"Well, you didn't start off being nice to me." She made her voice gruff. "Stay away from Anita. Don't corrupt Paul.

You're not welcome at my house."

He winced. "I was an ass."

"You were protecting your family. I'm no threat, but I understand. I...I would do a lot to protect my sister and my dad."

Carrie showed up table-side with coffees and they pulled apart. Grace instantly missed his hand holding hers. When had he become so important? Why him, this man who wanted her in his bed but not in his family's lives?

Carrie set down the coffees. "Two black coffees, but I brought cream and sugar for you, Gr—Lexi. Oh, for heaven's sakes." She shook her head. "This is like grade school."

"I'll take the rancher's special." Mike chose bacon over sausage, pancakes over waffles, American fried potatoes over hash browns, and ordered his eggs sunny-side up. Then he added milk and orange juice.

The way her stomach jumped with nerves, the mere thought of all that food made Grace gag. "Just coffee."

"You need more than that," he said. "It might be a hard day."

"What's hard about today?" Carrie asked.

"Nothing," Grace and Mike answered at the same time.

Carrie narrowed her eyes at them.

"I'll have two buttermilk pancakes, please," Grace rushed in before Carrie could question them further.

"Huckleberry syrup or maple?"

"Neither."

Mike stared. "How can you eat them without syrup? I'll have maple."

Other customers came in and Carrie rushed to their tables. Grace kept her face averted, hoping no one would approach. As she drank her coffee, she felt gazes on her but didn't turn. "People are staring, aren't they?"

"You should be used to that," Mike said, "as pretty as you are."

Surprised, she stared at him. His distraction, though obvious, worked. "You don't act like you think I'm pretty."

"I do, though. Even when I warned you away from my family, I considered you the most gorgeous female I'd ever seen outside of the movies."

She raised her eyebrows. "Really?"

"Marilyn Monroe has you beat, I'm sorry to say. And Selma Hayek. And maybe Eva Mendes, although that might be a tie. And Grace Ke—"

"Okay, you can stop now." But she couldn't stop smiling. Maybe that response to Mike drew her the most. Men flattered her, but few made her laugh. He also challenged her. She wanted to be a better person around him, worthy of his company. Worthy of his siblings' affections.

Could she possibly have fallen for Mike already? Just a month ago, she'd been prepared to enter into a suitable marriage with another man.

"Hey, Lexi."

Grace shot upright and stared at the woman next to her table. Marsha, a childhood classmate turned into a rancher's wife. Her figure had filled out with her three squares a day, which Marsha hadn't had growing up. Now she looked downright voluptuous.

Grace peeked at Mike to find him giving the woman a polite smile. She automatically infused Lexi into her tone, though the change was so minimal, Marsha wouldn't notice. "Hey, Marsha."

"I heard you left town. Didn't know you were back." Her gaze went to Mike. "Or with company."

Before Grace could reply, the woman stuck her hand in his direction. "I'm Marsha, obviously. I've heard about you, of course, but I didn't hear a name."

"Mike." He shook her hand.

"Welcome, Mike." She leaned closer. "Are you going to be in town long?"

"I haven't made plans yet," he said.

"Oh," Marsha breathed. "I think drifting around is so romantic. You know, like the old time cowboys, blowing where the wind took them."

Grace rolled her eyes. "How are John and the kids?"

Marsha straightened and shot her a look loaded with triumph. "My husband is fine. Wonderful. So are my children."

"Give him my best."

Marsha smirked at Grace and winked at Mike. "No need. I already give him mine."

She pivoted and returned to her table as Grace gaped. Noticing heads turned their way, she drew in, trying to disappear.

"It's okay," Mike said. "I'm not taking her up on her offer."

"What offer?"

He opened his palm to reveal a scrap of paper obviously torn from a placemat. Numbers in ink filled the space with Marsha's name.

Speechless, Grace glared at Marsha across the room. Then anger powered her voice. "She gave you her phone number? She's married."

Mike held her gaze and extended the paper to her. "Not interested."

Her outrage deflated. She took the scrap from him.

Carrie arrived balancing their food, and the moment—

whatever it meant—was lost. They ate quickly. Less time in the diner meant fewer questions, fewer visitors to their table, and fewer lies she'd have to tell. After laying down cash for their meals, Mike ushered her out, only giving her time to wave as people hailed her. Or, rather, as they hailed Lexi.

"Thank you." She climbed into her car as he held the driver's door open for her. Once he sat beside her, she pulled away, not wanting anyone to come out and talk. The only down-side to having an open convertible in town was the inability to avoid being seen. "I appreciate you getting me out of there so fast."

"What's the plan for today?"

"We go back to my place, change clothes, and go to the wedding."

"After the way people treated you in there, is that wise?" A frown line formed between his eyebrows. On him, it looked good.

Boy, she'd really lost it.

"Good idea or not, it's why I came home. You can wait at the house if you prefer."

"And miss meeting your fiancé? Not a chance."

She scowled. "Not my fiancé. My brother-in-law."

Mike just laughed.

Grace talked her dad into revealing the details but couldn't convince him to let her head over to Judge Simmons' house by herself. She changed into a lacy mauve sundress, and Mike into slacks and a sports coat. His white dress shirt and charcoal tie added another layer of sexy.

With her father on one side and Mike on the other, she marched up to the three story, white brick house, climbed onto the wide, white-railed porch and knocked. Mrs. Simmons opened the door, her polite mouth-stretch turning into a genuine smile.

"Why, Kevin, I wasn't sure you were going to get free of the animals in time. And Grace?" The woman eyed the three of them, sensing a juicy story, but after thirty years as a judge's wife, she knew better than to ask.

Grace gave a short nod. The best defense was... An indifferent air? She could only hope it would work. "Good morning, Mrs. Simmons. This is my friend, Mike."

Mike touched his fingers to his forehead as though tipping his hat. "Ma'am."

The bony, wrinkled woman blushed as Mike turned on the charm, and Grace hid her amusement. Having him by her side might be useful with the female population.

"Are Lexi and Jack here yet?" Dad asked.

"Everyone else is in the back parlor. We keep it nice for ceremonies. Though this wedding" —she eyed Grace— "is somewhat unusual."

Not knowing what the woman had been told, Grace bit back words and stepped into the house. The cool interior with its dark wood wainscoting and original black and white tile floors lowered the temperature a good five degrees.

Mrs. Simmons swept open French doors covered in white sheers. Lexi turned, her questioning glance changing to surprise as she spotted her sister. Grace stood frozen, heart thundering, uncertain for the first time in her life of how Lexi would receive her.

Lexi's arms went wide. "Grace. Last night, I dreamed that you'd be here."

Grace rushed forward as Lexi did, their laughter edged with tears as they embraced. "I wouldn't miss it."

Lexi pulled back and searched her face. "You missed

my first one."

Grace leaned close to her ear and whispered, "I tried to arrange your first one. I'm guessing it worked out?"

Lexi studied her again. Then she nodded. Smiled. Laughed. Grabbed Grace's hands. "It's all worked out so well. He loves me, Grace, almost as much as I love him."

A ton of worry fell off Grace's shoulders. Tears of relief stung her eyes. It had been worth six weeks of exile. "I'm so glad."

"But how could you have guessed?"

"Later." Grace took her sister's hand and turned to Mike. While their dad stepped over and kissed her temple, Lexi checked out the man her sister had brought. The protectiveness in her gaze tickled Grace. "This is Mike T—"

"Pleased to meet you." Mike thrust a hand out to shake Lexi's.

Grace gave him a sideways look. Why had he cut off the introduction? "I met Mike while I was away."

"Congratulations on your wedding." After they shook hands, he stepped beside Grace and took her arm. "I hope you don't mind that Grace brought me. I rather insisted, since she was coming to see her fiancé again."

Grace scowled at him. "I came to see my sister get married. Jack is just... Is... Well, you know what I mean."

Lexi raised an eyebrow. "A bonus? Getting a brother who might someday forgive you?"

Grace's throat closed. "He hasn't? But everything worked out so well."

Lexi rolled her eyes and turned to their dad. "You should have spanked her more when she was little."

"I might have, if I could have figured out which one of you was which. It'd be a shame for you to always take the blame for her actions."

Grace frowned. "Hey!"

Lexi and their dad laughed. He could always tell them apart so Grace knew he meant that as a joke. But the last part about Lexi taking her punishment stung. Probably because it was too often true.

"Do you need help getting dressed?" Grace said to change the topic.

Lexi glanced down at herself. "This is what I'm wearing."

Grace held in a sigh. It wasn't a white gown, but at least it wasn't jeans and a tank top. If Lexi wanted to be married in a powder blue, tea-length dress with a handkerchief hem, so be it. The satin under-dress showed through the outer layer of blue lace. The slight hint of color enhanced her sister's eyes, which already glittered with happiness. The look was so Lexi, understated but charming. "You look lovely."

"This is more me." The hint of apology in Lexi's tone made Grace wince.

"It's perfect for you. We've never had the same style, despite picking out dresses to marry the same man."

"Speak of the devil," Lexi whispered, looking over Grace's shoulder toward the hall door.

Jack came to Lexi's side, placing a protective and hopefully loving arm sliding around her waist. He stared at Grace, who could do nothing but wait out his decision. Would he yell at her? Ban her from the wedding? Embarrass her in front of Mike?

He nodded. "Grace."

"Jack."

Lexi elbowed him in the stomach. "Now that we know who everyone is, maybe we should get started."

"Not sure everyone's met," Dad said.

Mike stepped forward, his bulk a wall of support at Grace's side. He extended his hand. "I'm Mike."

Jack's eyebrows went up even as he shook hands. He did a quick assessment, his gaze darting between the two of them. "Pleased to meet you, Mike. How long have you known Grace?"

Mike raised one eyebrow, a territorial look Grace had never seen. So sure of himself as he took Jack's measure in return. "Long enough. Congratulations on your *most recent* marriage."

The men eyed each other. Grace swore the air thickened with testosterone fumes. She and Lexi looked at each other and rolled their eyes. But Grace had to smile inside as Mike held his protective stance. Having him stand up for her gave her a thrill.

"Welcome to the madness," Jack said with a nod of acceptance.

Mike chuckled, and the tension in the room eased.

"Shall we get started?" Judge Simmons asked.

Grace looked around the room. Dad, Lexi, the judge and his wife, and she and Mike. "Where's Annabeth?"

"It would be too confusing," Jack said. "She's already seen us get married, and we've explained to her that I married Lexi. This ceremony" —he eyed her— "just straightens out a clerical matter. Our last license was issued to me and you, instead of me and Lexi."

Grace didn't understand all the ramifications, but she understood this would be the official story. Questions would have to wait. "How awkward."

"Very," Jack agreed with too much emphasis to pass for politeness. "Fortunately for me, Lexi consented to this second wedding."

Grace stared him down, feeling a bit territorial herself where her sister was concerned. "And you felt the need to marry her again because you're so in love with her?"

"I wanted her to be mine, legally, and with no doubt in anyone's mind."

She narrowed her eyes at him. "That didn't answer the question."

He narrowed his eyes right back at her. "I love her more than I thought I'd ever love anyone again."

Lexi huffed out a breath. "If you two are done battling over me like some piece of prime beef, I'd like to get married. Again." She turned to Mike. "Would you and Grace do us the honor of serving as witnesses to our marriage?"

He hesitated only the briefest second. No one but Grace seemed to notice. "It would indeed be my honor."

Did he not want to get mixed up in the family? Be a signature she'd regret seeing for the rest of her life, a life he didn't plan to be a part of? She made a mental note to ask him about it later. Once she worked up the courage to deal with his answer.

The judge stepped up to her. "While you're here, perhaps you could officially annul that first ceremony? Pave the way for your sister's wedding."

Looking in his stern eyes, Grace wondered if he suspected more "shenanigans" from her and Lexi—with the blame going to Grace herself. As usual. And maybe this time she deserved it. "I'd be happy to officially un-marry Jack, if you feel it's necessary, since I never married him in the first place."

The judge grunted and led her and Jack away to do a quick form. Whether that was any more valid than the wedding, she didn't know. As long as the paperwork made Lexi and Jack a couple and let Grace off the hook, she would sign whatever needed signing.

Jack smirked at her. "Our last act as not-husband and not-wife."

"Amen." Grace surprised them both by kissing his cheek. "Thanks for being decent about this, Jack."

He took her hand. "We both knew it wasn't a love match between us. I should be apologizing for accepting your proposal. You deserve better." He jerked his head to indicate Mike across the room. "Is he the one?"

"I'm not sure." She cocked a teasing brow at him. "But he's *better*."

Jack tugged a strand of her hair. "Come on, brat. Let's go get me married."

Grace wiped away tears as she watched her sister become Lexi Walker, officially this time. The love between the Lexi and Jack as they exchanged vows, looking into each other's eyes with promise and devotion, cemented Grace's surety. She'd done the right thing. Whatever else had happened, Lexi had found her true love and would live right here in Little Tree.

Close to Grace.

After the papers were signed and the judge released everyone, they gathered near the cars. The sisters looked at each other.

"I want you and Mike to come out to the ranch," Lexi said. "We're going to pop some champagne with Dad and Crusty."

Grace groaned at the man's name. "How has that been going?"

Lexi shot a flirtatious smile at her husband. "If Crusty

were a few years younger, Jack would have had a serious challenger."

Jack grinned as he slid his arm around Lexi as though compelled to touch her. "The old coot helped me see the light at a time when I was, at best, stumbling around in the past."

"Well, he must have changed then," Grace said, "because he never cared for me."

Warmth radiated along her back. Mike. She didn't have to look to know. "It was confusing," she went on. "No matter how I tried, he was just crusty, in name and attitude. How did you win him over?"

"He could see that I loved his nephew." Lexi smiled up at Jack, who hugged her tighter.

Grace nodded. "That's the difference then. Because, and I don't mean to be offensive, Jack, but I never loved you that way."

"And I never loved you that way, either." He held his arms open.

Grace stepped into his embrace. "Forgive me?"

He kissed her temple and set her very resolutely back at Mike's side. "Thankful to you."

She grinned. "As you should be."

"Grace," her dad admonished. "Let's not poke a gift horse in the mouth."

They laughed and headed out. Grace took Lexi aside to walk together. "I ran into Carrie at The Diner. She said something about you and a drifter?"

Lexi chuckled. "We spread the story I went off with a hot drifter to Vegas. People were questioning my absence at *your* wedding."

"Oh. I didn't think about that, but then, I didn't realize there would be a wedding. I only thought about getting you two together."

"Fortunately, it worked out. But how could you know it would?"

Lexi would be hurt to discover she'd been the subject of the town gossip.

"I didn't know for sure." Grace glanced around to make sure they weren't overheard. "I haven't said anything to Dad or even Mike about why I left. I just knew I couldn't marry Jack when I realized you loved him."

"It's a good thing he loves me back."

"That's handy." Grace's smile faded. "But what are you telling people in town about the bride switch? Carrie and Rachel thought Jack married me."

"You've been at Rachel's all this time?"

"Yes, and Jack's pesky brother keeps popping in, looking for me."

Lexi gasped. "Oh, no, I forgot to call Clint. We have to tell him. He's probably taken too much time off work looking for you. I didn't realize he'd be that diligent in searching."

They reached the cars, and Grace hesitated. She'd been too big a part of their relationship already. The couple needed some time alone. "We shouldn't come over for champagne."

Lexi frowned. "It won't be official if you're not there. You're our matchmaker, right?"

Finally someone understood. "If you're sure. Let me check with Mike."

"I want that whole story. Soon."

Grace tried to smile. "I'm not sure what the whole story is yet."

"Can I give you some advice, from an old married lady?"

"After being married for fifteen minutes?"

Lexi teetered her hand back and forth in front of her. "And about six weeks, give or take."

"I guess that qualifies you as a relationship expert. Go ahead."

"I've seen the way you are with him and he is with you. It didn't take me the entire past half hour to see that you're together as more than friends."

"It's complicated. We aren't dating or anything."

Lexi put her hand on Grace's arm. "He looks at you like you're a dessert he can't have."

Grace's body heated. He could have her, though. That was what scared her. What came after the sex?

"And you," Lexi continued, "just beam when he's near. When he stood behind you before, you relaxed. All your tension evaporated. I've never seen you lean on anyone else. I'd almost be jealous if I didn't understand it perfectly. I have that with Jack. We're a team."

Grace's chest tightened. "I can't say that. I just met him last month."

"Is there a time requirement on love?"

"You know what I mean."

"Jack couldn't admit he loved me because of his first wife. It took him a while to acknowledge how he felt. I look at Mike looking at you, and I see some kind of struggle. He wants you, Grace. Maybe he's just not sure what he'd do with you once he wins you."

"We Marshall women are a handful."

Lexi nodded. "And we deserve men who can appreciate that. I found mine. Haven't you?"

Grace watched her walk over to Jack's car, kiss their father, and slide inside. Jack climbed behind the wheel. "I expect you all to be right behind us," he called, making eye contact with Grace before including the others. "The family should celebrate together."

Gratitude made her knees weak. Jack was a hell of a guy. His forgiveness underscored his love for Lexi.

"I'm going over," her dad said. "You?"

She nodded. "Mike, would you drive please?"

He took the keys but waited the others to drive out. He glanced at Grace in the passenger seat, as though trying to gauge her feelings. "They seem happy."

"Yes, and I'm so relieved."

"I don't know that I would have been as forgiving as your fiancé."

"My *brother-in-law* has Lexi, the woman he really loves, which is the way it should have always been. He never would have proposed to me."

"What?"

CHAPTER TEN

Mike stilled as his heart stopped pumping blood. At least it felt that way when he couldn't catch his breath. "Hold on. You asked him to marry you?"

"Oh. Uh, yeah."

That changed everything. "You never said you were in love with him. Why didn't you marry him?" He looked down the road where the two vehicles had gone. "Did your sister come between you?"

Grace sighed. "You're not going to start the car? The judge and his wife probably have their noses pressed to the windows."

"I don't care." But he started up and pulled out, keeping well behind the vet's truck. Not only did he need time to process this information, he didn't want Grace pelted with rocks and dirt through the open roof. "So. Perhaps you'd like to catch me up?"

"Not really, but here's the short version. I never said I loved Jack. I liked him very much. Still do, maybe even more now that he's going to make my sister so happy."

"But you proposed marriage to him."

"His uncle threatened to take the land away from Jack, just because Jack didn't have a son, or a wife to produce one. He's worked the ranch his whole life expecting to inherit. I considered that unfair, so I said we were getting married."

"I think pieces of the story are missing, but go on. Why did this uncle believe it?"

"We were dating, but I knew Jack didn't love me. I thought he was hung up on his first wife, who died a few years ago. Turns out, he was really in love with Lexi." She grinned. "Lexi. Who, it turns out, was in love with him."

"Pieces still missing, but I'm getting the picture."

"I didn't know about Lexi's feelings when I proposed. But I did know on the wedding day. I couldn't marry him without either of us being in love."

"And you couldn't have told him this before he stood at the altar?"

"No, I couldn't."

He drove in silence. So many elements to this tale she hadn't told him yet, but he believed her. She'd done nothing but go toe-to-toe with him. She didn't lack courage. If she could have found a way to tell Jack, she would have.

Hearing that it had been her idea to link her life with Jack's chafed, but it helped ease the burn in his chest that love hadn't entered into their relationship. How Jack could have missed his chance with Grace, Mike didn't know. He could only be thankful. And promise himself he would not be as slow if given a similar opportunity.

How that would all work out, he had no idea.

Champagne bubbled in her glass as Grace toasted the happy couple once again. Crusty and Jack's daughter Annabeth rounded out the party. Crusty had harrumphed on seeing her and stayed across the living room since. Had the sharp glance from Lexi influenced the old geezer? Her sister must have more power than Grace imagined. She overheard Mike and

Jack talking about horses and cattle, the two main topics here.

Little Annabeth stayed nearby Lexi as they sampled from plates of hors d'oevres. Grace's heart softened witnessing their bond, an attachment she doubted she could have brought about as quickly.

"Here." Mike thrust a glass in her hand as he suddenly appeared before her. "You're pale, so I found you some of the girl's sparkling juice."

"Adrenaline crash, coupled with champagne at ten a.m. Thanks for thinking of this."

He just looked into her eyes before he walked off. Given the family watching and the questions an embrace would have raised, that gaze was better than a hug. Almost.

Suddenly the six-year-old appeared at her side, munching on a carrot stick. "Hello, Aunt Grace."

"Hello, cutie. This is a crazy party day, huh?"

The girl nodded. "I thought Daddy married you. But now Lexi is my new mom. And she has been since the wedding. I called her Grace and she answered, like she was you."

Grace floundered. Hadn't this all been ironed out already? Jack had said a second wedding would be confusing, but Annabeth seemed confused about the first one. "Well. I was supposed to marry your dad, that's true. Then I didn't, so Lexi did."

The girl nodded, expression expectant.

"Then, I guess it was hard to explain what happened, and so they pretended Lexi was me for a while. We used to switch places like that a lot when we were younger."

"It would be so cool to have a twin. Or just a sister." She glanced over at her dad and Lexi. "Do you think they'll have babies?"

Grace tightened her grip on the glass stem. She definitely didn't want to explain the birds and the bees to her new niece. "Oh, well, that would be sometime in the future. I guess we'll have to wait and see."

"I'd like a brother too. Maybe Mom could have a twin boy and girl."

Mom? Wow. Looked like Lexi had won over every heart on the ranch. Grace's heart filled near to bursting with joy.

"I have to go," Dad said, coming to her side. "It doesn't seem right to send Lexi out on her special day." He glanced down at Annabeth. "I'll see you tomorrow, though. You're still helping me in the office, right?"

Annabeth nodded enthusiastically before looking up at Grace. "I'm going to hold all the puppies and kitties for Grandpa so they'll be calm."

Grandpa. How the family had grown. "That'll be a big help."

He kissed both girls on the forehead and said his goodbyes to the others. Annabeth wandered away. Her family had found happiness. Now she just had to figure out her own future.

She glanced at Mike and saw him laughing in the corner with Crusty. That didn't bode well, so she meandered over. Sure enough, as she drew closer, she heard her name.

"Then," Crusty said, "Grace had to stay after school for a week, repainting the walls."

Grace cringed. Not that old story. "I was nine, Crusty," she said as she approached. "Don't you think it's time to let it rest?"

"You were a good speller for nine."

She shot him an ironic look. "Thank you. Besides, that

teacher deserved it. He called me a cheater in front of the entire classroom. And I wasn't cheating."

Mike nodded, his glass suspiciously close to his mouth considering he wasn't drinking it. Hiding a smile?

"I wasn't," she insisted. "I let Jimmy Krause copy off my paper. But I had already finished the math test. And Jimmy didn't get in trouble at all."

"That hardly seems fair," Mike murmured.

"That's what I thought."

Crusty leaned closer to Mike. "Now, did I tell you about the time Grace got in trouble for—"

"Stop." She glared at the old man. His shining blue eyes and sweet old man beard didn't fool her one bit. "Mike has heard all he needs to hear about my misspent youth."

"But did you tell him about—?"

"Crusty, I'm serious. Just stop, okay? It was a long time ago, and I learned my lessons."

"Maybe covering over those bad words started your painting career."

"I didn't mind being up on a ladder for a week. Mom had made sure I couldn't sit down anyway."

"That woman was a saint."

"Agreed." Witnessing her parents' disappointment had been the harshest punishment. "I think it's the last time she had to spank either of us."

"Why would she ever have to spank Lexi?"

Grace leaned forward. "Who do you think helped me with the spelling?"

Crusty held his belly, laughing so hard he nearly toppled over. "What a spitfire."

"Wait a minute. How come she's a spitfire and I'm a troublemaker?"

He poked a gnarled finger toward her. "Cuz you got caught."

She watched the old man totter off, hitching and limping his way across to the bar. "I'm ready to go if you are."

On the way home, she noticed Mike glancing at her. As they neared the house, he spoke. "It doesn't matter to me that you had a wild childhood."

"I'm not proud of it, but I'm not ashamed of all of it, either. It's just my past. Lexi grew up loving animals, and I grew up getting in trouble." She ran a hand through her hair, lifting if off her temple. "No one lets me forget it."

The townspeople still saw her as that wild child. That she'd become a painter instead of a grocery clerk or waitress didn't surprise them. They just shook their heads at yet another of her oddities.

"Lexi grew up loving animals," Mike echoed. "You grew up to become a famous artist."

She scoffed. "Like that makes a difference. In this town, paint is for barns. It's as though they're waiting for me to do something crazy again."

"Like leave your groom at the altar?"

She winced. "I'm not sure what story they told everyone in town. Lexi got side-tracked and never told me."

"You should call her later."

But the landline rang as they walked into the house.

"Oh, hey, Carrie. Lunch?" Grace panicked but could only come up with one reason not to. "I have a guest this week."

"That hunk won't mind if you spend a little time apart. It'll be good for him, make him appreciate you more."

"Are you sure you want don't want to wait until Lexi's available?"

"I'll have lunch with her another day. It's time we got to know each other better, now that you're back in town. You are back, aren't you?"

"Yes. Okay. Let's do this."

Carrie laughed. "Your determination to get through a meal with me warms my heart. I'll meet you at Kerr's at 12:30."

Grace set the phone down with a groan. "Why did I agree to that?"

"What?" Mike asked.

"Lunch in half an hour with Lexi's friend, Carrie. She was our waitress at The Diner this morning."

"Why wouldn't you go? I can find something to do."

"If you drop me off, you can use my car. Tour the valley."

He nodded. "I like looking at land."

"Just don't forget to pick me up in an hour. If I decide to leave early and walk home, I'll let you know."

"I'll come get you."

"Sounds better." She wanted a cold cloth for her head. "I need to change. This is a little dressy for Kerr's Grill."

He watched her go. She felt his gaze, and almost turned around to find comfort in his arms. But that wasn't really their dynamic.

Problem was, she didn't understand their relationship, at all.

Grace sat in the booth at Kerr's with her mouth agape, staring as Carrie finished the story in a whisper. Outrage, pain, and shock ran through Grace's veins. "Why didn't someone tell me my sister was attacked?"

"Well, you'd know the answer to that better than I

would."

Grace cringed. Right. No one had known where to find her. She'd turned off her phone for most of the time she'd stayed at Rachel's. "They should have called our cousin. She would have told me."

"It wasn't like Jack came out and announced his wife was attacked. News just spread."

Grace's stomach contracted like a lead ball had dropped into it.

"You need to explain how Jack's wife wasn't you, when I saw you guys get married."

"I'll tell you when I can."

Carrie took a breath. "All I know is Jack's wife was grabbed and terrified, but not hurt. Then Darryl Peters got the bejeesus beat out of him."

"It was Darryl? And Jack beat him up? Good." Grace couldn't believe it. Darryl was a slimy no-account, but his parents were decent folks.

"That's the story. Not from the Rocking W, of course. No one from there has said a thing. Even Lexi. The sheriff arrested one of their ranch hands, but I don't know the story on that. Could be unrelated."

"I have to go see her. I mean, I know she's okay. I just saw her this morning." Grace put her hands over her face. "This is all my fault. I should have been home."

"I'm willing to listen."

"Ask Lexi. Or…wait." Grace studied Carrie. As Lexi's friend, the brunette had been a mainstay in her life since forever. Not quite another sister the way Rachel was, but Carrie could be counted on in whatever adventures required a third person.

"You can't tell anyone, okay?" Grace waited until

Carrie nodded then leaned in and lowered her voice. No one was close enough to overhear, but this wasn't just her secret. She couldn't be too careful. "I didn't marry Jack. Lexi did." She ignored Carrie's gasp. "She's been posing as me until they could figure out if they were married or if I was married to him. Her being Alexis Grace and me being Audrey Grace led to some mix up. Now they're in love. They got married, or re-married, this morning."

Carrie fell back against the seat. Gaze fixed on Grace, Carrie took a gulp of her beer. She shook her head. "I'll be damned."

"Is that all you have to say? No questions?"

"This story is so like you. Like both of you. One does something crazy, and the other backs her up."

Grace grimaced but couldn't deny it. "I'm relieved to tell someone and glad you're not asking for more details. I don't want to answer questions." She toyed with the straw in her water glass. "You can ask Lexi. I'll give her the heads-up that you know."

After a moment, Carrie shrugged. "Okay, we'll leave it at that. So, what can you tell me about your friend from breakfast?"

Grace lifted her gaze. Carrie only looked curious, not interested in Mike. Good thing because— Well, just because. "He's a friend. Maybe more. We haven't figured anything out yet."

"Are you staying in town? Is he moving here?"

"No. I mean, yes, I'm staying. But Mike has a family, a whole different life in Colorado."

Carrie raised a brow. "A family?"

"Siblings," Grace amended. "Not a wife. Responsibilities."

"Ah." Carrie scooped an onion ring through the chipotle dipping sauce. Licking her fingers, she added, "So what are your plans?"

"Maybe you could help me, but let's keep this between us for now. I'm looking for land. Do you know any for sale?"

"How much land? And for what? I can't see you ranching."

"No." Grace had to smile. "I want to open an art center."

"That's...different."

"It would bring people to town, where they'd spend money. So the townsfolk ought to be happy." At least she hoped so. She'd finally thought of a way to win them over. "There would be classes and cabin studios for retreats. Get away from it all and paint. So many artists need that dedicated time. We'd bring in experts to teach different techniques, and I'd like to open a gallery in town eventually."

Carrie frowned. "Would people really come here to paint? I mean, it's pretty country, but Montana's not everyone's cup of tea."

"Right. It's rugged and dry and full of interesting characters. The colors in the West aren't like anywhere else on the planet."

"I'll take your word for that, seeing as how I've only been as far as Yellowstone Park." Carrie tapped her chin. "I have an idea, but I need to talk to Adam."

Grace kept her expression neutral. Adam Moore couldn't even manage the ranch he and Carrie had inherited from their parents. Unless he heard gossip in a bar, he wouldn't exactly have his finger on the pulse of the county. "Why Adam?"

"It has to do with Hannah, so let me get back to you."

At the mention of Carrie's deceased sister, Grace dropped the subject and asked after Hannah's husband. "What's Ryan doing these days?"

Carrie frowned and wiped condensation from her glass. "He's still bronc riding. Chasing the championship belt. I don't follow rodeo so I don't know if he's doing well or not. And it's not as though he checks in with us. Not even any updates on Samantha. I miss her so much."

"No word on when he and Sam are returning?"

Carrie shrugged. "When he wins, I guess. Or gets hurt. Or Samantha graduates from home schooling."

"Graduates? Isn't she just a toddler?"

"She's five. She should be in a real school."

Here. The word echoed in the silence.

Carrie cleared her throat. "Adam and I have been keeping an eye on his family's ranch. It's the least we can do. Plus, it borders our land, so it's not a big deal."

Grace's mouth went dry as a possibility occurred to her. "Do you think Ryan would be open to selling?"

"His parents' place? I don't know." Carrie drew a pattern on the table. "I'd hate for him to cut his last ties to Little Tree. And it's Samantha's future."

Grace sat back, dejected. Ryan would have to be really hard up for cash to sell Windy Glade. "Maybe he wants to sell it and invest the proceeds for Sam's college."

Carrie kept her gaze on the table surface. Her mouth drooped as hopelessly as her shoulders. Could Carrie have feelings for her deceased sister's husband?

Maybe she and Lexi had bonded over that. Wanting their sister's guy. Except Jack had never been Grace's.

"Sorry to bring that up." Grace patted Carrie's hand, feeling awkward with the gesture. "Fine way to start our newfound, adult friendship."

Carrie smiled. "Being the third in your group was always fun, if hazardous at times. I wish I'd gotten close to you like I did to Lexi."

"You two are soul mates, and yes," she added as Carrie's eyes widened, "it does kill me a little to say that. We were all 4-H but you were the girls interested in animals. I only cared about Visual Arts."

Carrie chuckled. "And every time you entered a painting, you won."

"It may seem silly now, but those county and state fair wins gave me a boost of confidence."

"You? Since when did you need confidence?"

Grace shrugged. "Being a painter is fine here if you're looking to fix up houses or barns. An artist is considered odd. Competing with others across the state showed me I could hold my own. That my paintings had worth."

"We always said so. Even if the townspeople didn't understand how talented the paintings were, we knew you were special."

"Special." Grace blew out a laugh. "I've been called worse. I want to fit in. Bringing money to the town via the art center and retreat might help."

Carrie's eyes were wide. "Fit in? You're the vet's daughter. Damn, girl, you're like royalty in this town."

"*Dad's* like royalty. And now Lexi, too. I'm still looking for my place." Grace sighed and stared at the last inch of water in her glass. "I don't want to leave again. I'm done traveling."

"What about the new guy?"

Grace shook her head. "I told you. He has a family and a job in Colorado."

"Would you go back with him?"

"What kind of a question is that? I just said I want to stay here."

Carrie wagged a finger at her. "You're answering a question with a question. I can pick up on these things since I once dated a cop."

Grace frowned. Carrie had dated a cop because other than her ranch hands, she mixed with cops the most. They kept arresting her brother for Public Drunkenness. "It's not like that between us."

"And now you're avoiding a direct answer." Carrie leaned back, shaking her head. "New girlfriend, you've got it bad."

Mike drove Grace home from her lunch date, wondering why she was so quiet. Either something worried her or she was cooking up some plan. Neither option put him at ease. "Good lunch?"

"Hmm? Oh, sure. Carrie's a lot of fun and has some interesting views on things. It was nice to touch base again *now that I'm back*."

Was he imagining the emphasis? She'd been home from her travels for several months, and this stay at Rachel's had only been six weeks long.

"What did you do today?" she asked.

"I drove around, looked at the land. Talked to a few ranchers."

Grace's brows rose. "About what?"

"Ranching. It's nice country. Drier than Longmont. It would be harder to feed a herd of horses." Nor had he heard of any land for sale outside of town, let alone anything suitable for a horse ranch.

"A herd of horses? This is cattle country."

He nodded. "I heard that view today. Several times."

Mike stopped the car in front of the house and extended the keys to Grace. "Driving this little beauty didn't help my credibility any."

She followed after him, two hurried footsteps for each of his, all the way to the house and into the kitchen. "Why do you need credibility here?"

Mike opened the fridge and scanned the contents. He closed the door and pulled down a glass from the cupboard. "A man always needs a standing in a community." He filled the glass with tap water. "Got to know where he stands, and let the other men know where that is. Maybe it's a guy thing."

He eyed her as he drank.

"Why here, though?" She had the cutest furrow across her forehead, which he knew better than to mention. "What do you care what these ranchers think of you?"

Because you live here. He'd also become part of their community if he stayed here and built a horse rehabilitation ranch. He was leap years, and hundreds of thousands of dollars, from affording that. Buying land; then building corrals, fences, and barns; then buying horses, feed, hay, and help. There was no sense getting into details now

He shrugged. "Little darlin', a man always cares what other men think. We want respect and need to establish our place in the world."

"Well, in the world, sure. I get that. But in Little Tree?"

He tapped her nose. "It's part of the world. Don't you want these people to respect you and your art?"

She blinked. "Yeah, of course. But these are my people. This is my town."

"And maybe that's precisely why it's important to me,

too."

He walked off having said more than he'd intended.

"Mike." Those quick tapping steps came after him.

He grinned. Should have known she wouldn't let it rest.

"Carrie asked me something today."

He turned at the guest room door. "I would hope so. You were together for two hours."

"Very funny. She asked if I would go back with you to Colorado. And it got me to thinking…"

His breath caught in his chest and he had to cough out a blockage. Was she saying she'd go back with him? "What were you thinking?"

"When are you going back? You have a job, and the kids. They need you."

"I have a job, yes, and the kids need me." He swallowed. "You've said you wanted to stay here. To come home for good."

"Right. I said that. I meant that."

His chest pounded. "I have time still. As the kids told you, we never go on vacation, so I've accrued quite a few days."

Grace glanced away, pursed her lips as she thought. His gaze fixed on her mouth, on what he wanted to do. Those lips, puckered up like that, drove all thoughts from his head except one.

"So." Grace lasered him again with her blue eyes.

He thought he might swallow his tonsils, his mouth was so dry.

"Carrie asked what we were doing."

"Doing?" Dammit, he sounded like a parrot.

"I mean, I guess it was me wondering. Why did you come with me?"

He took a step backward, his bootheels loud on the hardwood floor. "I told you. I'm taking a vacation."

She shook her head and stepped in after him. "No one vacations in Little Tree. Not yet, anyway."

He wasn't sure what "yet" meant, only that he had to sidetrack her. It was too soon for this conversation. "I'd never been here, so I didn't know that."

Her hand landed on his chest. Surely she could feel his heart racing.

"How long is your vacation going to last?"

"A few more days." If all went well.

Somehow his arms had circled around her, snugging her up against him, raising her on her toes. Her hands lay flat on his shoulders, partly for balance, and partly, he hoped, for something else. Something like need. Acceptance. Anticipation.

His lips brushed hers. Electricity zipped between them, racing in spikes up his arms.

"You never said," she whispered, "why you came along with me."

This he could answer truthfully, though it would only be part of the reason. "I couldn't let you come back to face your fiancé alone."

Her body melted against his. "You thought it might be hard for me? That's why you came?"

"I knew it would be hard for you." That half truth didn't sit well with him so he decided to 'fess up. "And I didn't want you to look at him and wish you'd married him, after all."

"Wasn't going to happen." She took a breath that pushed her breasts into his chest. "But why would that bother you?"

The look in her eyes threw him. Was that hope? With

her breasts pressed against him and that glitter of something in her gaze, he didn't have words to convey what he felt.

So he kissed her.

CHAPTER ELEVEN

Grace gasped as Mike's mouth closed over hers. He dove and took, and she reveled in it. He didn't ask, didn't wait. His fingers gripped her; his hot palms pressed her body to his.

She slid her arms around his neck, pulling him closer. Kissing him with the passion churning inside her. Tasting him. Wanting to devour him.

"Oh." She tried to speak around his kiss, around her lack of breath.

"What?" His tongue trailed up to her ear.

"I probably taste like onion rings."

His chuckle reverberated along her ribs like fireworks. His lips returned to hers. "You do. And chipotle sauce." He backed her up until her knees hit the side of his mattress. "And I want to taste all of it. All of you."

She tightened her arms around him and toppled backward.

Mike's eyes went wide with surprise but he got one hand out to break his fall on top of her. "Give a guy some warning. I could have crushed you."

She arched a brow at him. "That's the idea."

He grinned. "I wouldn't want my buckle to tear your pretty dress."

"You are so thoughtful." She kissed the corner of his

mouth and inhaled the fresh male scent of him. "I guess you better take off that belt then."

"Or we could take off your dress."

"Or we could take off both."

Mike nodded. "A wise woman."

She freed her hands from around him to unbutton the bodice. What bra did she put on this morning? She'd shaved yesterday, so—

His hands stilled hers.

"Let me." His husky voice sent shivers through her and her hands fell away. She'd get to his clothes soon enough. For now, she let him take over, let him uncover her. She watched his brown eyes go ever so much darker as he slipped each button from its enclosure. He parted her collar down past the vee of her cleavage, and his breath caught as his fingers trailed along her skin, over her chest, along the tops of her breasts.

She shivered, and gooseflesh rose as her belly tightened. She wanted him. Had for a long time.

She drew him down into a scorching kiss. His tongue thrust into her mouth, and she opened for him, inhaled him. Heat flared where their bodies lay against each other, him pressing, her accepting.

She went to work on his buttons, not as patiently as he'd done hers, but a lot more adroitly. His shirt fell open to the waist in seconds. She tugged at it. Mike dipped his head and licked her breasts and she gave up undressing him for the moment. The suck and pull of his lips, the wet trail of his tongue, the thrill as the edge of his teeth slid along her skin— all these distracted her. She held him to her, pushed up to give him access as his fingers peeled down the lacy cups of her bra.

Thank God, I put on something pretty was her last thought before his mouth found her nipple.

He growled as she tried to maneuver off his shirt, eager to touch him, to please him in return. Every tug of his lips drew her tighter, made her ache to have him inside her. She'd had lovers and experienced passion, but her body reacted to Mike as though he were sustenance long denied. Desire and need combined with something in her, something new. Her heart soared and her body quivered with anticipation. She wanted to shout with triumph to the world, and at the same time, hide them both away. To savor this first coming together, just for the two of them.

She yanked off his shirt far less kindly than he pulled off her blouse. She pushed at his opened pants, less concerned with the jeans falling off than getting her hands inside them. When he sat up to remove his boots and jeans, she growled. Her greedy hands wanted access but her eyes took their turn, her gaze roaming over his dark skin and hard muscles. A working man with the body to prove it. She smiled, thinking of his stamina and how she'd put it to the test.

He stretched out beside her and slid one arm beneath to pull her against his warm body. His other palm cupped her face. She needed him close, sought to connect in the most elemental way. Driven by a hard burst of desire, she only wanted him inside her, becoming a part of her.

Mike opted for gentleness.

She swallowed down emotion and took a calming breath. Never would she have chosen this moment to slow down, but it was perfection. She gazed into the endless depths of his brown eyes, losing herself, becoming more.

She tried not to be unnerved.

He bent and nuzzled her cheek, whispers of words drifting across her skin. His tongue followed the path, making her shiver, goose bumps forming, making her taut and needy.

Mike pulled back, his gaze traveling down her body. His hand cupped her breast, fingers teasing. "You are so beautiful."

Her body shook, whether at his words or his touch, she didn't know. Or care. She wanted to stretch out for him, like a cat being petted, expose more of her body for his touch and admiration.

At the same time, frustration raced through her at his slow, thorough loving. She wanted him. Now.

With a hand on his nape, she pulled his mouth to hers, trying to communicate the urgency of her need.

He wouldn't be hurried.

Still kissing her, he slid his hand downward, fingers gliding along her belly, over her mound, lower. She nearly shot upright in a spasm of need as his fingers encountered her most sensitized flesh.

"Easy," he murmured. "I've got you."

She wanted to tell him she was ready, her body wet enough and eager to take him inside. Words wouldn't form past the sensations churning in her, building to something not just sexual. Something…more.

Something a little frightening. Unexpected and new. Had she ever felt this building, building, building tension suffusing her lungs, her blood, her very skin until she thought she might explode with… Love?

She shied away from the thought and hooked a leg over his, pulling him as best she could. He stopped to sheath himself then levered over her, guiding himself into her. Grace tensed, not with pain, but with the joy of uniting.

His mouth consumed hers as he pushed into her, her slick passageway aiding his entry. He paused, eyes tight.

"Don't stop," she managed to say.

Mike shook his head. "I want to remember this moment. This feeling."

A laugh breezed out of her. "It's a great feeling, I agree. But there's more."

He began to move.

Grace met him, thrust for thrust. Mike had forgotten about slow, but not about tenderness, one hand against the mattress keeping him from crushing her while the other explored and drove her crazy with longing. She stroked his skin, tightened around him, sought to please as he pleased her. Kisses landed wherever she could reach, teeth pulling gently, encouraging.

He lowered against her, hot skin to hot skin. His chest hair brushed her breasts, tightened her nipples, made them ache for his touch. He didn't disappoint as his hand cupped her breast, kneading, his fingers finding her aching tips.

Desire tightened her body. She didn't want to climax yet, didn't want this to end. She grasped him closer, legs around his hips, holding him to her. Yet still he thrust, still he drove her on, drove them both on, upward, climbing, peaking. One moment of perfect fullness then she shattered as Mike pumped his own release into her. She grabbed at him, clutching, trying to hold on to the moment, to him. His hands glided over her, arousing her when she would have said she had no more to give.

Whatever she had to give, she'd give to him. Again and again. For as long as he asked.

Being so vulnerable made her tremble.

Being able to bring him pleasure made her soar.

They lay quiet afterward, she in his arms. She smiled against his chest.

"What?" His fingers drew patterns on her skin.

"A month ago, I would never have imagined you like this."

"You didn't think I was a cuddler?" His voice held amusement.

"You couldn't stand me."

He levered up on an elbow. "A month ago, I was still running."

"Running?"

"From what you made me feel."

"This?" She indicated their bodies in the bed.

"When we met, you were hours away from having almost married another man. You intended to return home, to Montana, but my life was in Colorado. Neither of those infused me with confidence."

A smile grew on her face. She trailed her fingers along his chest, flicking his nipple then venturing lower. "Feeling confident now?"

He swooped in on her, taking her mind away from the conversation, losing all thought but pleasure. It wasn't until much later she realized he hadn't fully answered her earlier question.

What did he feel for her?

Grace sat in the kitchen of the Rocking W the next morning and waited for Lexi to come downstairs. Grace had been up early, painting the sun rising over a field of sleeping cattle. Or that had been her excuse. She'd just been too restless to sleep, too excited by this change in her relationship with Mike, and she'd wanted to talk to Lexi.

Her sister had not just been up even earlier, she'd been out on a call. When Lexi returned, according to Crusty, she'd "stunk to high heaven" of hay, manure, and afterbirth.

Grace doubted the truth of that, since her father and sister were religious about hygiene before and after treating an animal.

"Just de-scustin'." The old man cradled a mug of coffee, keeping Grace company, as he put it.

Grace cut a smile at him with clenched teeth, trying to keep the peace. She'd like to have asked what he thought veterinarians were supposed to smell like—roses and baby powder? But she bit her words back. He'd become her twin's uncle by marriage, and as an elder deserved her respect.

Not that he made it easy.

"Whatcha here to talk to our girl about this early? Don't ya got nothin' else to keep ya busy? Like makin' breakfast for that man ya brung to town?"

She closed her eyes and counted to ten, focusing on his fond tone when he referred to Lexi as "our girl." Her sister had found the way into the old geezer's heart. Probably through a wormhole.

Oh, wait. She was trying to think nice thoughts. "*That man* can make his own breakfast."

Crusty harrumphed.

"And quite happily too. Mike doesn't expect me to provide for him."

"Ain't about expectations, ya daft girl. It's about the doin' for without the askin'."

He made her head spin. "What?"

"A man shouldn't have to ask."

"And a woman? Can she expect to have breakfast made for her without asking?"

Crusty grimaced. "What's the point in that? Women do for their men. Men do things—other things—for their women. Thought the Doc woulda taught ya how to get along in this world."

Grace scrubbed a palm over her cheek to ease the ache in her jaw. It was too early in the morning to argue equality rights with Crusty.

Lexi bounded into the kitchen, clean and shiny, her wet ponytail swinging behind her. "Hey, Grace. Sorry about that. Judy's foal couldn't wait till daybreak. They didn't have any problems, but they like me or Dad on hand, just in case."

"Judy?"

"Cal and Maria Schmitt's mare."

Grace nodded as she recalled the couple. In their sixties, they ran a dude ranch, but the lack of visitors to Little Tree kept their stable small.

The germ of an idea ignited hope and made her heart race with excitement. Maybe they had a few unused acres where she could build her retreat. People could come to paint and ride. The dude ranch would keep their families occupied while the artists attended classes or enjoyed uninterrupted studio time. She made a mental note to call on the Schmitts.

"So they have a new filly?" Grace drew a seemingly idle doodle on the island counter, imagining how much land she'd have to ask for and how she could phrase it to sound mutually beneficial.

"Yep. I had to talk them out of naming her Alexis."

Crusty grinned, or so Grace guessed, as his white mustache parted from his bushy beard. "Ya shoulda let 'em. They'd be proud to honor ya that way."

Lexi laughed and opened the fridge then removed a covered plate. Popping it in the microwave, she said, "If Dad and I let everyone name their animals after us in a moment of gratitude, we'd have several hundred Kevins, Lexis, and Marshalls in this county by now."

The timer dinged and Lexi gingerly lifted the hot plate. Short toothpicks held up the plastic wrap, which she removed to reveal scrambled eggs with cheese melted on top. "Thanks, Crusty."

He grunted at her and buried his face behind his raised coffee mug.

"Why are you thanking him?" Grace asked.

"He saved me some eggs."

Grace spun on him. "You made her breakfast?"

His brows lowered nearly into his mug.

"He's a wiz at scrambled eggs." Lexi winked at him. "I wouldn't touch his brownies, but he has a few other specialties."

"Man can't survive on bread and milk," he growled. "Ever'body knows that."

Grace narrowed her eyes. "What was all that about earlier?"

He shrugged. "Weren't talking about me then."

"What were you talking about?" Lexi asked. "Same thing you came to see me about this morning?"

Grace glanced at the old man. No way would she discuss her relationship with Mike in front of Crusty. Especially as that relationship now included sex. Lexi usually had some insight into how men thought since she spent so much time around them. "Nothing in particular."

"Early for a call about nothing." Lexi scooped up some eggs. "Early for you, I mean."

"I had to get up to paint the dawn. What would you think if I move in with Dad while Mike's here? It is technically your house. Do you mind having someone who's a stranger to you in it alone?"

Lexi set her fork on the counter, frown lines between

her eyebrows. "If I can trust him with my sister, I can trust him with my house. Are things not going well between you and Mike?"

"Don't be surprised," Crusty interrupted, "if the Doc don't want you movin' back home."

Grace put her hands on her hips, bracing to spar with the old coot. "What's that supposed to mean? Why wouldn't he?"

"Your daddy weren't always your daddy or just the town vet. He's a man, too. Was one long before you two came along."

Some of her footing shifted. At least it felt that way as Grace tried to absorb the old man's words.

"Crusty," Lexi warned him off.

"No," Grace said, "let him talk. What do you mean?"

"Are ya bein' deliberately dense, girl? He's got a woman friend."

"Well, sure he does. Dad has lots of friends who are…" She trailed off as Crusty shook his head.

"A *woman friend*. Ain't the same."

Her mouth went dry and that familiar sense of panic made her palms damp. "A girlfriend? You mean someone he's dating?"

Crusty snorted. "If you call that dating, then sure. She's a little long in the tooth to be called a girl, though."

Grace shot a look at Lexi for confirmation. Her sister concentrated on her plate a little too intently. Had everyone known but her? "Who?"

Lexi cleared her throat. "Remember Iris Browning, the librarian?"

No words came. Hearing who had stolen her father's heart didn't make a difference. Grace couldn't wrap her mind around it.

Grace wanted her dad to be happy. She just never thought he could find someone to live up to their mom.

"How long…" She cleared her throat. "How long has this been going on, and why didn't you tell me, Lex?"

Lexi rose and hugged Grace. "I just found out myself while you were gone. I'd have told you, honest."

"But I didn't have my phone on." Grace nodded, her mind abuzz. "Okay. I understand that part."

How had her dad gotten over their mother?

"Iris is important to him," Lexi said. "Dad brought her to your wedding, to introduce her to us as his date, but neither of us went to the reception. I would have invited her to my wedding yesterday, but it was a little confusing. Although, I'm sure Dad told her all about it."

Great. Another person to blame me for screwing up Lexi's life. But this time, she'd fixed things for her sister, so she should get some credit.

"Have you…seen them together?"

Lexi shook her head.

"They don't parade it around," Crusty put in, "like they won a prize at the state fair, or put them selfies up on Tweeter."

"Twitter," the women said in unison.

"I don't understand young people and their obsession with putting up pictures of ever' darn last thing they do. I mean, who cares what strangers are eatin', anyway?"

Grace took a breath for patience. "I'd liked to have known he was seeing someone. We'd have been blindsided at the wedding. What was he thinking?"

"If'n the Doc thought it was any of yore business, he'd have told ya."

Lexi put her hand on his arm. "I'm sure Dad will

appreciate knowing you took his side in this."

The old man reared back as if burned. "I ain't doin' no such." He rose and limped out, his stomp-step louder than usual.

Grace watched until Crusty left the room. "That's handy to know."

"If you want to offend him, catch him doing something nice." Lexi's eyes twinkled. "Or tell him he is, even if he isn't."

"What's with him and Dad, anyway?"

"Dad never put up with his BS. I think Crusty might have taken a shine to Mom, back before she married Dad."

Grace goggled at her sister. "The old geezer would have already been old. Like twenty years her senior."

"When does love make sense? Besides, it's just a rumor." Lexi rinsed her plate in the sink. "Speaking of love, why are you really here?"

"Oh. With all the news about Dad and that woman, I nearly forgot."

"Her name is Iris Browning. She's important to Dad, so be nice."

Grace sulked for another minute. All the things she wanted to say had logical counter-statements.

I'm home now to keep him company. A man wants romance, not companionship. A man wants intimacy. Neither of which he can get from his daughter, especially since that daughter won't always be home.

How could he love someone else? Mom died a long time ago. He deserves happiness.

Wasn't talking about him loving someone other than Mom, she groused to the logical voice in her head.

Tired of fighting with herself, she said, "I guess I know

now why Dad didn't want me and Mike staying there."

Already putting me second to Mrs. Browning.

"We haven't sold my old truck yet if Mike needs to borrow a vehicle."

"You have a new truck?"

"A Jeep. It's a long, but pretty darn cute story."

"Thanks, Lex. Mike mentioned my car isn't manly enough, though he likes the speed."

"Men." Lexi rolled her eyes. "You're okay staying at our house, though, now that you know about Dad dating? You and Mike each have a bedroom." She raised her eyebrows. "If that's what you want."

"Up until yesterday it was."

Lexi tried to restrain a grin, but her eyes sparkled with humor. "Oh, man. You made it one whole night alone without jumping that hunk? I'm impressed."

Grace frowned her down. "I've known him for six weeks."

"Well, that changes everything. You deserve a blue ribbon." Lexi let a bubble of laughter escape. "I've never seen you so in tune with anyone before. The way you were at the wedding, I knew it was more than casual."

"What way were we?"

Lexi shrugged. "Together."

"Gee, that helps."

"Anticipating each other's thoughts. Watching out for each other. Protective. Clearly attracted, but also attached. Like I said, together."

"Well, the clearly attracted part has been proven."

"Oh, my gosh, are you blushing?"

"No."

"Audrey Grace Marshall, you've fallen in love." Lexi

bounded across the room and hugged her tight.

"Stop that. I have not."

"You can lie to yourself." Lexi smiled into her face. "But when you lie to me, I feel it in my DNA. You're in love."

"Stop saying that. He's leaving. He has a life in Colorado."

"That's not on Pluto, for Pete's sake. It's about, what, a nine hour drive?"

"It's too far for a long-distance relationship."

Lexi shrugged. "Then go with him."

Pain pierced Grace's heart at Lexi's casual suggestion. She could barely catch her breath. Leaving the family again would tear Grace apart. "You think I should move away?"

"No. I think you should pursue your happiness."

"I just got home."

"You can paint anywhere. Rachel will be close by, and I'll visit. You can come home anytime; it's not that far."

"It sounds so logical when you say it."

"Grace, I'll miss you like you're half of me." Lexi smiled at her twin joke. "I always miss you when we're apart. But since you *are* half of me, we can't ever be separated, no matter the space between us. Not really."

Tears pricked the back of Grace's eyes. "I know." She swallowed down her emotions like a chunk of under-chewed steak. "This is a little premature. I don't know how he feels. Or when he's leaving. Or if he even wants me to come with him."

"He loves you," Lexi asserted. "I don't know if he's at 'forever' yet, but I could see it in his eyes, in the way he was with you. You can ask him what his travel plans are. And who said you had to wait to be asked to move to Colorado? You can live with Rachel until things are settled between you."

Her mood lightened as Grace remembered their

cousin's plans. "Oh, lordy, Lex. I can't believe I forgot to tell you about Rachel."

"What about her?"

Grace grinned. "We're both going to need coffee for this story."

CHAPTER TWELVE

Talking about Rachel took Grace's mind off her immediate problem until she drove home. Maybe Lexi had the right idea. Wait and see.

"Hi," she said as she spotted Mike in the kitchen with bread, meat, and condiments littered over the counter.

His gaze stayed on her too long for comfort. He was assessing her, but for what? Signs of picking up where they'd left off last night? Grace hoped not. Hearing about her dad and Mrs. Browning, she just couldn't work up any enthusiasm for sex right now, even with Mike. And that was saying something.

"Hi," Mike said. "What do you want on your sandwich?"

Grace chuckled. Crusty would have a fit if she let a man "do for" her.

"Didn't you have breakfast?" A little guilt crept in. *Not* because she was a woman and he a man, but because she'd been lacking as a host to her guest.

"I walked in to town." He looked up at the clock. The rooster's short leg pointed towards nine, and its longer foot toward six. The timepiece displayed more accuracy than elegance. "But it's been four hours since breakfast."

"You're on vacation, you know. No need for you to get

up that early."

He leaned down and kissed her, sending a thrill of happiness over her skin. "Habit. You were already gone, so there wasn't any reason to stay in bed."

She ducked her head. Staying in bed with him had been tempting, but she'd been confused. Still was, but stressing about it would ruin their time together.

"I thought we'd go for a ride," Mike said, "and take lunch with us."

"We can ride at the Rocking W. We need to go out there anyway. Lexi offered to loan you her truck. Shoot." Grace remembered Lexi's comment about it being a cute story. "I never heard why she got a new one. The one she's loaning you runs just fine."

"Sounds great. Thanks for asking."

Had she? Grace had had enough half-truths for the year. "It was her idea. I didn't know she had a spare vehicle."

"We can swing by later, right? The Rocking W horses will be working today, but I heard about a place while I was at The Diner. A riding stable, dude ranch, something like that. Sound good?"

A tingle went over her skin. Was this a sign? "The Schmitts'?"

"Sounds right. Go east of town, then a little south, then down the gravel two-lane till you get to the old pine, then turn." He grinned. "People here give terrible directions."

"Whereas, I know exactly what that means."

"You'd have to live here to understand all that, but if you lived here, why would you need directions?" He replaced everything in the fridge. "You didn't say if you wanted to go riding. Feel up to it?"

What did that mean? Did she look sickly? "That's

exactly what I need right now. I have a bag ready."

He looked at the counter and back at her. "Food?"

Grace shook her head. "Art. It's still in the car. I take supplies and a camera everywhere. You'll have to get used to—" She caught herself and cleared her throat. "Anyway, it sounds fun. I'll go change into riding clothes."

Her current attire, shorts and a T-shirt from Australia, would have served for riding. If he called her on it, she could claim she'd needed her boots. But while in her bedroom, she changed into long pants.

In the front room again, she tossed Mike the car keys. "You should drive, since you have the directions."

His white teeth flashed in a smile. Was that a dimple on his left cheek? Surely, she'd have noticed by now. But then again, only in the past days had he demonstrated this lighter, carefree side.

Mike made her laugh as he drove, emphasizing the directional oddities, and relating a story from The Diner he'd heard that morning—not one about her, thankfully. When he drove up to the old pine, he took the only turn onto the long road to the Schmitts' ranch.

"It hasn't been very active as a dude ranch since I was a kid." Grace studied the place with dismay as she climbed out of the car. It looked like all the dirt from the past few dust storms had wound up here, covering the grass, equipment and every stationary surface. If the owners didn't maintain the property better than this, people wouldn't want to bring their families here.

On the bright side, if they didn't have customers, maybe they'd sell her the land. In a very long-term, very low interest rate agreement.

"Not sure about this." Mike stood beside her holding

Lexi's picnic basket.

"Dad and Lexi have never said anything about them not taking care of their animals. Let's go see what the horses look like."

"Should we call a hello up to the house first?"

She shook her head and started walking toward the barn. "They'll come out and find us. Besides, I'm the vet's daughter."

"What does that mean?"

Grace looked at him. "It means I'm always welcome."

"Must be nice."

She shrugged. "It's just the way it's always been."

"Even when you were a mischievous young girl?" Mike chuckled. "I've been hearing stories about you at The Diner."

She grimaced. "I bet."

"Let me guess. They're highly exaggerated. I shouldn't believe everything I hear."

"Nope." She gave him a tight smile. "I'm sure I did whatever they told you. And more no one found out about."

He stopped her with a hand on her arm. "I only meant to tease you, not hurt your feelings."

"It's no big deal." She pulled her arm free—or tried, anyway. Mike held her in a firm grip. "Really. It doesn't bother me anymore."

"Are you sure?"

"I was a rebellious kid. I had a blast, most of the time. Sooner or later, the town will notice I've grown up and they'll stop telling those stories."

"I don't think so. I hope not."

Surprised and a little miffed, she asked, "Why?"

"It shows how much they love you."

"That's plain crazy."

"You might have been the town terror, Grace, but these people talk about you like you're royalty. Maybe part of it is the privilege that comes with being the vet's daughter." He swept his other hand out to indicate their surroundings. "But part of it is pride. You're theirs. They talk about you like you're world famous. They knew you back before your paintings became popular. This is where your talent started, and they're proud of you."

She opened her mouth to refute that notion, but no words of her own emerged. What a crazy theory. She glanced around. It had never occurred to her to call up to the house first when she visited a ranch. Sure, in the hills, that practice might keep her from getting shot, but most of the sane ranchers in the area knew her well enough not to think twice about her presence.

But the rest of it? Grace put it down to Mike being from out of town. He didn't know the history she and the town had. Famous? More like infamous. Proud of her? More like bemused by her. A painter who'd never applied a brush to a barn? In these parts, that was just plain weird.

Mixed up by his theory, she walked on to the barn. As she'd guessed, she spotted Maria bent over the tractor, parts on the ground around her feet.

"Hey, Maria."

The woman straightened, a hand to her lower back. In her late fifties, Maria looked ten hard years older than when Grace had last seen her. Her weathered tanned skin formed crow's feet as she squinted to identify them. "What are you doing back, Lexi? Judy and the foal are fine, aren't they?"

"I wouldn't know. I'm Grace."

Maria tipped her head to study Mike. "That ain't the young groom, so you better not be Grace, off with some other fella so soon."

This was the second time someone mentioned Jack's bride not being able to socialize with another man—and half-expecting Grace to be doing Jack wrong. She forced a smile. "It turns out Lexi married Jack, not me. And Jack has no reason to worry about Lexi, even if she is out with another man."

"Hmph. No one's ever had to worry about Lexi." The unspoken comparison echoed silently. Lexi wasn't the troublemaker; Grace was. "I'm almost certain I heard it the other way around. Are you sure you didn't marry Jack Walker?"

"Very sure."

Maria shrugged, her stained T-shirt shifting loose around her body. Come to think of it, the woman appeared to have lost twenty pounds. Were things so hard she had to miss meals?

"Maria, this is my friend, Mike. And this is Maria Schmitt. She and her husband Cal are the owners."

He extended his hand and shook hers. "We'd like to ride out, if it's possible, ma'am."

"Do you still rent out trail horses?" Grace asked.

"Well, we don't rent out Thoroughbreds. Sheesh." She waved a hand and walked off.

Grace and Mike shared a grin and followed after her.

They admired Judy and the unnamed foal which Lexi had delivered that morning, then Maria stopped in front of the corral fence where five horses stood. "I'll get Cal out here to saddle them for you."

"I can do that, ma'am," Mike offered.

She gave him the once-over. Twice. "I just bet you can."

Grace rolled her eyes.

"Watch out for the sorrel," Maria continued. "She's had a wasp up her butt for the past week. Won't let Cal anywhere near her without kicking."

Mike sauntered up to the fence rail to study the horses and choose which he'd bring in. Grace and Maria stepped into the shadow cast by the barn and watched. Neither woman pretended they were admiring anything but him.

"Maria, are you still running the dude ranch?"

Maria lifted a corner of her mouth. "So the sign says, anyway. We're open for business. There just ain't that much business."

"Oh." Grace took a moment to digest that. "Have you thought about partnering with someone, offering more than the ranch experience?"

"Expand, you mean?" Maria's voice rose in incredulity. "Girl, we're barely making ends meet. We'll keep these horses till they're dead, though we'll probably sell that foal. We're not taking on more responsibilities at our age."

"You and Cal aren't old."

"Cal just turned sixty-three. We're old for ranchers. We'd turn the place over to our kids if I could convince my son or daughters to take on these horses. I'd like to travel and see something of this planet before one of us is buried into it."

Maria stopped talking and stared. "Would you look at that?" she said in a reverent tone. "You didn't say the man was a whisperer."

Mike patted the sorrel's neck as the mare head-butted his face, the horse's way of nuzzling his cheek. Another conquest.

Mike was a horse whisperer? "I couldn't tell you. I didn't know."

"That damn horse has about kicked Cal to the next

county and has barely let me near enough to drop feed. Damn, your friend has skills."

Grace needed to finish this conversation about the land before Mike overheard them. If he learned she planned to stay here might, it might prevent him from asking her to go back to Colorado with him. Not that Grace knew what she'd say if he asked. "Would you consider selling?"

The older woman's eyes went wide. "Now I'm sure you must be Grace. Lexi would know better. No rancher sells their land. My kids will want it once we're gone, just like Cal wanted it when his mama and daddy passed on."

Frustration mixed with disappointment. "I thought you said they aren't interested in the horses."

"Doesn't mean they won't want to inherit the land."

Mike had captured two horses' bridles and was leading them to the fence. Although it appeared more as though they simply walked over together, like old buddies meeting up after years apart. The sorrel trailed behind Mike like a hopeful lover. Grace had about two seconds to change the subject.

"Were you thinking of buying it?" Maria asked.

"I was just curious."

"Even if we had the money to take on a partner, I wouldn't. We don't want to make changes that the kids will have to deal with. Which is fine by me. I want to travel. Like you did."

"Traveling is fun."

"How long are you going to be home this time before you head out on more painting adventures?"

Mike's head shot around like that little girl in the movie with the devil inside her. "You're going somewhere?"

Grace tried to look innocent. "Just riding with you. Let me help."

Together, they saddled the horses and headed out on the worn trail through the scrub grass and sage. The sun beat down, turning everything around them dry and hot. Grace relaxed as they traveled away from the lies she had to tell the town, the lies she had to un-tell the town, and her worries over the future. She'd have to find another place to buy. Tomorrow. For the moment, she just enjoyed the familiar sway of a horse beneath her.

After half an hour riding in the heat, she'd nearly wilted before they spotted the small creek bank with its few trees and soft green grass.

The shade lowered the temperature at least ten degrees. With the addition of the water trickling by, it felt like fifteen. Mike unpacked the basket with their lunch and she found two water bottles in a bag with ice. If he wasn't there, she'd have poured the melted water over head and let it steam off her. With him nearby, and with the way she wanted him, she didn't consider a wet T-shirt a good idea.

"Maria was impressed with the way you won over the sorrel."

He slanted her a look. "Just Maria?"

She shrugged. "I haven't seen the horse misbehaving, so I can only take her word for it. Is that what you do back home? Are you a horse whisperer?"

Mike shook his head. "Whisperers exist, but I'm not one. I don't perform magic. I just pay attention to the horses, watch their behavior, try to read them and then adjust to what they'll accept."

"That's your job at the ranch in Colorado? Breaking horses to saddle?"

"Taming, not breaking. Helping them accept their role as partner to their rider. Training them to work cattle."

He could get work anywhere…even in Little Tree. "You could travel throughout in the West and find work. Sounds like a dream job."

Mike took a bite of sandwich. Then a drink of water. She waited, hoping he'd mention wanting to move here. To be with her. Come to think of it, she could use a swig of water to get rid of the lump building in her throat.

"My dream job? No. Someday, I hope to have a horse ranch. I already own a horse, Libre. My plan is to buy more wild horses from the BLM when I can afford to. I'd also take in abused horses to rehabilitate."

The Bureau of Land Management held horse auctions in Montana. Would reminding him be too obvious?

"That sounds interesting."

"I'd have to have a sideline to bring in the money. Boarding, training, riding lessons, something like that."

"Dressage?" she teased.

He slanted her a look. "You've figured me out."

"Carrie used to barrel race. Her sister Hannah became the bigger star. Carrie quit, but she might teach some classes for you."

"What about Hannah?"

"She moved from barrel racing to the chuck wagons. One rolled on her, and she died."

Mike winced. "I'm sorry to hear that. I don't know if we'll teach rodeo riding, but I'll keep Carrie in mind."

Grace's heart thudded like a horse's hooves during competition. She'd just suggested he hire someone from Little Tree to work at his ranch/boarding stable/school—and he'd agreed. Why else would he keep Carrie in mind? She wanted to point it out and lock him into a firm commitment. But if he corrected himself, she'd be crushed. Better to let the idea steep.

She demolished the ham sandwich and half her water. "Thanks. I guess I was hungry, no matter the time on that stupid clock at home."

He stretched out on one elbow and propped his water in front of him. "You looked a little ragged when you got back."

Grace took a sip to stall. "I got up early. That never sits well with me unless I'm going out painting. I did some quick watercolors while the sky changed colors."

"I don't think it was just rising early. Something else is wrong." He studied her for a moment. "I'm a good listener."

She hooted with laughter. "You are not. For instance, I've told you time and again I'm not going to hurt Anita or Paul, but you haven't heard a word."

He held up a finger. "Not true. I heard you. It just takes me a while to lower my force field when they're involved."

"So you listen, but stubbornly stick to your own beliefs, anyway?"

Mike shrugged a shoulder. "I'm working on it."

"I'm sure Anita and Paul will appreciate that."

"And you?" He trailed one finger down her forearm to her hand. "Do you want to tell me what was bothering you?"

She shook off the shiver his touch evoked and looked away. It would sound silly to him.

After another minute passed in silence, he asked, "Was it me? Because we had sex?"

She looked at him with surprise. Was that what worried him? "No. I don't have any problems with that."

With a hand to his chest, he fell back on the blanket in overdramatic relief. "Phew. Nothing a guy wants to hear more than his partner saying she didn't 'have any problems' with the sex."

Grace laughed. "You're such a joker."

"Oh, no, I'm seriously relieved. I've spent the whole day worrying that you regretted our night together."

Was that all it was to him? A night together? She pasted on a weak smile, knowing it probably appeared insincere. "No regrets."

She determined not to have any. Just enjoy him and see what happened. If they were meant to be, it would work out. If not… She swallowed. If not, she'd get over him.

"Grace, what's wrong?"

She wasn't about to confess her thoughts, so she broached the other subject bothering her. "You'll think I'm silly. Or selfish. Or some other thing."

"Maybe. Maybe not." He sat upright and crossed his legs, sitting as though he had all day to listen. "Let's find out which."

"My dad has a girlfriend," she blurted.

Mike's brows rose. "His first?"

She nodded then shrugged. "First I've heard of."

"Ah."

"And he's serious about her. She's been the librarian in this town since I went in there as a little girl. Can you believe it?"

"Which part is unbelievable? That she's had one job so long or that you used to read books?"

She swatted at his shoulder. "Ha ha."

"Is she a wild divorcée?"

"No." She took a moment to remember. "I think Mr. Browning died a few years after my mom."

"How old were you?"

"When he died?" When Mike shook his head, she realized what he meant. "When Mom passed? Twelve."

"That's a hard time for a girl. For a son, too." His gaze

dropped. "My twin brother and sister were just about that age when our parents died."

"Why didn't you tell me you had twin siblings?"

"At first, I didn't want to include you in anything."

Ouch. Not a surprise, but still. "Has that changed?" She held her breath, waiting for his answer.

Mike stared into her eyes, his brown ones dark and sexy. "Didn't you notice the change last night?"

She nodded, and then shook her head. "That's just sex."

"It didn't mean anything to you?"

"Of course it did."

"Then—" He leaned over and kissed her gently. "Why do you think it wouldn't have meant anything to me?"

His words sent happy beams of hope speeding through her veins. His kiss made her head fuzzy with desire. Off-balance, she waited for more. More words. More kisses. More both.

"So, tell me. What's upsetting about your dad dating this woman?"

Grace blinked as he switched back to the former subject. "I thought everything would settle back to normal. I'm home now. Lexi is married, so, while that's a change, at least she won't be moving anywhere."

"And you don't want anything to change?"

She shook her head. "It's not that. I don't mind change. I just thought everything would…stay the same."

Only the corners of his mouth twitched.

"I know," she said. "That sounds stupid. Everything changes."

He covered her hand with his. "Yes, it does."

"I just don't know why Dad needs… I mean, I want him to be happy, but… Oh, never mind."

"Your dad needs a female companion his own age." Mike pulled her onto his lap. "It's quite an adjustment, huh?"

She snuggled against him. "I don't know how he could love anyone else. Mom always understood me, even the art. Especially the art."

Mike pressed her closer in a comforting hug.

"Then she passed and Dad did his best. He found a way to pay for summer art camps. Being away from him and Lexi tore me apart, especially right then, but it was necessary for my future."

"And then you went to Australia."

"To art school then Europe and then Australia."

"And your dad found someone to spend time with."

"He had Lexi."

"Sorry. I meant, your dad found someone to love."

She stiffened, panic trying to smother her. "I don't know if it's love. Maybe it's just two old people spending time together."

That's not what Crusty implied.

Mike hugged her. "How long will it take for you to adjust to this?"

He said it as though he knew she would, once she got used to the idea. "I just got home. I pictured us all spending time together finally. But Lexi's married, and Dad has someone *important* to him."

Dad dating meant a woman other than Mom taking part in the family activities. Them making new memories with her, not Mom. Grace wanted her dad to be happy, but... "This is such a huge change, so quickly. I've just finally gotten back home. We were supposed to be together. The three of us."

"How did your marriage fit into that plan?"

"Oh, that." Grace waved a dismissive hand.

Mike snorted.

"Jack only wanted to inherit the land. Crusty wouldn't have come to our family's events. Annabeth would have been a delightful addition, though."

"That's true," Mike said into her hair. "Things have changed. But them loving you hasn't changed. It never will. If you got married, would you love them less?"

"Of course not, but I'd be putting my husband and family first before them." She swallowed. "That's the way it's supposed to be. Now Lexi has Jack and Dad has Mrs. Browning." She gave a helpless lift to her shoulders.

Mike hugged her closer, finally understanding. She feared being left alone. Had she been testing her family and her town, all these years, wondering when they would forsake her?

He'd never considered himself abandoned by his parents when they died, but he'd heard some people couldn't overcome that kind of loss. It amazed him to think Grace suffered from doubt. She grew up feeling she didn't fit. According to her, her mom had been her anchor. Now her father was moving on. No wonder Grace felt adrift.

How could she have believed anyone would give up on her? That her childhood hijinks were too much? Those antics he'd been hearing about had been her natural spirit coming out. And from what Grace had implied, Lexi wasn't all innocence. She just hadn't been caught as often as Grace had.

"I'm sorry." He kissed the side of her head, feeling protective.

"For what?"

Mike held her close, not wanting her to move. He enjoyed the feel of her snuggled on his lap, her head on his shoulder. Trusting him. "For taking so long to show you how important you are to me."

Wrong words. She bolted upright and stared with wide eyes.

"Important?" It came out as an adorable squeak.

He couldn't help but grin, despite the serious subject. "Were you not paying attention last night?"

She deflated back onto his shoulder. Mike frowned. What had he said wrong now? "Look, Grace, people are going to move on, but that just gives you more family. My sister's husband Jimmy has become another brother to us. Jack wouldn't have forgiven you so quickly if he didn't care for you. Now you have him and his daughter and the old man as family."

Grace scoffed. "Crusty is *not* my uncle."

"Under that gruff exterior, deep down, he likes you."

"Right. Really, really deep down." But her body softened against him as she contemplated his words.

Would she accept someone else's family as part of her own?

Would she accept his?

On the ride back, Grace thanked him. "It's been an upsetting few days, news-wise. Learning about the attack on Lexi upset me, and hearing about Dad dating was just the last thing I could take."

Mike reined his horse to a stop. "What attack on Lexi?"

"Oh." Grace turned around and came back to his side. "Carrie told me about it during lunch. While I was in Colorado, someone in town caught Lexi unawares at the house. She delivered a swift kick to his privates and got away."

Mike's jaw tightened. "She's okay?"

Grace nodded. "It was about two weeks ago. I'm not sure if Dad knows."

"And the local police caught the guy?"

"Not sure." Grace frowned. "I know he was severely beaten. Word around town is that was Jack's doing."

Mike grunted. "As it should be."

"I agree. I'll have to remember to thank him."

Mike settled easier in his saddle, searching her face with his gaze. "Why didn't you tell me?"

"I just found out yesterday. When I came home, well…" She grinned. "I guess you side-tracked me."

His lips twitched. "Or you side-tracked me."

"Let's call it mutual side-tracking."

"Want to go home and see who can side-track the other first?"

Hiding how the idea tickled her, Grace rolled her eyes and turned her horse to face in the same direction as his. After two steps, she urged her horse into a run. "I bet I'll win," she yelled over her shoulder.

His laugh followed her down the trail as his horse galloped behind hers. In that kind of adventure, they would both win.

CHAPTER THIRTEEN

Grace perked up when Carrie walked into Kerr's Grill the next day. She had to set this retreat plan in motion. "Thanks for meeting me."

"I only have time for a bite." Carrie set her battered leather hobo purse on the seat of the booth next to her. "We're moving cattle today to Windy Glade, and I need to check on them."

"To Ryan's?" Grace watched Carrie's face for a flicker of emotion. She didn't want to hurt Carrie, no matter how perfect Windy Glade would be for the retreat. What emotions did Carrie's bland expression cover?

"Yep." Carrie signaled the waitress. "He said we could graze over there while he's off at rodeo."

They ordered tea and fajita salads.

"What's up?" Carrie asked.

Grace took a breath. "I thought about what you said the other day, but I want to ask Ryan about selling Windy Glade. Give him the opportunity to decide. He might want to sell it and invest the money in a college fund."

Carrie sat back in the booth. "I don't have any contact information for him. Like I said, I'm sure he plans to come home after rodeoing."

"That land would be perfect." She drew it out in the air.

"Here's the house. I'd put the retreat cabins over here near the horse pasture."

Carrie quirked a brow. "Horses, huh?"

"Or something." Grace forced herself not to squirm under Carrie's scrutiny. "I'd want activities for the families, too, to free up time for the artist to paint or take classes."

"We have a dude ranch in town already."

Grateful when their drinks arrived, Grace sucked down some tea. "Maria wants to retire."

"And are you retiring, from painting, I mean? Because running a retreat is going to be time-consuming."

"I don't have all the details worked out yet." Like if Mike would stay in town. If they'd become serious. If Paul and Anita would move here.

The waitress came and plunked down their salads before rushing off.

"I could so teach her a thing or two," Carrie muttered, straightening the dislodged cutlery.

Perfect opening. "Would you consider teaching barrel racing, if I open a school?"

Carrie's eyebrows shot up. "I haven't raced in years. Decades. Hannah was the racer."

"Your sister was better," Grace agreed, "but you were darn good, Carrie. Maybe consider a beginner class, okay? See how it goes."

Carrie smirked. "Right. In my spare time. But, sure, I'll keep an open mind. You're not talking right away, are you?"

"I don't even have land yet."

Carrie took a bite of salad, and Grace let her mull it over. Selling land always hurt, even when one planned to move away. Staying and seeing the property in someone else's control could turn a person bitter.

"I still need to talk to Adam, but maybe we can help each other."

Grace's heartbeat sped up. What influence would Adam have on Ryan's decision? "Help how?"

"We have some land. There's a flat area that might work for a training school." Carrie stirred her tea, despite not having added any sugar. "It's the great-great-great Moores' property. The old homestead is there, but a little bit falling down. Hannah had wanted to do something with the building, so Adam and I haven't had the heart to touch it."

Grace could barely breathe. "It sounds perfect."

"Far from it. I rode out with Matt a few months ago. I'm not sure an artist would stay there, but you could use it as an office or a bunkhouse, if you don't mind roughing it."

Grace fought back a grin. "You and Matt just rode out there, eh? Were you making moves on your foreman, Carrie?"

"We were searching for Adam."

The wind left her sails. "Oh." She put a hand on Carrie's arm. "I'm sorry."

"Me, too. He was gone for a week before he called." Carrie quirked an eyebrow. "Sound familiar?"

Another punch to the airstream. "You talked to Lexi."

"Yep."

"Hey, I left a message at Dad's as I drove out of town. It's not the same." Grace shook her head. "I know you'll keep our secret."

"And in the name of fairness, I'll share one of mine. I am dating Matt. Neither of us has much free time, but it's good to have someone to dance with on a Saturday night."

"Is it serious?" Grace finished her salad.

Carrie shrugged. "I don't have time for serious, but it's fun."

Grace raised her glass in a toast. "Here's to fun."

After drinking, Carrie pulled her wallet from her purse. "I'm going to have to scoot." She set some money on the table and slid out of the booth. "And I'll talk to Adam."

The mention of buying Ryan's property had sure lit a fire under Carrie to find an alternative.

"Thanks, Carrie. I appreciate your help."

Carrie crossed her fingers. "Here's hoping."

Mike made his way through the hardware store on Monday, back toward the pick up area where this Darryl character worked. Anger still simmered under his skin. He needed to keep it in check. People in the store glanced at him sideways and moved discreetly away.

Spotting the swinging doors, he slammed one open with the heel of his hand and stalked through. His boots stirred up dirt on the concrete floor. Motes of dust and grain floated in the air.

He spied the dickweed on the far side of the open floor, his eyes wide. Darryl sported a sling and a greenish yellow bruise on his face. Mike smiled with satisfaction. Jack had done a bang-up job on this asswipe.

Darryl straightened. "Do you have an order coming in?"

Mike waited until he was within swinging distance to answer, watching as the other "man" tried not to flinch. But Mike recognized panic in his eyes. How often did the jerk have to face up to his actions? "You Darryl?"

He nodded then puffed out his chest. And immediately winced. "I'm the manager of this department. How can I help you?"

"You can keep your damned hands to yourself."

Darryl skittered back, bumping into the row of feed sacks behind him. "What are you talking about?"

"See, now, it's pitiful that you have so many offenses you don't know which one I mean."

"I didn't do anything. That's why I don't know what the hell you're talking about."

Mike shook his head. "I wouldn't take that line if I were you, Darryl." He let the R roll, guessing his Spanish accent would add a layer of intimidation. "You went to the Marshall sisters' house a few weeks ago. Where I come from, forcing yourself on a woman doesn't sit well."

"I'm not saying I did, but if I did," Darryl whined and held up his slinged arm, "don't you think I've paid for it?"

"A few bruises of your own? Not even close to what you deserve. This is just a warning, scumbag. Keep away from Grace and Lexi. You don't want me to have to visit again." Mike started to leave then turned back and stepped nearer. "Which woman did you think you were assaulting—or didn't it matter?"

"Well..." Darryl's Adam's apple bobbed as she swallowed. He eyed Mike, calculation clear on his face. "Grace, of course. Lexi had run off with some dude to Vegas."

Wrong answer, asshole. Not that there was a right one. Grace would be devastated. Mike pushed away that thought for later. He leaned in and spoke low and clear. "I'm with Grace now. You even *think* her name again and this beating will be a fond memory."

A flash of something Mike hoped was fear flashed in the scumbag's eyes. Then Darryl recovered and smirked. "You got a ranch hand to come beat on me too, the way Walker sent his flunkie?"

Mike hoped he covered his surprise. All of Little Tree

had supposed Jack took care of this bastard himself. He layered on the accent he'd fought so hard to suppress a decade ago. "I don't want anyone else to do it for me. It'll be my extreme pleasure. *¿Entiendes?*" When the other man didn't respond, Mike said, "Do you understand me?"

Darryl nodded.

Mike turned and left, the click of his bootheels punctuating his threat.

Thursday afternoon, Grace poured a cup of flour into the bowl, hoping Mike liked banana bread. She didn't have many supplies in the house by way of baking, but the urge to do something domestic had nagged her all day. Maybe a week's worth of great sex with Mike had triggered some dormant urge to feed her man.

Mike had gone out somewhere earlier, as he did every day, putting the loaner truck from Lexi to use. He hadn't specified his mission and she hadn't asked. She wasn't his keeper.

But she might want to keep him, she thought with a smile, as she smashed bananas with the beaters. Their lovemaking thrilled her. They'd spent five amazing nights in bed, giving her hope for the future. She knew lovemaking didn't equal love and forever after. She'd lost that naïve view long ago. Sometimes great sex was just sex.

But she had hope. Mike had lost his reservations about her, although she couldn't very well corrupt his sister and brother from Montana. That doubt caused her to falter in her mixing. Was she just "safe" here, away from them?

No. Grace pushed away the traitorous thought. She and Mike had grown closer, understood one another better now. She could feel the connection between them, and while they hadn't made any promises, she felt pretty sure they had some kind of future together.

She froze, then slid a stool over and slumped onto it. She hadn't made any promises to Mike yet, either. Not verbally. But, surely he knew how she felt. Surely he *felt* how she felt. Her…what? Attraction? Admiration?

Well, crap. If she couldn't name it, how could she expect Mike to realize she… *Okay, spit it out.* That she was falling in love with him.

Grace sucked in a breath. There. That wasn't so hard to admit. To herself. In her head.

Maybe she wouldn't declare her love. She didn't want to scare him off and she wasn't one thousand percent sure herself. It was early yet. But somehow, probably in their next intimate moments when he was all snuggled up and fond of her, she'd ask him to stay in Little Tree.

Great plan, except for the kids. She sighed heavily. Why couldn't anything ever be easy?

Tires crunched on the driveway and adrenaline shot through her. Maybe she wouldn't wait for that mythical "right moment." Maybe she'd just fling open the door and launch herself at him. *Stay with me*, she'd whisper in his ear. And he'd laugh with surprise, then delight, and say *of course*.

She dusted off her hands and wiped at the flour on her shorts from pulling over the stool. She had no time to primp. Her gut churning with nerves, she flung open the kitchen door and stepped outside.

"Surprise!" Anita called out. Paul waved with his free hand, the one not holding his duffle bag.

Anita launched herself at Grace. "I've missed you so much," the girl said with a laugh of joy. "I was so happy when Mike called and said to come as soon as my summer classes ended. So we did. We drove all day. I could really use your bathroom."

Before Grace could blink, Anita bolted inside.

Paul studied her. "You didn't know we were coming, did you?"

"Mike mentioned inviting you up, though he didn't say when. But I'm so glad you're here, Paul. How was the drive?"

He shrugged. "I let Anita drive partway. Better not tell big brother that. He'll have a fit."

A smile spread over his face, as though in anticipation.

Grace barely kept from rolling her eyes, exasperated. *These two.* They'd better come to terms—soon—or they'd never be close. In the not-too-distant future, Paul would strike out on his own and not look back. Not feel he had much to look back on.

"I'm glad you could get off work. How long are you two able to stay?"

Paul slid her a sideways glance. "A couple of days." He held open the kitchen door for her. "Where should I put our stuff?"

Where, indeed?

Anita emerged from the hallway just then and her crestfallen expression indicated she'd overheard the question, witnessed Grace's bemusement, and drawn the correction deduction. Her shoulders slumped. "You didn't know we were coming."

Grace considered denying it. Paul wouldn't rat her out, knowing the truth would hurt Anita. The girl's dull tone screamed disillusionment and Grace re-considered. No sense starting out with half-truths or outright lies.

"That doesn't make you any less welcome; it only makes me less prepared."

Anita's gaze moved past her to Paul. "Should we go?"

"No." Grace didn't give him time to answer. She stepped up and hugged a very stiff Anita. "You're staying here and I'm thrilled." She glanced at Paul, including him in her statement. "Stay."

He gave one short dip of the head. "We drove all this way."

Grace's knees almost gave out in her relief. If he'd gone all moody, he could have ruined everything. The hot-blooded man-child was unpredictable. She'd take his agreement, grudging though the nod might have been.

"We have two bedrooms." Grace turned to Anita. "I hope you don't mind sleeping with me, and the guys can share the other room."

The young man's shoulders hunched up to his ears. "You got a couch?"

Mike pulled up to the house, his eyes going wide with surprise and pleasure upon seeing Paul's blue truck with its yellow door in the driveway. The kids were here!

And on the heels of that thought came another. *Oh, crap.* He'd forgotten to tell Grace he'd invited them.

He'd called them every day but he hadn't pinned down when Anita and Paul would leave. He thought they'd want a day to pack, and he'd have that extra day to prep Grace for their arrival. Obviously, he'd been wrong not to verify their plans. They must have started driving before daybreak.

He hadn't known Paul could get up so early. Come in from a night with his friends at that hour, yes. Rouse himself out of bed? Not as likely.

He'd missed those bratty kids. Their absence made him ache like he'd left behind one of his limbs. He swung open the kitchen door with a grin and a hint of misgiving over Grace's reaction.

Mike caught sight of Paul shoving doodads together on a shelf. "What are you doing?"

Paul turned. Smirked. "Hi to you, too."

Mike shook his head and crossed the room. He yanked his brother to his feet and into a hug. The boy returned the brief embrace, making the breath catch in Mike's throat. "Good trip?"

Paul stepped back. "We made it."

Mike glanced toward the hall, about to ask about Anita. But wasn't that what he always did, worry about their sister? "How was the drive?"

Paul studied him for a minute, assessing. "It wasn't too hard. Mostly because I let Anita drive part-way."

"You let—" Mike bit back the rebuke. Closed his eyes for a moment. "How'd she do?" he asked like a mature adult instead of an over-protective parent.

His brother's eyes widened. "We didn't die. She's got to get her speed up on the ramp before merging onto the highway, but otherwise, not bad."

Mike squeezed the muscles at the back of his neck. "Thanks ."

Paul took a surprised step backward.

"I never made the time to take her driving," Mike said. "I guess I didn't want to."

"She's old enough. Wants some freedom."

Mike heard his brother clearly, and Paul wasn't talking about Anita. "I'm well aware. But it's not just the license. She'll want a car to exercise that freedom."

Paul's face went blank. "Oh. Right."

"I didn't want to have to deal with sharing the two

trucks between three of us, and I don't have the money for another vehicle, more gas every week, insurance and maintenance."

Paul's chin dipped as he studied the floor. "I didn't think of that. You know I'd do the maintenance and fix anything I can."

"I know. You've always kept our truck running." Mike debated realities. "I have some money saved to buy another horse, but I can't afford to have more money taken from my pay for boarding, if the boss'll even let me board a second horse at the ranch."

Paul nodded, still not looking up.

"But," Mike continued with a sigh, "Anita's going to want a job once she earns her license. That means a vehicle of some sort. Her salary might pay for gas and oil changes, but not much else. So I guess I can use the horse money for a vehicle."

"The price of freedom." Paul raised his head then. "Maybe we can work something out. Share my truck for a while. I could pick her up from school and take her to her job." He stopped to swallow. "Or I could get a different job, work days, and she could drop me off before school. One of you could pick me up afterward."

Mike's throat closed. When had his brother ever compromised? "That'd be great. Let's get her that license first, then you both figure out your job situations, and we'll go from there."

Paul shrugged and turned back to the bookcase.

"You never said what you're doing."

"Making a shelf for my clothes."

Mike cursed silently. He hadn't thought of where the kids would sleep. "I'm not using all the drawers in the dresser in my bedroom."

"I'm going to sleep in here, on the couch. Sharing is fine for Anita and Grace, but I'm not likely to fit with you."

Mike grinned at the image. "Yeah, I'm really sorry. I should have thought this through, planned better before you got here." *Planned anything at all.* "You can keep your stuff in the room I'm in. You'll want a place to change. And we'll figure out the sleeping arrangements. I should have done it before."

"You should have told Grace we were coming."

Mike winced. "Was she mad?"

Paul stared at him. "You don't know her at all, do you?"

"What's that mean?"

The boy shook his head and turned away to squat before the shelves, his shoulders set in the resentful line Mike had seen too many times. "Go find out."

Giving up on his brother offering any insight, Mike headed down the hall, easing his way, feeling the air for a hostile vibe. Nothing. He tapped on Grace's half-open door. "I hear there's an adventurous young maiden in here, fresh from braving dragons on the highway."

The door opened and Anita smashed into him, arms tight around his neck, and planting a loud kiss on his cheek. "I'm so glad we're all together."

Hugging his little sister, spying Grace's smile over her shoulder, and knowing Paul was settling into the other room, Mike's chest ached, like he'd just come home.

It was unnerving. He understood Grace's difficulty adjusting to her dad's dating. This feeling overwhelmed him. Too much, too fast.

He set Anita to her feet, keeping his hands on her upper arms. "What's this I hear about you driving?"

The child—for that's what she was, the baby of their family—nodded with a huge, proud grin. "I did. I was good, too. Tell him, Paul." She raised her voice to be heard in the front room. "Tell Mike how good I can drive."

"Did you get that call from our insurance company?" Paul yelled back.

Mike started, heart galloping. "No."

"Well, there you go."

Anita scowled. "He's joking. So not funny, by the way," she yelled to her brother in the front room. They could hear Paul chuckle.

Mike smiled over at Grace, sharing the moment. Just a second too late, he remembered she might be upset with him. But she smiled back. All was good in his world.

Since his talk with Jack that afternoon about a job at the Rocking W, he'd been riding on that "cloud nine" everyone talked about. Pretty view from up here. Not one he'd experienced before.

He glanced at Grace again. *She* was the pretty view. Lovely and funny. Sexy and kind. Talented and smart. His entire perception of her had changed since meeting her. Had it only been two months ago? Less? His heart thudded in his chest. Would she be glad he was thinking about staying?

Staying.

He glanced down at Anita, thought about Paul in the front room. Robbie's summer job would keep him in Bozeman. June and Jimmy were settled in Colorado. They all needed him. Frank was secure enough in New York City, and Mike couldn't do anything to help Lilly.

His parents wouldn't be proud of his failure with her, and with a wrench to his gut, he wondered what they'd think of him moving to Montana. He looked at his baby sister. Was he doing the right thing? Would she and Paul fall in step with the plan or strain against the rope? His future depended on their opinions of the small town and his half-formed plans.

He flashed back to a decade before, making plans blindly and ignoring the nervous dread cramping his gut. He believed his family would benefit. He'd known it then; he hoped it now.

"We're starving," Anita said. "Can I make us a snack?"

"Sure." Grace waved her on. "Whatever's in the fridge. We'll have to go to the grocery store later."

"Of course. I'll go." He shut the door most of the way but not against the jamb, so it wouldn't make noise. No sense alerting the kids to their private conversation. They'd assume it concerned them. Worse, they'd be right. He crossed to Grace and lowered his voice. "I'm sorry I didn't ask about inviting them. I should have talked to you first."

"They're your family. Of course they're welcome."

He shot her an apologetic grin. "But a little notice would have been welcome, too?"

She sighed. "We could have gotten a second bed or bunk beds into your room. For both rooms maybe. Paul shouldn't have to sleep on the couch."

"It's not going to hurt him for a night or two." He cupped her upper arms and squeezed. "Thanks for being so great about this."

"I happen to like them. They can stay as long as you want, as long as they can, but we can't have Paul on that old sofa for a week."

He hesitated. "I don't know how long they're staying. Can we leave it open for now?"

"If it's longer than a day or two, we need to borrow a daybed for the living room. Paul shouldn't feel like he's in the way. He also needs a place to go to be by himself. I know he's not a teenager, but everyone needs privacy."

Mike leaned in and kissed her quickly, mindful of the kids in the other room. "Thank you. I'm sorry this is going to cut into our private time."

She put a palm against his chest and pushed him back half a foot. "I wasn't talking about that kind of privacy. And this isn't going to cut into our private time, buddy. It's going to cut it off."

He winced at the phrase and would have replied but knuckles rapped, pushing open the door.

"Hey, not bothering you, I hope." Paul's snarky tone indicated the opposite, as though he'd caught them in the act. "Thought me and big brother should talk. Outside."

That put a lead ball in his gut. Mike followed his little brother out through the kitchen.

"Where're you going?" Anita asked. "I'm making sandwiches."

"I'll be back in a sec," Paul called, easing Mike's heartburn. "No mustard on mine."

"Have I ever?" she retorted.

Paul stopped at the garage door and turned, running a reverent hand over Grace's convertible, eyes wide. "Ho-ly God, this is beautiful."

"Don't blaspheme," Mike said automatically before he grinned. "And, yeah, she is. Looks like a kitten, drives like a tiger. The power is unbelievable."

"I'd like to see under the hood. And..." Paul chewed his bottom lip for a moment. "Do you think I could drive it?"

The kid never asked him for anything, and Mike ached to give him permission. Yet, at the same time, could he trust Paul with that much car, both powerful and expensive? "You'd have to ask Grace."

Paul nodded, gaze lingering on his new beloved.

Grace no doubt understood that Paul driving this car was a bad idea, and he felt like a heel for making her say so. But, dammit, being the one to always say no didn't help his relationship with Paul. "What'd you want to talk to me about?"

"Oh." Paul stepped back to the garage and leaned his hip against the doorframe as though he didn't have the strength to stand upright on his own. "How long did you plan on us staying here?"

And there it was again. Mike being forced to have answers about the future. "How long can you stay?"

"I got two nights off work, then my two weekend nights as usual, but I gotta give them some idea when I'll be back."

Mike ran a hand over the back of his neck. When did these muscles start tightening up on him? Oh, right, since meeting Grace. "I wanted to talk to you and Anita after you'd had a look around town. See how you like Little Tree."

"What are you saying?"

"I want to make sure you and Anita are happy. Settled. If you don't like Little Tree, maybe you could bunk in with June and give her a hand with Jimmy for a while."

Paul's mouth dropped open. "You want us to stay here? Move here?" He looked around as though the rock driveway and old wooden garage encompassed his future. "Here?"

Granted, it didn't look promising. "If we move to Little Tree, I'll need a place to live and a place for Libre. Or money to board her. We can use the money from the sale of the house in Longmont. I have a possible job here and some money saved, but land isn't going to come cheap."

"This is the middle of nowhere." Paul gestured wildly with his hands then slapped his fists on his hips. "There's nothing here. Not for us, anyway."

"You haven't even looked around yet. It's a good town. Maybe a little limited in its—"

"A little?" Paul cut in, his voice carrying to Colorado. "You're joking, right? There's not a single AutoZone or McDonald's. Where am I supposed to work?" He cursed, low and vicious under his breath. "I can't believe you're doing it again."

Mike ignored the cussing. "What am I doing again?"

"Making all these decisions without asking us. Taking our home away."

Mike felt like a boulder sat on his lungs.

Paul glared at the house, eyes narrowed. "Are we going to have to change our names again too? Is Thompson not good enough for Grace?"

"No, we don't. And Grace has nothing to do with this." Mike took a breath to calm down. "That's not true. Of course, I'd be staying here because of her. But it's also a fresh start for all of us. Anita will probably balk at moving for her senior year, so I'd appreciate your help convincing her it's a good idea."

Paul's mouth dropped open. "You want my help? Hell, I don't even have a place to sleep."

"We should fix that," Grace said from behind Mike.

The men turned as she advanced from the door toward them. The tension eased from Paul's shoulders as he dropped his aggressive stance. Mike let his muscles relax. They'd revisit that crack about Mike stealing their lives later. The little ingrate.

"Sorry for interfering, but I couldn't help overhearing." She gave a lop-sided smile. "No one in town could help but overhear. I want you to stay, Paul, you and Anita. If you want to move here, that would be fantastic."

Her voice quavered on that last word.

"But whether it's a week or forever, I want you to be comfortable. My dad has a set of bunk beds I'm sure we can borrow. I just need you two to follow me over in the truck. Does that sound all right?"

Paul blinked then nodded. Mike felt the same loss of footing. Coming down from being mad drained a guy.

"I need to check with Dad, but it should be okay. He's using our rooms as guest rooms. No one's ever in there." She stopped for a minute and pursed her mouth as she thought.

Mike wanted to swoop in and kiss her. Only Paul's presence kept him in check. He couldn't believe how every small move of hers distracted him.

She continued, bringing his wandering mind back to the problem. "You guys should probably take Lexi's bed to Dad's house in order to make room here. Let me check if he's going to be around."

"Thanks." Paul gazed at her as though she'd just stepped out of a spaceship. Grace could be a force of nature, apparently. With a few words, she had the two of them ready to do her bidding.

"Are you sure you want to go to all this trouble?" Mike asked. "It's only a few days. And if it becomes more, which—" He turned to include Paul. "I hope it does, then we can make changes."

They turned to walk inside, following Grace.

Crap, he should find his own place for his family. If he planned to stay.

He'd tentatively lined up a job with Jack. He'd gotten the kids here to look around. He had a relationship forming with Grace. All in all, a pretty great start.

But he hadn't realized he'd have to make such an important, literally life-changing decision in the span of ten minutes.

What if he and Grace didn't work out as a couple? Did he really want to live in Little Tree, Montana? He saw the town through his brother's eyes. Small. Limited. Smothering. Far from June and Jimmy and Mike's secure job back in Longmont.

Then he recalled the past few days. The welcome of the Marshalls and Walkers. The friendly townspeople. The warm handshakes when he introduced himself. The cautious gazes weighing up an outsider.

The wide-open spaces. The possibilities for his own ranch.

This could be a new beginning for him, a different life. For Paul and Anita, too. Paul, especially could turn his life around, get away from his low-life friends and mend his wild ways.

"Grace." Paul held open the kitchen door for her. "Can I drive your car sometime?"

"How about now? You can drive me over to Dad's."

Mike frowned. She'd been around Paul long enough to know he didn't have the maturity to handle that much responsibility. That car probably cost as much as a house in this town.

What was Grace thinking?

CHAPTER FOURTEEN

Grace looked up ten minutes later when Mike walked into her bedroom. She paused with a handful of underwear then stuffed it in her overnight case.

He frowned. "What are you doing?"

"Moving out for awhile. Giving your family space."

"No."

She raised an eyebrow, surprised at him. Surely he knew better. "I didn't ask for your permission."

"No, anyway. I don't want to run you out of your own house. The kids will feel awful if you leave."

"I'll explain it."

"Where would you go?" His eyes narrowed. "Not to Jack's."

She eyed him. What was with that steely tone? "To Lexi's."

"No."

"You keep saying that."

"No, you're not moving out, and no, you're not leaving me and going to live with your ex-fiancé."

She blew out an exasperated breath. "It's my sister's house, too."

He crossed the room and took her by the hands. "Grace, think of how it would make me feel. I don't want to push you out of your own place, and I'm sure as hell not going to pick you up for a date at your ex's house."

"Stop calling him that. He's just my brother-in-law now."

"Who you were going to spend your life with."

She pulled her hands away. "You're going to have to get over that."

"I might, someday." He arched an eyebrow. "But since your wedding was last month, you'll have to give me some time."

"You're overreacting. I'm not interested in Jack, and it was never a love match, for either of us."

"That's the only reason I can stand the guy." Mike kissed her, softly but still possessively. She couldn't say she hated it. He gazed into her eyes, turning serious. "Are you moving on with me or not? Because I thought we had something going here. Something good."

Her knees went rubbery. That was as close as he'd come to a declaring his feelings so far. "It is a good thing we've got. And I am moving on with you, and moving on with my life in general, with all sorts of plans." Now wasn't the time to discuss the artists' retreat. She didn't have anything solid to tell him, just a pipedream.

"I'm glad to hear it." He kissed her, long and slow and deep, arms secure around her as he pressed her against him. Her body felt boneless. "I'm relieved you're not stuck on Jack," he continued as he nibbled her ear. "But it doesn't matter tonight, since you're not going anywhere."

She pushed at him. He conceded some space between them.

"I am." Would she get used to his bossiness? Fortunately, she'd never been accused of being a doormat and could stubborn him right back. "You and the kids need your own space. You need to talk and plan. And you don't need to worry that I'll get my feelings hurt. They may not like Little Tree."

Mike dipped his head, unable to hide his flush of guilt.

"And that's expected. Some of our town kids grow up and get out, only returning for holidays or family events." She drew him to the bed and sat next to him. "Mike, I'm not leaving because your family is too much or too many. I want to give you time together, and I'm not going to sleep with you while they're in the house, anyway."

He jerked back as though she'd slapped him. "Do you think that's all I care about?"

"No, I don't, or I'd have said go to Miles City and get a hotel."

"That's an hour away."

"And that's my point. Paul and Anita might not want to live in a place where the nearest decent motel is an hour's drive away. I love it here. I want to make a home here."

She swallowed. Carrie's question came back to her: would she move to Colorado if Mike asked her to go back with him? "I could live elsewhere, I guess, but for now, *unless something changes*, this is my plan."

Could her meaning be any more plain? Well, yes, she conceded, but she wasn't likely to propose marriage a second time.

After the bunk beds were set up in Lexi's room, Grace let herself back into her dad's house. He wouldn't mind her staying there for a bit. She hadn't been able to reach him, but since suppertime was rolling around, she figured he'd be rolling in himself soon.

She was proved wrong an hour later as she ate a quick sandwich and cleaned up without her father appearing. Whose ranch had he been called to? Had Lexi been enlisted to help? She hesitated to call either phone, knowing they couldn't respond if an animal needed them. Restless, she settled into a comfy chair in the living room with a mystery novel.

Just as the killer snuck up behind the victim, Grace's phone rang. She jumped, just barely holding on to the book. Heart pounding, she checked the screen. Carrie Moore. Her first thought was *Lexi's hurt.*

"Hey, bad news," Carrie said.

Grace could barely squeeze out a word. "What?"

"I talked to Adam. He doesn't want to sell."

"Oh." Grace took a relieved breath. *Not Lexi.* Then Carrie's words began to make sense in her head. Grace slumped in the chair as disappointment crashed over her like a tsunami. "Oh."

"I'm sorry. I'll talk to him again. We could use the money." Carrie sighed. "But you've got to understand where he's coming from. No one wants to sell land. It would be hard for me too, no matter how practical. It's been in our family for over a hundred years."

"I know. I'm sorry I asked, Carrie. Thanks for trying."

"Don't give up yet. I'll keep at him. Like I said, the income would be welcome."

Grace closed her eyes as she disconnected, unable to face her dream collapsing. She'd been so hopeful. Despite Carrie's reassurances, Grace couldn't imagine Adam changing his mind. She couldn't blame him. As Carrie said, no one wanted to face the defeat of losing their family's land.

They'd surely feel the way she did now, having her dream dissolve.

***

A little after nine o'clock, Dad's front door opened and Iris Browning walked in, her face going stiff when she spotted Grace. Her soft gray curls appeared dark charcoal in the dim light. An aqua crocheted shawl draped over her shoulders and lent her face a summery glow. "Hello, Grace. Kevin, you didn't mention your daughter was here."

"I didn't know it myself." Dad walked over and kissed the top of Grace's head. "Hey, honey. What are you doing here?"

"I tried to call." Grace stood, wiping sweaty palms on her shorts. Her dad was on a date. Her stomach knotted. He'd brought that date home to his supposedly-empty house.

Jiminy Christmas.

He studied her face. "I saw that you'd called, but you didn't leave a message, so I didn't think it was important. Are you and Mike having trouble?"

Mrs. Browning took a step backward in her sensible, low-heeled black pumps. "Maybe I should go."

Dad turned with a frown. "That's not necessary, Iris. Maybe we could use some coffee, though?"

How familiar was Mrs. Browning with Mom's kitchen?

"Not for me." Grace couldn't swallow coffee. She couldn't have swallowed spit, though her mouth had gone so dry, she couldn't test that. *Dad's on a date.* Right in front of her eyes stood proof her father had moved on. Had someone important in his life, as Lexi had tried to warn her.

He wore slacks, which he never did, and Mrs. Browning had on a flowery pink and aqua dress. Dinner, Grace thought, feeling her own ham sandwich sinking heavy in her gut. They'd returned here after dinner for...a drink? Her dad rarely drank.

Oh, God. She winced as other possibilities occurred to her frozen brain. Please let them only be here for a drink. "I'm in the way."

"Don't be silly." Her dad waved her back toward her chair and drew his date into the room beside him. "What's going on?"

She looked at them in turn then focused on her dad again. "I didn't mean to intrude on your evening with Mrs. Browning. I was going to stay here for a few days, if that's okay."

Dad's face went slack with surprise, and then scrunched with concern. "What's going on with Mike that you can't stay at your own house?"

Mrs. Browning pushed her forearm into his. "What your dad means is of course he wants you to stay here."

Dad looked at her. She raised an eyebrow at him.

Grace almost smiled. She didn't want to think how cute they were together. She didn't want to know that Mrs. Browning could keep her dad in line with just a look. She didn't want to admit they might be good for each other.

Mrs. Browning could never replace Mom. It hurt to watch them together.

"Do you want me to leave so you can talk?" Mrs. Browning asked. When Dad started to speak, she added, "I can wait in the kitchen."

"No, Mrs. Browning, it's nothing secret."

"Good." The woman gave a gentle smile and sat on the couch, hands folded in her lap. "Then I'd love to help if I can, but you must call me Iris."

"Oh, uh, sure. I'll try. Iris." Grace groped for the chair cushion and fell onto it, none too gracefully. This woman had ruled the library for Grace's entire life. Granted, Grace hadn't seen much of her. By the time she'd exhausted the meager holdings of children's mystery novels, Grace had become too entrenched in painting to spend much time reading. Her dad put a lot of money toward her supplies, training and art camps. Time spent doing anything other than developing her craft felt like a betrayal. And she hadn't wanted to do anything but paint.

Dad sat beside Mrs. … Iris on the couch. "What's up, honey?"

"It's nothing. I mean, it's nothing bad. It's great, really. Mike's sister and brother are in town. Staying at the house."

"Oh."

"So it's kind of crowded. We swapped out the bunk beds from upstairs in the guest room for Lexi's bed. I left a note in the kitchen."

Dad shook his head. "I must have missed it. I rushed in to get cleaned up for our date. Bob Jenkins brought his dog in, bursting with a litter. He shouldn't have moved her."

Grace hadn't seen that look on her dad's face often, but she knew what it meant. "Oh, no. What happened?"

"Blue and three of her pups died. I saved the other two, but one probably won't make it. Had to resuscitate the runt."

Missus Br— Iris patted Dad's hand then kept hers atop his. Her lightly tanned skin glowed against his darkened, rough hand. When had Dad acquired those age spots? Grace dragged her gaze away.

"I'm sorry, Dad. Why would Mr. Jenkins move Blue at such a time?"

"She'd injured her leg, and it got infected. Scared Bob, thinking she had a fever, so he brought her to me." Dad clapped his hands together. "Enough about that. Tell me about Mike's family."

"I met them in—"

Dad's phone chimed. He glanced at Iris as he pulled it out of his pocket. Whatever the display read made him grimace.

"It's Lexi. She's on another call and the Millers have a heifer in distress." He turned to Mrs. Browning. "I don't know how late I'll be."

The older woman glanced at Grace. "If Grace can take me home later, I'd like to stay and talk awhile."

Something caught in Grace's throat, like a hairball of apprehension. What could they have to talk about? "S-sure. No, uh, problem."

Crap.

They saw her father off and Grace busied herself making tea. Decaf, given the lateness of the hour. She didn't plan to drink it anyway. She just wanted something to do with her hands while she stalled.

Talk to her dad's girlfriend? Was there a quick podcast she could listen to on this? At least, she didn't have to worry about them producing any half-siblings.

Grace suppressed a fit of laughter. She couldn't let the events of the day make her hysterical.

Maybe if she gulped down her tea, Mrs. Browning would get the idea. Then, *bingo*, time to leave. There'd just be the excruciatingly long, six minute drive to her house, and Grace would be able to breathe again.

"Shall we go back to the living room?" Grace asked.

"Here is fine." Mrs. Browning remained at the kitchen table. Did she know that all important family discussions took place there? Had she and Dad sat there making plans for the future?

Grace eased onto the wooden chair at the head of the oval and stared at the old scarred table. She couldn't gulp the tea until it cooled, and she didn't know how else to rush the woman out of the house.

"I'm sure this is awkward for you," Mrs. Browning said.

"Oh. Uh, no." Grace didn't look at her as she lied. "I mean, it's Dad's house. I'm the interloper."

"Is that how you see me?"

Oh, double crap. Grace glanced at her.

Mrs. Browning had her head tilted in inquiry, a little frown around her eyes. "I'm sorry to hear that, Grace, but I understand your view. I'm not your mother."

The moment drew out.

Grace realized she was waiting for a response. "No. You're not."

"Kevin has said you and she were close. I'm rather envious."

"Of what?"

"Your mother. I served on a few committees with her, you know. We were friendly. Town this size, you know everyone. And your dad came out to tend our animals. My husband saw him more than I did since I was usually at the library."

"Right." The tea had barely cooled. Grace stirred in some sugar, stalling again while she worked up the nerve to ask. Gaze on her cup, she ventured, "Were you... interested in Dad back then?"

Mrs. Browning laughed. "Good Lord, no. Not that I was blind to him, of course. He's always been a good-looking man."

Grace would take her word for that. "So you didn't..."

"No. I was in love with my husband, just as Kevin was with your mom. Do you remember my husband?"

Grace thought about him and shrugged. "Sure, a little. Small town, like you said. But he was a just another grown-up to me."

"And not interesting to a young painter." Mrs. Browning sighed. "He was a wonderful man, Grace. I loved him with all my heart."

"Then I don't understand. Why did you envy my mom?"

"Because she had you."

Grace stared. "Me?"

"And Lexi. Harold and I were never blessed with children, though we kept hoping." She winked. "And trying."

A smile slipped onto Grace's face. She beat it down.

"A child might have made it easier on me when Harold died. I was so alone. And…angry."

Grace's mouth went dry, her heart stuttering. "Angry?"

The woman stared at the cup clasped in her hands as though drawing comfort from its warmth. She nodded. "I know it's horribly selfish. He died, so what did I have to complain about?"

Grace said nothing. She would have consoled the woman if words would have formed. But nothing came to her.

Mrs. B had been angry at her dead husband.

"It's awful, isn't it?" Mrs. B shook her head. "I lived on, healthy and not in debt, but I was all alone. I felt abandoned."

Grace's breath caught in her chest, cold and sharp, like an icicle jammed into her lungs. *Abandoned.* The word echoed in her skull. Pumped through her blood stream. Throbbed in every cell.

Her secret shame—resenting her mother for leaving her.

Her secret fear—Lexi and Dad leaving her, too.

Tears stung her eyes and clogged her throat. She sipped some tea, trying to force down her churning emotions.

"Are you all right, dear?"

Grace nodded.

"Is this upsetting you, hearing what a selfish woman I am?"

Grace shook her head.

Mrs. B sighed. "Harold would have been mad at me for pulling away. I quit all my committees. I would have quit my job at the library if I could afforded to." Her faint laugh held disbelief. "Can you imagine? Me, not working at the library? But that's how bitter I felt at being left behind."

Grace understood all too well. She hadn't given up painting. Instead she'd made trouble, pushed the limits. Expecting, she realized now, that her dad and Lexi would give up on her. Walk away. Abandon her.

But they hadn't. Lexi had been her sidekick in crime. While Dad hadn't been happy with her antics, he hadn't left. Or stopped loving her.

Grace swallowed some tea to wet her throat. "Was it Dad who helped you get over your anger?"

Mrs. B blinked, her brown eyes clearing. "Your father? No. One day, I looked at the calendar and five years had passed since Harold died. I couldn't count a single accomplishment or bring up a memory that stood out from any other day."

"I don't understand."

"It was a wake-up call. I was wasting my life. I had no child and was too old to adopt. Not enough energy. So I could die a lonely, bitter hermit, or I could get my act together."

Grace had to smile at her gumption. "So you did."

"You bet I did. Joined some groups who were helping

other people. There's nothing like helping others to end your own pity party. I packed care boxes for the military. Ran food drives. I even learned to knit and then sent scarves and caps to charities."

"That's wonderful."

"Do you know why I'm telling you this?"

Grace shook her head. *Please, God, don't let her say she knows I've felt the same way about Mom.*

"I started enjoying life again. I was content. When your dad and I started dating, I was concerned you girls might be upset. That's why we kept it quiet."

Wait a minute. "How long have you been dating?"

"Two years. The thing is, I hope to be part of your family. My goal isn't to replace your mom, Grace, but I'd like for us to be friends. If you think that might be possible someday."

Grace mulled it over. This woman might be the only one who'd ever understand. "Can I tell you a secret?"

"Of course."

"I was mad at my mom, too." Grace could only whisper the words. "For the same reason. She left me."

Mrs. B reached across and held her hand. "It's awful to feel angry at someone you love. You're ashamed, and then you get angry at the world because you can't admit you're angry at your loved one."

"That's it exactly. Dad and Lexi were so sad, but neither of them felt…abandoned." There, she'd admitted it out loud. The ceiling hadn't fallen down nor had lightning struck her dead. Screwing up her courage, she declared in a stronger voice, "I was mad at my mom."

Mrs. B laughed. "Feel better?"

"Much. Thank you for telling me about your

experience."

"Your dad means a great deal to me. A great deal."

Grace nodded, hearing the emphasis.

"But I would give him up if I'm coming between him and you girls."

Pierced with guilt, Grace slumped back in her chair. Silence buzzed in the room like an old fluorescent light rod.

This woman had guts. She'd laid her faults at Grace's feet, declared her feelings, and given Grace the power to tell her to step away. Grace could only think of two women she admired more—her mom and her sister.

Mrs. B only wanted to be part of the family. To stop being lonely. She'd basically said she loved Dad.

Mike had mentioned something along the same vein when they'd gone riding. More family meant more love, not less. If Dad loved Iris, he would still love his daughters, for Pete's sake. Obviously, since they'd been dating for so long already and nothing had changed. There was love enough for all.

She smiled, fully at peace for the first time in fifteen years.

"Can I get you a refill, Iris?"

CHAPTER FIFTEEN

Grace woke determined to move the world.

Buoyed by a good night's sleep after her talk with Iris, and realizing her feeling of abandonment wasn't abnormal, she decided to make some inroads into her plan for the future.

A plan that included Mike. And Anita and Paul.

She rose from her childhood bed and sketched out some details. Then she talked to a few gallery owners. Sales were small but steady. She gave the okay to reduce the price to sell her Australian series. If she bought land in Montana, she'd need money. If she moved to Colorado—and her heart still gave a small squeeze at the thought of leaving her family— she'd need money.

While dressing for the day, she called Carrie to find out where she could track down Adam. Carrie's foreman/boyfriend Matt answered her cell phone. Thrown a little off-balance, Grace hesitated. Did he know she knew about them dating?

When she asked about Adam, Matt's voice went on reserve. Adam was also his boss, technically. "He usually eats at Buck's if he's in town, which he is today. I'll send you his number."

Oh, Adam would love that. "Thanks, Matt. I'll try to catch him there."

Buck's Bar. Great.

She closed the front door and turned, nearly tripping over Paul sitting on Dad's front steps. Even while catching her balance on the porch rail, she glanced around for Mike.

"I came alone."

"Want to come in?"

Paul glanced at the house.

"No one's home."

He shrugged, rising like he was doing her a favor. She admired the patience Mike had built up dealing with Paul. Even Anita, a teenage girl who should be the drama queen, wasn't this taxing.

She led him to the kitchen. "Lemonade?"

He shrugged again.

Grace set her spine and raised her brows. "Yes or no?"

He flushed and dropped onto a chair. Hopefully he'd drop the attitude, as well. "No, thanks."

She poured herself a glass of water and sat. Last night, it had been Iris at this table. Now, another almost-family member. She'd have to give the old table a good waxing after all its extra duty. "What's up?"

"Mike."

"That was my first guess. Can you be more specific?"

"He's talking about staying. About the three of us moving here."

Staying? Her stomach lurched with excitement at the news. Then it pinched with nerves. Had Paul come here to veto the suggestion?

Carrie's question came back to her: *would you move to Colorado if Mike goes back home?* Grace no longer feared the choice. Her family would love her, no matter the distance between them. They always had.

That realization had made gaining the town's

acceptance less important to her. The retreat wouldn't bring in much money, anyway. So if she had to move to Colorado, nothing stood in her way. She'd just prefer to have everyone in Little Tree.

"I'm glad you're thinkking about it," she said. "Any decision yet? What does Anita say?" *Please, let her be on my side.*

"She hasn't made up her mind. Doesn't want to leave her last year of high school. She might choose to move in with June and Jimmy. Or sometimes Anita says she would move here if this is where Mike and I end up. Her answer changes with the wind."

Grace smiled at the old-fashioned expression. "And you?"

"I haven't decided."

"Are you here to debate the choice?"

"No." Paul studied the table. "It's something else."

She sipped the water, her throat so dry with nerves she almost couldn't swallow. He hadn't been in town long enough to be in trouble yet. Was the "something else" a girl back home? Did his heart pull him in two directions?

"It's something Mike said, about us using the Thompson name here. We need to decide, so just introduce us by our first names for now, okay?"

"Sure." But he'd lost her. "What about the Thompson name?"

"Our birth name is Torres." He shrugged. "Don't feel bad for not knowing. We don't use it."

"Why not?"

His mouth tightened. "Mike changed our names when we were kids. Bought us fake birth certificates as the Thompsons." Anger threaded through his voice.

Good Lord. Had she entered another dimension? Not yet woken or risen from bed? This dream world didn't look like anything she would ever conjure up. "What are you saying? Are you undocumented?"

His dark brown eyes flashed hot. "No. Why would you assume that?"

"Because you're Hispanics using fake birth certificates."

He slumped back. "Oh. Yeah. It does sound like that."

"Why else would you do it?"

"Can I?" Paul took her water before she could give him permission, and he drained the glass. "Long story short. Our parents died, *boom-boom*, like two months apart. We lived in New Mexico—where all us kids were born." He shrugged. "Our parents were from Mexico. I don't know if they were legal."

"I'm sorry to hear you lost them so close together." Grace concentrated on absorbing the story. It was a lot to digest at ten in the morning. Her whole perception of Mike changed. Was he a criminal? Was that why he hadn't told her any of this? Her heart ached. Didn't he trust her? "Why did he buy you fake birth certificates?"

Paul shrugged. "He made us move to Colorado and start using Anglo names. I became *Paul*." He said it with a sneer. "I hated it. We all hated it. Juana cried a lot. That's my sister, June. She's second oldest after Mike."

"How old were you?"

"Fifth grade."

Grace tried to make sense of it all, barely hearing Paul talk about entering school, not knowing anyone, and not recognizing himself. "I hated the school. I almost flunked 'cause my old school didn't teach me enough. I only got through 'cause Miss Rachel saved my butt tutoring me."

She nodded and some of it sank in, but she couldn't shake the feeling some aspects of the story had fallen through the cracks. And Paul's recounting left pretty big cracks.

What would motivate Mike to do something illegal? "You haven't said why Mike did that. It's like you were on the run."

The man-boy looked at her. "Our parents had died."

"I understood that part."

"Mike got it in his head we had to." He spoke as though she were dim-witted. "So we wouldn't be split up."

"But why did he think you would be?"

"Because he thinks he knows everything."

Impatient, Grace snapped, "Paul."

He shrugged, his go-to answer. "He said we had to. Move. Change our last name. Pick new first names close enough to our real ones that we could remember. Except Anita. She was only six, and her name would work."

"So this was ten years ago?"

He nodded.

"How old was Mike?"

Another shrug. "Seventeen."

Stunned, she couldn't form words. Or sit upright apparently, as she fell against the back of the chair. Seventeen. "And he's the oldest? Of seven?"

Paul shrugged.

She was going to get a straight jacket for the kid if he didn't knock it off.

Grace blew out a breath. Her heart ached for the boy Mike had been. The boy he'd had to stop being—overnight, from the sound of it.

Her whole understanding of Mike changed for the

second time that morning. He'd become responsible for six younger siblings at seventeen years old. She couldn't fathom it. While it hurt that he hadn't told her, she understood he'd been protecting his family for ten years.

"So," Paul continued, "if we stay, we all have to have the same last name. I think Mike's been using Thompson here already, but it's time for me to be a Torres again."

Grace just looked at him, still dazed. "Why?"

"I don't want to be white-bread anymore. No offense."

She smirked. "None taken. What do you want to be?"

"Myself. A *Mexicano*."

"What's stopping you?" She gestured at him. "You look the part. No offense."

He grinned for a split second then his gaze returned to the wood grain of the table. "I'm not sure I remember how."

Grace's heart ached for the confused and conflicted young man. She reached across and put her hand on his arm. "Paul, just be yourself. Having a Mexican heritage can mean whatever you want it to. Adopt the culture or don't. Adopt some of it or all or none. Just do what feels right for you."

"Says the white girl."

She tightened her hand when he tried to pull away. "I don't have all the answers. I'm not even sure I understand the problem. What I do know is *you* have to live with who you become. And if you don't like the results, then you change again until you're happy. You're American. You can be whatever you choose."

"Says the white girl."

This time a smile played around his mouth.

She cut to the heart of the matter. "Choosing to be American doesn't mean turning your back on your parents. Mike made those changes for the good of your family. Now you have to find your own way, for your own reasons. Just know that we're all going to support you, whatever the choice is."

"My brother is luckier than he deserves." Paul rose and kissed her cheek then disappeared out the door before she could reply.

She sat, letting it all run through her mind. Good Lord. What an amazingly brave and risky thing Mike had done.

Grace checked the wall clock. 10:45. If Adam went to Buck's Bar to drink his lunch after errands, she still had time to talk to Mike. She didn't have a clue what she'd say; she just wanted to see him.

It shook her to think of a seventeen year old taking on such an overwhelming responsibility. Feed, clothe, house, and raise six children. Six *other* children, as he'd been one himself. What had she done at seventeen? Studied painting. Pursued her dreams, while Mike had shelved his and become a man. A family man.

She wanted to hold him, and she wasn't sure if she needed to console him or herself. The drive to her house took three minutes. An eternity.

Mike was in the kitchen. She didn't take time to admire his backside as he bent before the fridge or his front side when he turned at her entrance. She just launched herself at him.

Fortunately, he caught her. Her mouth smothered his laughter, which quickly turned into a kiss so hot neither could breathe. She gripped him to her, and he responded in kind, holding her closer, molding her body to his. Her feet left the floor. She wanted to wrap her legs around his waist.

"Where are Anita and Paul?" she panted out the words.

His flushed face grinned and his eyes sparkled down at her. "A little late to worry about them watching, don't you think?"

She wiggled herself to the floor, peeking out of the corner of her eye to the living room. Empty. "Very funny."

"They're out. So, what brought this on? Not that I'm complaining."

"You." She shrugged and realized why Paul found the movement so useful when words wouldn't come, or in this case, when too many words overlapped. "I've missed you."

"It's been one night."

"Maybe you're irresistible."

He snorted. "Wish that were true."

"How long will the kids be?" She ran a finger around one of his shirt buttons with a naughty smile. "I could show you how irresistible you are."

His kiss rewarded the idea. "They went for a drive. Paul walked somewhere this morning. Hopefully looking for a job. Then he came back and took Anita to practice driving the truck."

"You sound less than thrilled."

Mike blew out a breath. "She has to learn sometime. I'll take her when she's more confident." He looked at the rooster clock. "I have to leave for an appointment myself in fifteen minutes."

She conceded the point. "Not enough time to do it right."

"I think we could manage a satisfying quickie."

"Be still, my heart. We'd be listening for the door the whole time. And there's not enough time to go somewhere else."

"Rain check?"

"You bet." Grace decided to backtrack to the point he'd glossed over. "Paul's looking for a job? Did he say that? Do they want to stay in Little Tree?"

If so, that was a fast turnaround from Paul's attitude when he'd shown up an hour ago.

"They haven't said. They've only been here one day, Grace."

"I know."

"And Paul's been a little touchy." Mike took her by the shoulders, his brown eyes serious. "I have something to explain to you about our past. I want to, whichever way the kids decide."

"Is this about your name being Miguel Torres?"

His mouth dropped open and eyes went wide. It was freaking adorable. "I've never seen you at a loss for words."

"I'm sorry I didn't tell you. How did you find out?"

"Paul and I had a talk. He's confused."

Mike grimaced. "He's angry."

"He feels that he can't claim his heritage. He's Mexican-American but doesn't feel like either."

"That's stupid. He's both."

"No, *you're* both. He's twenty, just past being a teenager. His native language is Anger."

Mike sat at the table. "Did he tell you the whole story?"

Grace had to smile. Maybe all kitchens became conference rooms. "Yes. And what you did was incredible."

"I did what I had to do to keep my family safe. To keep us together. Oh, and I have a birth certificate saying Thompson, so my signature on Lexi and Jack's license is valid. It may not be legal, though."

She laughed. "So that's why you hesitated."

He nodded.

She waved away his concern. "They've overcome worse. If it's necessary, they'll be tickled to have a third wedding. But how did you manage? You were only seventeen."

"I couldn't lose them to the foster care system."

"I understand that." She took his hand. "I would do anything for Lexi—I *have* done something outrageous for Lexi. But, Mike, that was such a big risk."

"The system would have split us up. Our parents' friends helped me hide the family from the government."

"But you're all citizens, right?"

Says the white girl.

She conceded Paul's echoing reminder. Maybe there were things a person had to experience in order to understand. But she wouldn't let that come between them. "The system wouldn't have been tracking you down because you're Hispanic. It was because you were so young."

"Right, a seventeen-year-old *Mexicano* can't provide for his family."

She shook her head. "No. A seventeen-year-old *boy* can't provide for six younger children. And you shouldn't have had to. You gave up so much."

His brows drew together and he looked genuinely perplexed. "What's too much when it's your family?"

And just like that, she knew.

She loved him.

She wasn't "falling."

She was a goner.

The realization rammed into her chest and stole her breath. She understood why people said love hit them like a sledgehammer.

Now the question was what to do about it.

And she thought she knew the first step.

"Are you mad at me," Mike asked, "for not telling you

myself?"

"I was. Hurt more than mad. But…" *I love you.* "I get it."

"You're pretty amazing. I won't keep anything else from you."

"You need to get to your appointment." She kissed his forehead as she rose, evading his hands. "And I have to meet a man myself."

"You've met a man." He stood and swooped her into his arms for another soul-lifting kiss.

"I have. Quite a man." She patted his chest. "Don't worry. This meeting is strictly about business."

And dreams for the future.

Five minutes later, Grace spotted Adam's truck parked in front of Buck's Bar. Maybe he wasn't too far into his cups to be reasonable. Grace swallowed. Selling the family land wasn't *reasonable.* It hurt. It smacked of failure. She was asking a lot of Carrie and Adam.

While she screwed up her courage and practiced sales pitches, Adam emerged from his truck two parking slots down. He hadn't been inside, which meant he probably hadn't started drinking yet. She couldn't be sure, however. Grace scrambled after him. "Adam. Hey, wait up."

He turned. His expression, never easy to read, went from curious when he recognized her to blank as he no doubt realized why she chased after him. But he'd stopped. Old West courtesy had been drilled into him. "Hey."

"I need to talk to you."

He scowled. "Didn't Carrie call you? I'm not interested in selling."

"Yes, she called me last night."

"Then why are you wasting my time?"

Grace narrowed her eyes at his rudeness then jerked her head toward Buck's. "You seem to have time to spare."

Adam studied her for a minute. She refused to squirm.

He shrugged. "Won't take me two minutes to tell you no."

"Do you want to talk here?" Grace indicated the faces in the windows of Buck's and Krause's Bakery next door.

"You don't want to be seen talking to me on the street?" Adam took her arm and hurried her along the side of the bar. She quick-stepped alongside him, determined not to be cowed. A sober Adam Moore would never hurt her, no matter how angry she made him. Grace only worried about convincing him.

They stopped in the alley behind the bar. The grit of the road and parking lot mingled with smashed wooden crates and bottles. Trash perfumed the air, overlaid with grease from the grill and alcohol.

Adam released her arm and looked at her, maybe waiting for her to object. To run like a coward.

Grace tilted her chin up, partly in defiance, partly to meet his gaze. "Is this the conference area where you conduct all your business?"

A slow grin washed over his face and took Grace aback. She'd forgotten how handsome he was. He had inherited his dark hair and eyes from a Native ancestor, but gotten his father's height and stubbornness.

He leaned closer to her with a mischievous grin. "I remember a time you raced me back here, looking for trouble."

Heat flooded her body. He might have blackouts, but of course, he'd remember that. "It was one kiss."

"Because you were underage."

"I was going off to college two days later. Almost eighteen. You were only, what, twenty-two?"

"That age difference saved you. 'Cause that was one long hot kiss, Grace." He winked. "You're not a minor now, though. And here we are."

She might have stepped back from anyone else. Might have been affronted or nervous. But this was Adam Moore, and he had that twinkle in his bloodshot eyes that assured her he was yanking her chain. He wanted her to run, but only so he didn't have to have this conversation.

"I have a fella in my life, but thanks, anyway. And it's him I want to buy the land for."

Adam's expression blanked out again. "Your boyfriend is an artist?" When Grace shook her head, feeling puzzled, he continued, "Carrie said you want to build some sort of artsy retreat. A place to paint."

"That's my plan, and I've been working toward it for a while. I can show you the property layout I've sketched."

He held up a hand.

She shook her head. "My two minutes aren't up yet."

"Ticking away."

"Okay, then I'll say this simply, and you'll have to forgive my bluntness."

He dipped his head in acknowledgement.

"Carrie told you about the retreat. What she wouldn't have mentioned is what a relief to her selling would be."

"A relief?" Adam sounded skeptical.

"Weren't you surprised Carrie wanted to sell? She said you don't use the old homestead acres anymore for cattle. You're grazing them at Ryan's."

"Doesn't mean we want to sell it."

"Carrie is basically running your ranch."

The corners of his eyes tightened—anger or conscience?—but he showed no other sign of hearing her.

"Your ranch could use the influx of cash from this sale. Carrie has cattle to feed and men to pay."

Adam leaned his shoulder against the wooden wall of the bar's storage shed and crossed his arms. She might get more than two minutes.

"I could build a classroom in town, sure, but I'm interested in the scenery for the artists. Maybe we can have day trips. For inspiration."

"Has Carrie told you she needs money?"

Grace hesitated. "No. But you know she does. The ranch does. And she doesn't need the extra worry of looking after the old house. She said she and—" Maybe she'd better not mention Matt in case Adam didn't know about them dating. Or if he did know, he might not like it. "She rode out last month to check on things. Took up most of a day she didn't have to spare."

Adam shoved his hands in his pants pockets and rocked back on his boots. He studied the ground, deep in thought.

Grace held her tongue and let him stew it over. She summoned up other arguments, but she'd just played the ace up her sleeve. Now he had to decide his priorities—hang on to his pride or take some burden off of his sister.

Which totally over-simplified the matter.

He pulled at his ear. Rubbed his cheek. Finally spoke.

"It would be good to see cattle roaming over there again. We haven't had the feed to expand the herd in a few years."

Exhilaration raced through Grace. Then evaporated. She paused before and inhaled. She might as well be honest upfront; he'd find out anyway. "We're not going to run cattle,

Adam. Just so you know. My..." What should she call Mike? Her boyfriend? "Friend wants to rehabilitate horses. Train the wild ones he buys from the BLM auctions."

Adam stared at her, eyes unreadable. After a minute, he said, "You know you're taking a risk telling me that. I just said the old homestead should be a cattle ranch again. You're jeopardizing this deal."

She nodded. "I don't want to be dishonest."

"You've changed."

A chuckle escaped her despite the serious conversation. "That's a backhanded compliment. Implying I was dishonest in the past."

He scratched at the day's bristles. "Nah, not dishonest, exactly. But you'd have nodded and charmed me into thinking you were ranching, and I'd never have known the difference until the papers were signed and the horses started fertilizing the valley."

"I don't know when we'll have the money for the retreat once the horses, barns, corrals, and our house are built. The artists' retreat would only be a small income source."

Adam nodded. "A very small income source. You talked this all over with the horse man?"

"It's a surprise."

"It sure as hell will be." Adam shook his head and looked away, went deep into thought. When he focused on her again, he wore a smile. "Damn if you weren't always setting this town on its ear. I'd sure like to see the reaction to the idea of an *artists' retreat*."

She couldn't help chuckling. "Not the most admirable of reasons, but are you saying you'll do it? You'll sell me the land?"

"I think we can come to some agreement. Why don't

you and me and Carrie all sit down around five at the house and discuss this."

"Thank you, Adam." Hope zinged through her veins like caffeine.

"Do you want to invite your boyfriend along?"

"Not this time." She held out her hand.

Adam gave her a knowing glance as he shook her hand. "You don't want to ruin the surprise?"

Oh, it'll be a surprise all right.

CHAPTER SIXTEEN

After meeting with Carrie and Adam, Grace curled up in her old bedroom after the meeting with a sketchpad on her knees. She drew for hours, starting with where to place the buildings. After several messy attempts on the retreat idea, she realized her heart wasn't in it. Instead, she sketched out a corral and barn then added a second cabin. She renovated and redecorated rooms in the old homestead.

Then her mind and pencil wandered. Around a big wooden table in the homestead, she placed her family. Thanksgiving, she thought, and a roast turkey materialized on the page, luscious enough to make her mouth water. She and Mike, Anita and Paul, Dad and Iris. Jack and Lexi and Annabeth. With a scowl, she drew a chair and TV tray in the corner for Crusty.

Then horses formed on the next page. She drew the land as she remembered it, populated it with cattle. Drew it without livestock, just the heat of the sun, with the grass blowing in an unseen breeze.

A knock sounded at her door. With bleary eyes, she glanced at the clock as she called for her dad to come in. How did it get to be after two a.m.?

"Hey, honey. Did I wake you?"

"No." She pushed the papers aside and made room for

him to sit. "I've been drawing. Lost track of time. Are you just getting in?"

He nodded.

"Iris or business?"

"Iris mostly. Interrupted by business, but she understands. She let me come back after I finished."

Grace smiled, and it came more naturally than she'd imagined. "She just might be a keeper, Dad."

"Might be." He cleared his throat. "I've been think—"

The house phone cut him off. His cellular went off after a two second delay. "Darn it. I was hoping for a good night's sleep."

He answered, his gaze going wide and straight to Grace. Her stomach clenched. A late night call was never good news. "She's right here." He extended the phone toward her, and she took it with shaking hands. "Mike. Said he's been calling but you didn't pick up."

"Oh, no." She put the phone to her ear and told them both, "I turned off my phone for a meeting earlier. What's going on?"

"Is Paul there?"

She closed her eyes. "No. I'm guessing he's not home?"

"I've driven around town, everywhere I can think, but I can't find him."

"I'll be right over."

"That's not necessary."

"Two minutes."

She disconnected before he could argue and climbed out of bed. "Paul's missing."

Dad looked at the clock. "It's not that late."

"He doesn't know anybody in town. Has no friend's

house to go to." She slipped on shoes. "Will you call the hospital? I don't know if Mike would have done that yet, and I don't want to suggest it."

"I'll call. And I'll pray."

"Thanks, Dad." She kissed his cheek. "I'll let you know when we know."

The three minute drive didn't take her even two minutes. Anita flew into her arms, cheeks pale and wet.

"What's happened? Have you heard something?"

Anita shook her head. "I'm so worried."

"You didn't have to come," Mike said from the doorway.

Anita's grip tightened.

"I'll feel better if I'm here." She patted the girl and held her as they walked inside.

Mike gave her a run-down of where they'd looked. "The truck isn't parked anywhere I can see it. Unless he's driving on the far end of town while I'm on the near side, he's not out on the roads."

"Do you want me to try looking?"

Mike shook his head. Anita implored her with big eyes dark with worry. "Can I go with you?"

"I'll go back out," Mike said.

"You stay this time," Anita asserted. "I want to go. Please, Mike. I can't stand being here doing nothing."

He grimaced. "I guess it's my turn for that. Half an hour, though. That's all. I won't be able to sit here any longer."

"Thank you." Anita raced out of the house.

"I think it's time to call the hospital while Anita's gone."

"My dad's calling them."

He closed his eyes and nodded. "Thanks. And thank

him for me. I dreaded calling, but maybe I should have done it sooner."

"We'll know soon enough. Dad will call us either way." She wrapped her arms tight around Mike. "It'll be okay."

"I'm sorry I had to call you, but I'm glad you're here." He kissed the top of her head. "It will help Anita."

She gave him a hard squeeze. "Just her?"

"I'm always glad to see you, sweetheart."

He wasn't so glad when she returned thirty minutes later without Paul or any sign of him. Anita slumped in a chair, covering her face with her hands.

Grace's dad phoned and she relayed the information. "The hospital hasn't had any emergency calls or admissions with a patient matching Paul's description." She hesitated before adding, "The police reported a burglary at Krause's Bakery, but the man arrested wasn't Paul. We're not supposed to know, but Dad found out it was Doug Pearson. He's suspected of selling more than marijuana."

Mike grimaced, his fists tightening at his sides.

"His accomplice fled before the police arrived on scene." She thanked her dad and disconnected. "It couldn't have been Paul."

"He wouldn't break into a store," Anita insisted in a thin voice.

Mike rose. "I'm going back out."

As he opened the door, a truck pulled into the drive. Not Paul's pickup, though. It came to a stop and Carrie jumped down from the cab. "I've got something that belongs to you."

"Oh, thank God." Grace raced outside. Mike stood, arms akimbo, solid and unmovable as Paul half-fell from the passenger side.

Anita grabbed Grace's arm. "Is he all right?"

Carrie nodded. "Is now. Won't be in the morning."

Grace smelled the alcohol as the boy wobbled closer, one hand on his stomach. Beer, definitely, but also something stronger. Paul appeared a little green under the porch light.

He stumbled past them, a silent Anita on his heels.

"Thank you for bringing him home," Mike said tightly. He stood near the steps, too polite to go inside until Carrie left but too worried to move far from the house.

"Yes, thank you." Grace crossed to the truck where her friend stood. "Where did you find him?"

"Behind Buck's, puking his guts out in the alley."

Grace shivered as coincidence crossed her grave. She'd just been there that afternoon. "This is so good of you, Carrie. We've been looking all over."

"I was out anyway." She grimaced. "Adam's been gone since you left the house. I wouldn't usually worry yet. It's not just coming on three o'clock now. But given our meeting, I thought he might be upset."

Stricken, Grace stared at her. "I don't want that. I never wanted that."

"It's not on you, whatever the outcome."

"But if it's because—" Grace glanced over at Mike, who was staring through the screen door, and lowered her voice. "Because of what we talked about, it is my fault."

Carrie shook her head. "He makes his own decisions, for better or worse. Nothing you or I can do. Nothing he can do about it sometimes."

"Thank you again, Carrie." Mike walked over and shook her hand. "I'm more grateful than I can say."

"No problem." Carrie shrugged. "I'm used to dragging brothers home in the middle of the night. It's just usually my own."

***

"Give me a few minutes, okay?" Mike didn't wait for Grace's agreement. He rushed inside as Carrie's truck pulled away. Paul sat on the couch with Anita beside him, rubbing his back. He sat upright as Mike entered.

Anita stood and scuttled toward the kitchen. "I'll make coffee."

Mike barely restrained his temper. He ran his gaze over Paul, noting the yellow tinge to his skin. "What the hell were you thinking?"

"I'm just finding my way in my new town."

"Finding trouble, you mean."

Paul shrugged. "Gotta get the lay of the land. See where I fit in."

"And where you 'fit in' is with the local weed dealer?" Mike unclenched his fists. He had no intention of hitting his brother and didn't want Paul to think he would. The boy was too old to spank and too dear to beat the living daylights out of. Maybe it would straighten Paul out, but Mike couldn't do it.

Paul's eyes narrowed. "Weed? What are you talking about?"

"Do you know Doug Pearson?"

Paul nodded.

Dammit. Of course he did. "He was seen smoking pot with a guy matching your description. The police caught him breaking into a bakery looking for cash. Doug was arrested, and the other guy ran off."

"Matching my description? I'm not the only *Mexicano* in town."

That digression took Mike back a step. "So you weren't smoking pot with Doug either?"

Paul shrugged. "He said he'd introduce me around. We

had some beers and whiskey. And, yeah, we burned one, but it made me sick, so I left."

Relief washed over Mike like a warm shower. "You left."

"I didn't break into any store."

Weak in the knees with relief, Mike put a hand on the wall. "I should have known better."

"Yeah, you should."

"But you were still smoking pot and drinking."

"Three puffs."

Mike raised a brow. "You only stopped because it was crap."

His brother was stupid enough to grin. Mike's teeth ground together as he endeavored to stay on point. So much needed correcting in Paul's life but each would have to be handled separately or the kid would tune him out.

"Paul, you have a chance to meet a new kind of people to hang with. What you do these first days is going to make an impression. Getting caught smoking pot, drinking underage, and puking behind the town bar is the kind of impression that's hard to overcome."

"Grace did stupid things as a kid and she was forgiven."

Acid churned in Mike's belly. "This isn't about Grace. She's from here, and she wasn't held responsible because she was a child."

Mike took a deep breath, not wanting to come over too strong or he'd lose Paul for sure. "You want a job. You want to be accepted, make friends, date a local girl someday. So, make life easier on yourself, and stay out of trouble."

Paul glared then looked away but didn't stalk off.

Progress.

Mike held his peace. The boy in front of him had to

decide what kind of man he wanted to be.

"Okay." Paul rose, a little wobbly. "I might be sick."

Mike pointed toward the kitchen. "Out back."

Mike gave Anita a reassuring pat as he followed Paul out. "Go on to bed. Everything's okay."

He walked outside in time to see Paul wipe his mouth on the hem of his T-shirt. The light over the door lit the driveway and yard like high noon.

Paul leaned on a hand against the house. "Maybe Doug wasn't the best choice. He's kind of a dickhead, passing off bad weed as primo Kush."

Mike nodded, biting his tongue. "There's a family-style bar and grill in town that has dancing on the weekends. You can meet people. Drink pop. Maybe check out the young ladies in Little Tree."

Paul gave a small grin, his face still a little yellow. "I'm all for that."

Mike clapped him on the shoulder, leaving his hand resting there in comradeship.

"Maybe Darryl eats there."

Mike froze. "Darryl?"

"Doug's friend, Darryl Peters. I was going to meet him tonight, but I left."

Mike raised both hands in the air. He couldn't trust himself not to punch something, and he didn't want his little brother in the way when he did. "Stay away from Darryl Peters."

Paul's face set. "You can't tell me what to do."

"I can and I am. Darryl is shit too good for your boot. Doug, too."

"You don't even know them. At least Doug doesn't mind that I'm Hispanic. Not like you do."

Mike gaped, baffled by the lob from left field. "What the hell does that mean?"

"We had to change our last name and take on white-bread first names. What do you think Mamá and Papá would have said about that?"

Stabbed in the heart, Mike couldn't speak. Mamá would have hated it, but Papá would have understood he'd had no choice. At least, that's what Mike had been telling himself for ten years. "I...don't know."

"We don't speak the language. You don't even swear in Spanish, *Miguel*."

"We couldn't." Mike struggled for breath. He thought the kids had all understood the situation, even the young ones. "We had to make a new start, in a new city where they couldn't find us. Where they couldn't separate us."

"I'm sick of trying to be white."

Mike reared back. He couldn't have been more surprised if Paul had thrown a physical punch. "I never said we were."

"We're not the Torres family anymore. And if I'm not Pablo Torres, who the hell am I supposed to be?"

Mike grabbed Paul's shoulders before he could turn away. "Listen to me. I did what I thought was right. Okay, not right, but what I thought was *the only thing* I could to keep us together. I was seventeen, younger than you are now." He took a breath. "In Little Tree, you can have a fresh start. I've got our original birth certificates in the bank in Longmont. I'll go get them."

Paul brought his hands up between them and broke Mike's hold. "That's the thing you don't understand, Mike. I can't be Pablo Torres. I don't know how. I'm freaking Paul Thompson. Except that I'm not really him either."

"Maybe if we stay…" Mike paused, the implications for Anita running through his mind. "If we stay, we can all reclaim our family name. I'm old enough now, Anita should be safe."

Paul stepped back, off balance. "Anita? What are you talking about?"

Mike barely heard him, cogs turning. "Yeah, I think it should work. If it's important to you, and if we all stay here together, we can introduce ourselves as Torres. I haven't met that many people yet and I can explain to the ones who ask. I'll go back to Colorado and get our papers."

"Back up. What was that about Anita?"

"She'll be okay. The authorities can't—or shouldn't be able to—take her away. She's underage, but I'm legally her guardian, no matter our names."

Paul grabbed his arm. Hard. "What authorities?"

Mike blinked, distracted from planning. "Child Protective Services. Human Services. Whatever the agency is called here. Jesus, Paul, what do you think I've been fighting against these past ten years?"

"I don't know." His brother sounded hollow inside. He put his hands out like a traffic cop at an intersection.

"Why do you think I did all this—" Mike continued, disregarding the stop sign from Paul, "—changed our names, bought us new birth certificates, and moved our family from New Mexico in the first place?"

Paul backed away, eyes wide.

"Where are you going?"

"Gotta think." Paul didn't sound like he could form sentences, let alone think. But his feet kept backing up.

"We're still talking."

"I know." Paul turned and ran, across Grace's back

yard, through the hedge and gone.

The kid knew how to execute a speedy escape. Not a thought that gave Mike any comfort.

The screen door shut, warning Mike he had company. Grace walked over to him. "Anita's in the shower. I think she just wanted to be alone. Where's Paul off to?"

"Were you listening to us?"

"No. I just came out, but I was watching from the window. I saw his face crumple like he'd been Tasered."

Guilt ate at him. He'd been hard on the kid, but— "Dammit, he's not a kid anymore. He needs to stand on his own two legs and stop blaming the world. And me."

"He's still a teenager. I mean, practically."

"He's almost twenty-one. He'll be an adult soon. And it doesn't help if you make excuses for him."

Grace took a step back, blinking. "Me? What did I do?"

"Oh, no," Mike said in a falsetto. "You can't sleep on a couch. Oh, sure, you can drive my too-damn-expensive and powerful car." He blew out a breath. "You're always making his life soft. And he has to learn the world doesn't owe him anything."

She goggled at him. "Is this because I let him drive over to Dad's? While I sat in the seat beside him, if you recall."

"You give him too much. Starting with money in Colorado. He did a job because I told him to."

"My tire? Are we back to that? I said I was sorry."

"But did you learn?" His hand swiped through his hair in frustration. He paced away. "No, you're giving him beds and car privileges."

She glared at him. "I'm trying to be nice. It always backfires on me, but I keep trying for some reason."

"He thinks he can get away with anything the way you

did. You, with all your childhood antics that you make sound so charming."

"I don't try to make it sound charming. I've owned up to past mistakes." She shrugged. "People have to take me as I am because I'm just myself."

Mike walked away a few steps, trying not to hear those words. "But his life isn't going to be like yours."

"I know. I didn't mean for it to sound like—"

He rounded on her. "You're a bad influence."

Grace's mouth opened; her eyes went wide. The color leached from her face. She didn't even blink. "Do you really believe that?"

"Well, Jesus, Grace. Would you call yourself a *good* influence?"

Instantly sorry for hurting her, Mike turned on his heel and left. Angry at her. And at Paul. And at the world.

But mostly at himself.

After a horrible night spent crying and swearing at Mike, Grace called more galleries with small pieces and set new prices for her artwork. One message came in from Mr. Willard regarding the Ayers Rock series, which gave her hope. If he negotiated a decent price, she could build a new guest cabin. Or if things worked out between her and Mike—once he got his head out of his backside, that money would provide a down payment on the land and lumber for both a barn and a corral. Then she could fix up the old Moore homestead for her home and use it as an office.

With that thought in mind, Grace called Anita to do some negotiating of her own.

"We'd love to," Anita said after conferring with Paul. "Some spending cash would be great."

Assured Mike had driven off somewhere, Grace loaded up with cleaning supplies and swung by her house. The kids followed her out to the Moore homestead. Paul's pickup suited the bumpy, overgrown road better than her red convertible.

Grace ticked off a list of the things she needed to do.

Item One: buy a sturdier vehicle.

Item Two: grade the road and rock it.

Item Three: win the lottery.

For today, she'd tackle what she could handle, and she'd maintain a positive attitude.

The thrill of ownership ran through Grace as she stepped inside the cabin. She hadn't finalized anything, but she and Carrie and Adam had a verbal agreement. The place was as good as hers.

And good it was. Someone had recently cleaned it. Anita handed her a piece of paper from the one metal folding chair in the room. Grace took it, expecting to see Carrie's handwriting.

Instead she read in a dark slant: *Best I could do. A.M.*

Grace clasped the note to her chest in relief. Adam. The mystery of his disappearance had been solved. He hadn't been drinking last night, after all. He'd been here cleaning and saying goodbye.

The poignancy of the image brought tears to her eyes. She shook them off, and silently thanked God for Adam's safety.

Paul moved gingerly but overall seemed okay after last night's adventures, though he kept his sunglasses on even while inside. They unpacked the supplies and started in. Anita joined in when Grace hummed "Whistle While You Work," then left Grace behind singing "A Happy Working Song" from *Enchanted.*

"You have a beautiful voice," Grace told her.

"I have lots of chances to sing while I'm cleaning." Anita shot a hard look at her brother. "Since I'm always doing it alone."

Paul snorted. "Whatever."

"I'd like to talk to you outside," Grace told him.

They went to the edge of the porch.

"I don't know if you're staying or not. I don't know if Mike is, to be honest. But here's something I was thinking if you do. Would you consider staying out here in this cabin to oversee the work being done?"

His jaw dropped then he whipped off his sunglasses and stood straighter. "What?"

"I'm going to need an on-site foreman."

"I don't know anything about construction. Why can't you do it?"

She could. "I'm offering you a job until you find something in your field."

His eyes narrowed. "What do you think my field is?"

"Cars. Motors. Out here, you'd probably work more on tractors and ATVs. Horse trailers."

"What makes you think I'd like that?"

"The ease you had changing my tire back in Colorado. I've watched you with my car and noticed how your truck purrs." She raised her brows. "Am I wrong?"

He hunched his shoulders. "No."

"Working here will give you a start on your tuition for, what? Vocational school. Car mechanic school?"

He nodded. "That would be great. Thanks."

"If you're going to be my foreman, living out here alone, I need to be able to trust you."

"You can."

"If you wind up staying in Little Tree, that is."

His head tilted to the side. "Why do you say it like that?"

"Mike might have decided to go back to Longmont."

Paul shook his head. "I don't think so. We talked about it yesterday. He wants to stay. Of course, then he goes crazy when I try to make friends."

Grace arched an eyebrow at him. "Friends like Doug the Dealer? Gee, I can't imagine why that would upset him."

Paul gave a half-smile. "Okay, bad example. There was another guy, though. Really set Mike off, and I haven't even met him yet. He's just a friend of Doug's."

"A friend of his is probably a druggie too. Who is it?"

"Darryl Peters. Do you know him?"

Grace's head spun. All the blood draining out of it made her dizzy. She grasped his arm. "Don't get mixed up with him, Paul. I'm serious."

The boy's jaw dropped. "Why? Who is he?"

"When I was in Colorado, he assaulted my sister. He might have thought she was me."

Paul squeezed his eyes shut for a minute. "Dammit. I'm sorry, I didn't know. Is she okay?"

Grace nodded, sick at the reminder.

"No wonder Mike went ballistic when I mentioned his name. I just figured ordering me to stay away from Darryl was another one of his decrees from on high. I'm so tired of him making decisions for me."

"He's protecting you."

Paul crossed his arms and scowled. "Well, he can stop. I'm not a kid."

She elbowed his arm. "Going to stick out your bottom lip?"

Paul scowled harder then broke and chuckled. "That's not funny."

"Depends where you're standing."

"Exactly. It's easy for you, over there in those shoes, to say Mike did all this and I should be grateful."

"You're right. From these shoes that's what it looks like. It should look like that from every pair of sensible shoes."

Paul rolled his eyes.

"Why do you think he owes you a life?"

"He stole mine. Ours. We didn't have to move. We could have lasted a year in the system."

Grace smiled to herself. Such a tough-guy act. "A year? You still don't get it. Just because Mike turned eighteen doesn't mean you would have been processed out. Once you're in the system, they've got you. He would have had to prove he could care for you—for six of you, and himself—with a home that passed inspection, and clothes, food, and schooling."

"We could have made it."

"If you survived being bullied or abused by the other foster kids, maybe even by the caregivers. Anita was six. Would you have wanted to risk her being neglected? Bullied? Abused?"

Gaze on the ground, he shook his head.

"It's time for you to grow up, Paul, and stop blaming Mike for the past. Make your own decisions."

"I'd like to, but he's still taking charge of our lives. Making decisions for me, like moving here. Just like when I was a kid."

Exasperated, she blew out a breath. "But you know why Mike did that."

"To keep us together."

"Exactly. It would have been hard to hide a family of

seven from the authorities, you know. They would have been interested in your welfare since you were all minors."

"I didn't think of that."

"Sounds like you didn't think of a lot. Mike gave up his identity too, you know, and I don't just mean his name. He was a teenage boy, younger than you are now. Try to imagine someone Anita's age with six younger kids to feed, and house, and clothe. Could you do it?"

Paul swallowed.

She didn't give him time to answer. "So he buried all his dreams of the future and transformed himself into a father."

"He's not my father."

"He raised you, Paul. He took on the responsibility for all of you." She gentled her voice. "You forget, he was grieving too, but he didn't have that luxury." She gave Paul a pointed look. "Nor did he have the luxury of blaming everyone else for his problems."

The red blooming across his face indicated he received her message.

"You all would have been split up," she continued, "sent to foster homes. Even at six, Anita probably wouldn't have been adopted. Mike kept the seven of you together. Kept you a family."

"Saint Michael, defending us."

She might have snapped at him—or swatted his diaper—but she heard the layer of tears and respect mixed under the sneer. Still, she couldn't walk away on that note.

"It's time for you to make your own decisions." She leaned into his face. "And when an impossible choice arises, I hope you're a quarter of the man your brother is."

Grace turned and left him standing there, gawking. The kid could digest that or choke on it.

CHAPTER SEVENTEEN

The sunrise had found Mike ill-tempered. He'd tossed and turned for the few hours left of the night, gut-sick over what he'd said to Grace. What she'd said to him.

I'm just myself.

Could he claim the same?

Wouldn't it serve him right, after all the grief he'd given her, if she was the one leading an honest life?

Neither kid had risen, so he left a note and drove Lexi's truck out to the Rocking W. A ride would set his head straight.

Lexi came out into the yard as he pulled up. "Hey, Mike, what's up?"

"Good morning. I'd like to go for a ride or work with a horse that's acting up. Something soothing."

Her brows rose. "Is Grace making you that crazy?"

He had to chuckle. "I should say no, but, well, you know her. It's a combination of her and my brother."

"Bad news from home?"

"Not from home. He and my sister are here, visiting."

She lit up like fireworks. "I'd love to have you all out for dinner here. How long are they staying?"

"Two more days. My brother has to go back to work. Didn't your sister tell you about them?"

"*My sister?* Oooh, it's a bad fight when you won't even

say the other person's name. And no," she went on before Mike could comment, "I just want to invite everyone over. It'll be our first big dinner party."

While she counted attendees on her fingers, Mike debated telling her about the "bad fight" he'd had with Grace. He'd called her a bad influence. She'd never forgive him.

"Ten," Lexi announced. "We'll hardly even know they're here."

He didn't know how the three Thompsons became a party of ten, and he didn't want to ask. "Do you have a horse I can ride?"

She nodded. "Take any of them in the barn. We have a colt about seven weeks old if you want to do some hands-on. Or" —she eyed him with a nervous smile— "you can talk to me. Might do you as much good as riding."

He gave her a doubtful look.

"Okay," she said, "nothing is as therapeutic as riding. But what you said before is true. I do know her. I might be able to help you understand her."

Mike debated for half a second. "Maybe you can. There's something that's been bothering me since I met her. How can Jack forgive her for jilting him? How can you forgive her for leaving you to clean up the mess?"

Lexi stared at him, open-mouthed, then let out a shout of laughter. "Oh, Mike, my friend. Hasn't she told you what she did?"

He nodded. "She was very upfront about it. She left him at the altar, literally, with all your friends in the church."

"Well, yes. It sounds bad, put that way."

"What other way is there to put it?"

"Come sit on the porch for a second." She gave him no chance to refuse as she plopped down on a rocking chair that looked older than Jack's uncle and twice as sturdy. He eased onto a similar one, relieved it took his weight.

"Here's the part Grace hasn't told you." Lexi smiled. "She's protecting me, so don't be mad she didn't share the details. Do you know she's the older one of us? By three minutes and twenty seconds. I was in a hurry to meet everyone. Grace said I always hated missing out on the fun."

"Do three and a half minutes matter?"

"Of course. That's why she's the leader, getting me in trouble." Lexi laughed. "And why she's so protective."

"Maybe I haven't seen that side of her."

"Fair enough. So, the thing with the wedding." Lexi sighed. "You ask how I've been able to forgive her. The truth is, I don't know how I'll ever be able to thank her enough."

Thank her? He must have misheard. "What?"

"She found out I was in love with Jack."

His mouth dropped open in surprise. "I heard it was a fast wedding, but I thought you both fell in love after Grace left."

Lexi waggled her hand back and forth. "Sorta. He only realized it then, once we were forced together in an intimate situation. I knew, of course. I just didn't know how Jack felt."

"I see." But he didn't. It was hard to take all this in.

"And Jack didn't know how he felt either, so it's understandable that I didn't. He wanted me all along." She grinned. "But I was too scary for him."

"Scary?" This elfin-like delight in front of him?

Lexi nodded, looking very pleased with herself. "And I thought he was just a sexist hardhead. But because Grace left, I went through with the ceremony, we had time to talk, and" — she smiled— "stuff, and we realized it was love. Forever after and all that jazz."

Mike tried to process the information. "And Grace knew?"

"That's why she left. She and Jack weren't a love match. I didn't know that until right before she bolted."

"She told me."

"But somehow she knew I loved him. So she buttoned me into that fancy wedding dress she'd picked out, and *poof.* I don't think she intended for us to marry that day. She just wanted to strand me in the dressing room, thinking I couldn't come out looking like her, like the bride."

"But I'm guessing you did."

"I did." Lexi smiled. "We have the video. Jack and I watch it all the time and explain to each other what we were feeling at each moment, even though he thought I was Grace."

"So you watch him marry your sister?"

Lexi laughed with delight, rocking in the chair. "Yes. Except it's me."

He eyed her like she was nuts. "And this is fun for you?"

"So much."

"O-kay."

"We'll do this over drinks sometime. It'll make sense then. For now, all you have to know, Mike, is that Grace made a big sacrifice."

"Giving up Jack."

"No, although of course, *I* think that would be heart-breaking. For her, though, it was the scandal. She's tried to live down her childhood. And she knew leaving would only reinforce everyone's opinion of her. It would hurt Jack and Dad and maybe me. But she believed in her heart it would give me a chance to win Jack's love. And it did."

He just stared at her, mind whirling.

"So when you ask how I can forgive her, that's the wrong question. It's how can I *repay* her? Because of her, I have the life I only dreamed of."

Mike sat for a few minutes, letting it sink in. Grace had sacrificed her good name and reputation in order for her sister to find happiness. It was crazy. And so Grace-like.

"I need a horse."

He was going to have to beg.

Mike had a long ride, ran the jitters out of the horse, did some smooth-talking in its ear back in the corral, and readjusted his own head.

It was a pretty messed up head, at that. He'd hurt Grace.

The way that ate at him made his feelings for her clear.

After a call to Anita, he located Grace at her dad's. Alone, thank God. What he had to say would be impossible with an audience.

She pulled open the front door, mouth tight.

He swept off his cowboy hat and smoothed down his hair. "Hi."

She dipped her head in hello.

He might have to crawl before he could even start to beg. "Can we talk?"

She led him inside and sat in a chair opposite the couch. Message sent: don't get too close. But close was exactly what he wanted to be.

"I want to apologize."

Grace leaned back, gaze steady on him. "Go ahead."

"I'm sorry. I'm really sorry I called you a bad influence."

She looked off into the middle air and wouldn't meet his gaze.

"I was being an ass."

"Something we agree on."

Mike took it as an olive branch. She might want to switch his backside with that branch, but it was a start. "I was mad at Paul and at myself. I shouldn't have taken it out on you."

"You shouldn't have." She blew out a breath. "But you might have had grounds. Stories of past mistakes can sound like past glories to someone looking to rebel. I didn't realize he'd been hearing them around town."

"It's not your fault. He'd been to The Diner, and mentioning your name started the ball rolling."

She grimaced. "I never meant to usurp your authority. I should have asked before letting him drive my car."

"No, you shouldn't. It's your damned car, Grace, and he's twenty. It's not my place to say." He tested the waters with a grin. "If you want to give over your keys to a kid, it's your business."

Her faint smile rewarded his risk. "He's a good driver. Understands cars. Do you know he wants to be a mechanic?"

Mike grimaced. "I'd hoped for more for him."

"More? It's his passion. I could make more money in the corporate world doing graphic design or marketing than I can painting. But I'd be miserable."

Mike nodded. "I get it."

"Just let it percolate for a few days then talk to him. He's really interested. And if you stay in Little Tree, I can have Dad talk to the garages. They'll probably take Paul on while he's learning."

If you stay.

"Are you going to forgive me for being an idiot?" Mike held his breath.

"Idiot?" She snorted. "That's putting it lightly. But yes. I'm going to forgive you."

He fought back a grin—and a shout of relief. "Going to, huh? Just not at the moment?"

"We'll see. You were a pretty big idiot."

"I agree. Does it help to tell you I am planning to stay?"

A smile broke across her face, fast and probably against her will. She tried to force it down but gave up. "So the kids agreed?"

"I don't know."

"Oh."

"Come over here. Please."

She sat sideways, facing him. He took her hand. "If they stay, perfect. If they don't want to stay, they can go live with June and Jimmy."

"You'd let them go? Separate from them?" She looked skeptical. "How's that going to work?"

Mike squeezed her hand. "I'm going to let Paul be a grown up and make his own mistakes and achieve his own triumphs. And June will take care of Anita."

"It's not easy for you, though, is it?"

"No. Them leaving will be like losing an eye."

Her face screwed up. "Ouch."

"But it'll be good for them and probably for me."

"We'll deal with it together, whatever they choose." Grace studied him. "When's the last time you asked for help?"

He thought. And thought.

"Um-hm. That's what I figured." She squeezed his hand. "It's hard for you to trust anyone else. It's who you had to become, raising six kids. Making all the decisions. Putting up with their battles and your fears."

"What fear?"

She smiled. "Okay, suppressing your fear."

"You're probably right."

"You're going to have to trust me. If we're going forward together."

"We are. I mean, I hope we are."

"Okay then." She blew out a breath. "I forgive you."

He raised her hand to his lips, humbled. "I don't deserve you."

"Oh, yes, you do. I'm exactly what you deserve." She hugged him. "I just hope you're never sorry."

"Never." He tried to show how deeply he loved her with his kiss, but nothing could ever be enough. The words hadn't been invented yet to express his feelings. He'd have to show her every chance he had, with gestures big and small. Every day.

And he thanked God for the opportunity.

"Want to take a ride with me?" she asked.

"Oh." He'd had other ideas of how to celebrate their reunion. "I was thinking we try make-up sex."

She shot him a wry look. "I'm sure you were. But this is important."

"Babe, we need to reorder your priorities."

She batted her lashes at him. "Please?"

So he found himself riding along a road he hadn't seen yet in his explorations. The long road ran along dried grass where cattle grazed. Then fewer cattle. Then none as the grass became weeds. She stopped at the end of an overgrown lane, the tracks barely visible. "Whose property is this?"

"Wait and see."

Grace ignored his complaints about her ruining the car as she navigated the rutted trail. Butterflies bounced in her stomach.

"This car wasn't made for this road," he complained.

"Almost there."

Then the old homestead came into view. What had looked like a cute rustic cabin full of possibilities now appeared like a shack of problems, inhabitable. He'd hate it. He'd never bring his siblings to live out here. It was too far from town. Too run-down. Too—

"It's great."

She shot him a look. Was he making fun of her?

"I love the character this place has. Friends of yours live here?"

"Sort of. You remember Carrie, from the restaurant?" She waited for his nod. "This is her land, hers and her brother's. The old homestead."

"Can we look inside?"

"Sure." They went in and she watched his face. He didn't yet know he was viewing their possible-future home. "Three bedrooms. Needs a generator, but there's indoor plumbing."

He smiled at her. "Always a plus."

"So." She took a breath.

Mike took hold of her hand. "There's no bed for make-up sex, so why are we here?"

"I'm buying it."

His face went blank before he glanced around again.

"Carrie and Adam need the money. They don't even run cattle over here. I haven't signed the papers," she babbled on, "but we have a verbal agreement."

He took in every detail this time. Why didn't he say anything?

"Why?"

Drat. The one question she wasn't prepared to answer.

"There are a couple of options. An artists' retreat is one."

He didn't reply, just kept looking around. The original wood walls of the cabin had been insulated and covered in sheet rock. The kitchen needed updating, but it functioned.

"I'd either rent it out to artists so they could stay and paint. I'd give them lessons if they wanted. Or..." She took a breath. "We could build a corral and barn and whatever else you need."

His eyes went wide. "What are you saying?"

She borrowed one of Paul's convenient shrugs to cover her nerves. "We could build your horse farm."

Mike turned around, looking at the place with a fresh perspective. Grace crossed her fingers. "I know it needs renovations, but it's livable. Mostly. We'd need a new generator."

"Are you sure you want to do this?" He took her in his arms. "It's a lot. What about your artist retreat?"

She grimaced. "That was mostly to make the town happy. But I realized I don't need to win their approval." Her discussion with Iris had made that clear. She'd grown out of testing people's love, or in this case, trying to win the townspeople's favor. "I'd rather paint than teach, trust me."

"Babe, I can't even begin to fathom this."

"You want to board horses, right?"

He nodded.

"I also talked to Carrie about teaching barrel racing."

"You have been planning. I don't know about rodeo."

"We don't have to, but if you decide to have any riding lessons for children, keep her in mind. She's always been good with kids."

Mike went silent for so long she feared she'd overstepped. "We don't have to do barrel racing or the artists' retreat. Or even live here."

"Do you have your heart set on owning this place?"

Disappointment crashed over her, and she struggled to keep her voice casual. Her stomach cramped. He wanted to go back to Colorado. She went still for a minute, searching her heart.

And found she didn't mind. If he went, she went. "You don't like it?"

"I do. What I've seen is great. But what would you think about leasing it? I don't have to own the land, and I don't feel right taking it from someone's family. To me, it's the horses that matter, not whose name is on the deed."

Grace couldn't believe it. "That's so sweet, and the perfect solution. I thought you'd want to own the land."

"Not unless you do."

"No. It feels so right, I have goose bumps. It'll mean a lot to Adam and Carrie to keep the land in the family."

"We'll talk to them about a sixty-year lease or something. After that the next generation can decide whose name is on what."

"How would you feel about your name on this?" She went to the corner and brought over the initial painting she'd made from her sketch for Rachel's present. She'd nailed boards across plywood then sanded it smooth and painted it to see the effect. Once satisfied with the wild horses, she'd completed a more professional one for Rachel which included Curly.

His face went slack with surprise.

"Larger scale, of course. Dream Dancer Farm."

He made a face.

"Seurat to Trot? No? You don't like it?" She snapped her fingers, hiding a grin. "I've got it. Horses by Torres."

He lunged at her and she gave a laughing shriek as he swept her into his arms. His kiss said all he couldn't about the gift.

"I'm not a sign painter. We should have someone do it professionally."

Mike shook his head. "Only you can do justice to it. You're amazing."

"There are three bedrooms here, so it's already perfect for all of us. Or what would you think about the kids living in town at my house? Then we could use one bedroom here for my studio and one for your office."

He smiled. "Are you asking me to live with you?"

"Is that what you're...suggesting?" She wouldn't use the word *propose*. She refused to nudge him. Her breath caught in her throat, holding down nervous tears. Heart-broken tears would come later if he didn't ask her to marry him.

Ask her?

Hold up. When had she become a woman to wait for anything?

Oh, God, seriously? She'd have to do this again? She looked into his gorgeous brown eyes, at the face she wanted to see every morning and every night.

And laughed out loud, sure of her actions this time. "I can't believe I'm doing this again, but it feels right. Mike Thompson, will you marry me?"

He tilted his head and didn't reply. What was there to think about? Grace's breaths came shallow. It was a simple answer: either yes or—

"No."

The world went white and soundless. Grace feared she might faint.

"Let me do it." Mike dropped to one knee.

Color and sound whooshed back into her head in a dizzying rush. She blinked down at the solemn man who had taken hold of her hands. Excitement raced through her veins.

"Grace Marshall, you've confused and delighted me from the first day we met. I was born Miguel Antonio Torres in New Mexico. If you would do me the honor of becoming my wife, I'm offering you the Torres name as well as my family. In return, you get my heart. My love is all I have to offer."

"It's all I want."

He rose and cupped her face. "I want you to be mine. I want everyone to know. You're my world. I don't deserve you, but I love you. Will you marry me, honey?"

Tears came then, as she nodded, as she kissed him.

He wiped some away with his thumb. "Happy tears, right?"

"You've never called me 'honey' before. My mom used to call me that. It's like a sign."

"Did you need a sign?" He nodded to the one she'd painted. "Another sign?"

"No. I've been on the road to you for a while, without signposts. But it's so nice to know we have her blessing."

His face softened. "That's a good interpretation. I'm honored you think she'd approve of me. I plan to make you happy."

"I'm so glad you like this place. I was afraid you'd decide to go back to Colorado."

"What were you going to do then?"

"Stalk you until you gave in."

He chuckled.

"What? Do you think I'm kidding?"

"No, but while you were making plans to leave, I brought the kids here and got a job at the Rocking W."

Surprised, she gaped. "You're joking."

"We're destined to be together, Grace. I'll be a good husband, I promise. And if you want kids, I'll be a good father. With your help."

"I'm sure of it. You come with ten years' experience, after all." She kissed him. "And I'll show you I can be a good wife and mother and big sister."

"Woman, you don't have to prove anything to me. I fell in love with you over a glass of lemonade."

She froze, disbelieving. "That first day? You did not."

"Hand to God, I wanted to throw the glass on the ground and drink you up. You blew my plans to hell and scared me spitless. That's probably why I've been fighting it ever since." He kissed her, leaving no doubt he hungered for her. Loved her. "I need you, honey. By my side, helping me with this place, and my family, and our own kids. Marry me. Soon. Be mine."

His kiss was so sweet and heart-felt, tears pricked her eyes. When he gave her a chance to catch her breath, she said simply, "I love you."

"I love you. And I will. Forever."

EPILOGUE

On a sunny June day, Grace and Mike rushed into the church. Despite staying up most of the night watching Mike's new mare deliver her first foal, Grace couldn't miss her dad's wedding.

They'd leased the land from Carrie and Adam last July and moved into the homestead. Anita and Paul chose to live in the house in town.

Grace married Mike in August at Judge Simmons' house. She'd borrowed Lexi's blue wedding dress, which looked perfect with their mother's veil. She'd worn the silver necklace Anita and Paul bought her, and she'd put a penny in the grass-stained shoe she'd been wearing when she first met Mike.

All the Torres kids had attended, including Lilly. Tensions ran under the surface, but at least she'd come. Mike had wiped at his eyes when he saw her, then denied doing any such thing. Despite the room being crowded, they'd made space for Crusty. Afterward, Rachel had borrowed the penny for luck.

At one time, Grace wouldn't have been able to bear anyone replacing her mom. For too many years, she'd felt abandoned and hadn't trusted anyone to stay. Hadn't been able to give her heart. Then a big brooding cowboy had stolen it, and she couldn't be happier.

Now, with Mike in her life proving his love every day for the past ten months, in small ways and big, she only wanted her dad to be equally as happy and nurtured. She could feel the love surrounding her dad and Iris like a white light and knew her mother approved of the marriage.

Jack and Lexi walked over to Grace and Mike. The girls hugged while the guys shook hands. Grace was pleased her sister had accepted Iris, too, since Lexi and their dad were so close.

"Sorry we're late. I was helping Iris adjust Mom's veil. Her something old and her something borrowed."

Lexi nodded then tipped her head to the side, studying her. "Grace?"

Grace frowned at Lexi for a moment, then her eyes widened. She couldn't believe it. On the other hand, it made perfect sense. "Lexi?"

The men looked at each other, baffled.

Mike leaned over to Jack. "They have met, right?"

Jack grinned. "You almost get used to the crazy after a while."

Grace jerked her head toward Jack. "Have you?"

"No," Lexi said. "You?"

"Not yet."

The girls grinned. The guys shared another pained glance.

"Is this some sort of secret twin code?" Jack asked.

The sisters nodded, turned to their husbands and said in unison, "I'm pregnant."

Dear Reader:

If you read The Wedding Rescue, you know this companion book was also a labor of love. I conceived the idea at a conference in 2009. Some people doodle, but when a writer's mind wanders—watch out! A book could be hatching. It's been a long time coming, and Grace Marshall presented a challenge at every turn.

Now another book is calling me, and while I hate to leave the sisters behind, I know they're in good hands with Jack and Mike.

If you enjoy my books, I'd appreciate a review posted at your favorite retailer or book review site. Not looking for a school book report, just a few sentences will do, but no spoilers please. A review helps other readers find this book to enjoy and it helps me as well.

You can find my Reader's Group if you'd like to keep up with my releases. I promise not to bombard your inbox.

Thanks so much for reading. I do appreciate my readers!

Megan

Do Rachel and Clint have a future together?
Find out in
Baby Makes Three*, the next in the
Love in Little Tree series.

Authors live off reviews and if you liked
this book, I'd appreciate your
honest opinion.
This helps readers find this book to enjoy
and helps me as the author.
Just post it to your favorite retailer
or a book site like GoodReads.
Thank you!

FMI, please visit Megan's website.
http://www.megankellybooks.com

To keep up to date on releases and news, sign
up for her Readers' Group on the website,
or Follow her Author Page on Facebook.

Other Books by Megan Kelly

Love in Little Tree series

The Wedding Rescue

Runaway Bride

Baby Makes Three

Christmas in Stilton series

Santa Dear

Holly & Ivey

Returning Home Romance series

Fixer-Upper

Harlequin American Romances:

Marrying the Boss

Howard MO series

The Fake Fiancée

The Marriage Solution

Stand-In Mom

(reprinted in No Ordinary Family)

www.ingramcontent.com/pod-product-compliance
Lightning Source LLC
Chambersburg PA
CBHW070856180626
46817CB00003B/791